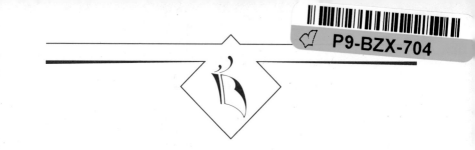

Home in the Hills

LETHA BOYER

CAPPER PRESS
Topeka, Kansas

◆

Published by Capper Press
616 Jefferson, Topeka, Kansas 66607

Cover Illustration and Calligraphy by Catherine Ledeker
Cover Design and Book Design by Kathy Snyman
Edited by Tammy Dodson ◆ Typeset by Karen Gomel

ISBN 0-941678-17-2
First Printing, November 1989
Printed and bound in the United States of America

◆

For more information about Capper Press titles
or to place an order, please call:
(Toll-Free) 1-800-777-7171, extension 107, or (913) 295-1107.

Capper Fireside Library

Featuring
the most popular novels previously
published in *Capper's* magazine, as well as
original novels by favorite *Capper's* authors, the
Capper Fireside Library presents the best of fiction in
quality softcover editions for the family library. Born out of
the great popularity of *Capper's* serialized fiction, this
series is for readers of all ages who love a good
story. So curl up in a comfortable chair,
flip the page, and let the storyteller
whisk you away into the world
of this novel from the
Capper Fireside
Library.

Contents

Home in the Hills

CHAPTER ONE

A New Name

"Miss Davis, I mean Mrs. Hilton."

I had to smile. I had been married for two months now but my students were still having trouble remembering to call me by my married name.

"Yes, Ruth," I said.

"Mama said tell you she'd be here for that meetin' Saturday evenin'. Is there anything you wanted her to bring?"

"No. Ruth, but tell her thank you. It's just a meeting to talk. I may serve refreshments but there's no need for anyone to bring anything. How many of the rest of you children think your parents might come to the meeting?"

About half the children raised their hands.

"Good," I said. "I'll send another reminder home with you on Friday. You may all clear your desks now and get ready to go home."

There was a sudden flurry of activity. I rose and walked down the last aisle between the desks of the older children, my eye on one boy in particular, Todd Johnson.

"You have homework to do," I reminded him rather sternly.

It had been one of his days to act up. He was not a bad boy, just high spirited and mischievous.

"I want a complete report handed in when you come in in the morning," I added.

"Yes, Ma'am," he said with deceptive meekness, looking up at me with wide, innocent eyes. I was hard put to suppress a smile.

"James, don't forget your spelling book," I said, continuing down the next aisle. "Mary, tell Nellie we missed her and I hope she's better soon. I'll send some homework when she's better. Andrew, there's paper under your desk."

I went back to the front of the schoolroom and stood behind my desk.

"All right. You're dismissed for the day. Be sure and button your coats. It's cold out there."

I spent the next several minutes helping the little ones with gloves and buttons and boots, all the time aware of the boy who stood alone at the side of the room, watching me and waiting. When the last small child was gone, he came forward.

"Well, Calvin?" I asked gently.

"I don't think Granny can come to th' meetin'," he said, looking anxiously up at me.

"It's all right. I know all the parents won't be able to come, so don't worry about it. How is your Granny?"

"She ain't doin' too good. She's mostly just been doin' a lot of layin' around."

"Do you think she's sick?"

"It's that gallopin' rheumatism she's got. She says th' cold makes her hurt all over."

"I'm sorry. Is there anything I can do?"

"Don't guess so."

"Who's cooking your meals, Calvin?"

"Granny makes lots of soup an' stuff. There's always somethin' around to eat," he answered indifferently.

I looked more closely at him. His face was thin and looked a little pinched. My heart went out to him. I put my hand on his shoulder.

"If there's anything you need, you be sure and let me know, all right? You'd better run along home now. Don't worry about the meeting Saturday. Maybe I can come over one day next week and tell Granny about it. Good-bye, Calvin. I'll see you in the morning."

I gave him a warm smile, which he returned. There was a special bond of affection between us, but I tried not to let it show in front of the other students.

He went out the door, and I cleared my desk and put things away in the drawer. Then I put my own coat and boots and gloves on, gathered up the books and papers I needed to take home with me, padlocked the outside door, and started walking in the direction of the cabin where my husband and I lived with his parents.

I was deep in thought, thinking about the meeting I was planning Saturday, and I didn't see my husband coming toward me until he was just a few feet away. My heart gave a little leap. I felt my lips curve in a smile. He covered the last few feet between us in a rush and grabbed me around the waist, lifted me off the ground and swung me around. I dropped my books and papers and clutched at him.

"Davy, for heaven's sake," I protested, half laughing.

He set me on my feet, hugged me tight and kissed me.

"How's th' best little teacher in th' world doin' this evenin'?" he asked.

"If you're talking about me," I said in faint exasperation, "I'm not doing so well at the moment, with my books and papers scattered all over the countryside."

I bent to retrieve them, and he squatted down to help me, rising then and pulling me up after him. He took the books and papers from me, tucked them under his arm, and put his other arm around me. I put an arm around his waist, and we started off again.

"And it's not evening," I said. "It's still afternoon, as

I have tried to tell you many times before. Evening doesn't start until five p.m. or so. Afternoon is the time period from noon until approximately five p.m."

"Yes, Teacher," he said meekly.

He looked down at me and smiled and tightened his arm. I had to smile back.

"How you doin', Sweetheart?" he asked softly.

"Fine. And you?"

"Okay. Better now, since you're here. Been missin' you."

"Have you?"

"Yep. You been missin' me?"

"Oh, not terribly. I keep busy."

"Me too, but that don't keep me from missin' you."

"What have you been doing with yourself today?"

"Been doin' some measurin' an' stakin' out our cabin, among other things," he answered.

"You've started then? Oh, Davy, that's wonderful."

"Soon's th' ground starts to thaw, I want to get started diggin' the foundation. Jim come by an' offered to help. With him an' Lewis an' John an' me all workin' at it, we'll maybe get it done enough to move into in a couple months."

"That would be great."

"You mindin' us livin' with Mom an' Dad?"

"No, not really, but it will be nice to have our own home. I can have my piano shipped out and I can perhaps give a few piano lessons. I have one girl that I feel is quite musical and should have some training. Then we could have my folks out and some of our friends over."

"An' here I was thinkin' you was wantin' to be alone with me," he said mournfully.

"That too, of course, but I'm looking forward to doing a little entertaining too." I gave a little skip of happiness. "It's so exciting to be able to plan our own home just the way we want it."

"You like bein' married to me, then?"

"I love it, Davy. I love you," I said giving him a little squeeze. "You're so clever, drawing up all the plans yourself, and building it and making most of the furniture. Not many women have husbands as smart as mine."

"You jist got through tellin' me I don't know th' difference between afternoon an' evenin'," he complained, though he was smiling down at me.

"Oh, well. One can't have everything, and I'll reform you yet, or my name isn't Anne Davis."

"It ain't. It's Anne Hilton."

"Oh," I said, my hand going up to my mouth. "So it is. I'm as bad as my students. They keep calling me Miss Davis, too."

He hugged me up against him. "Gonna have to see what I can do about that," he said grinning.

"Davy," I said after a minute of silence. "I'm worried about Calvin and Granny. I don't think she's feeling well at all. Calvin says she has galloping rheumatism. What is galloping rheumatism anyhow?"

"I think she's meanin' it moves around on her an' hurts in different places."

"Well, whatever it is, Calvin says it's worse because of the cold and she's spending a lot of time in bed. I'm afraid Calvin may not be getting regular meals and all."

"You worry a lot about that young'un, don't you?"

"I guess I do. Granny is old and not well and he doesn't have anyone else, and he's only eleven years old."

"He's better off than some of th' kids."

"That's true. I guess it's just because he seems so alone that I worry about him."

"Well, stop worryin' an' let's talk about our house. Come an' see what I done today, or are you too cold?"

"I'm not cold and I'd love to see what you've done."

"I want you to see how I laid it out an' see if there's anything you want changed. I tried to do it jist like th' plans we drew up, but I mighta missed somethin'."

We turned off the path and went in a southeasterly direction, down a long sloping hill. I looked down in the valley below and I could see the area he had staked off. I stopped and he stopped with me.

"It's a good location, don't you think?" he asked.

"Yes, it is. I like those trees to the north and west of the house. A house without trees looks so bare."

"It makes good sense, too. Them trees on th' north will be like a windbreak in winter, an' th' ones on th' west will shade it in th' afternoons in summer. Let's go on down an' I'll show you th' rest of it. I got it all figgered out, I think."

We went down and Davy laid my books and papers on a stump and eagerly took me by the arm and showed me how he planned to build our house.

"This'll be th' porch," he said pointing, "along th' front here an' around to th' south side. It'll be open at first but later I'll screen it in if you want me to."

"Oh yes, I'd like that. Then we could eat out here in summer and perhaps sleep out here some of the time, too."

"Th' livin' room will be here, an' th' kitchen there," he went on. "Then in th' back, bedroom, bathroom, bedroom, an' utility room."

"Did you remember about the closets?"

"There'll be a closet in each bedroom and one in the utility room. A door'll open onto th' side porch from th' kitchen an' utility room, an' a front door onto th' front porch from th' livin' room. That sound about right?"

"It sounds just about perfect."

"I'll have to build a pump house for th' 'lectric pump. Thought I'd make it outa concrete blocks an' put it east of th' house there. Th' septic tank will have to be over there, course that'll be covered up, so's you won't see it. I'll put th' toilet over there, jist where th' trees start."

6

"A toilet? But why, if we have an inside bathroom?"

"Don't all th' ritzy people have two bathrooms?" he returned with a grin. "Besides, don't ever know when you might need it. 'Lectricity sometimes goes off out here an' don't get fixed for days. I'll be puttin' in a hand pump for th' same reason."

"I see. You're right, of course. I hadn't thought of that. Do you think there's water here?"

"Should be a vein runnin' somewhere right along about here," he said pointing, "but I'll have to be sure before I start buildin'. I'll get Ol' Man Miller out here in th' next few days an' find out."

"I wish you'd say Mr. Miller instead of Old Man Miller," I complained. "It sounds so disrespectful."

"What? Ol' Man Miller?" he asked, eyebrows raised. "That's his name. Nobody'd know who I was talkin' about if I said Mr. Miller. He wouldn't know hisself."

I sighed and he grinned at me and came over to put his arms around me.

"Seen enough?" he asked. "You cold? You're shiverin'."

"I am getting a little cold. The wind seems to be picking up."

"We better get on up to th' house, but first give me a kiss Mrs. Hilton."

Obediently I raised my lips to his and he held me tight.

"Can't wait to get you all to myself," he murmured as we turned toward his parents' house.

CHAPTER TWO

The Reformer

*T*he meeting I had scheduled at the school was for two o'clock on Saturday afternoon. Davy and I were there an hour early to make sure the room was clean and presentable and to set out the refreshments I had prepared. I had baked two kinds of cookies and made punch and brought a large electric coffee pot to perk coffee for those who wanted it. The first to arrive were Lewis and Sue Proctor. Lewis worked for my husband, and we both liked the young couple very much. They brought their two daughters with them, first and second graders.

"I hope you don't mind our bringing the girls," Sue said in her rather shy way. "We didn't have anywhere to leave them."

"That's fine," I said. "I'm just glad you've both come, Sue. How have you been? I haven't seen you for awhile."

"We're fine. We've been wishing we could have you and Davy out some evening. Do you think, maybe — ?"

"Of course, Sue, that would be very nice. You just let us know when."

"Maybe in a week or two. I'll have Lewis give Davy a definite date, if that's all right."

"That will be fine."

"You look so happy, both of you. Marriage must be agreeing with you."

"It is," I said, my eyes going to Davy where he stood

talking to Lewis. His eyes met mine and he smiled a slow, intimate smile.

"I'm so glad for both of you," Sue said softly.

"Thank you."

There were more arrivals, so Sue went and sat down. By two o'clock there were some twenty adults there and about as many children. I was gratified that that many had showed up, though it represented only about half the parents.

"Thank you for coming," I said, standing beside my desk. "The reason I asked you to come today is because there are several things that are of concern to all of us that we need to discuss as a group. Afterward if any of you would like to talk to me individually, feel free to do so.

"As you know, there are only three months of school left this term. I should have called this meeting earlier in the year, I suppose, but I've been — rather busy."

There was a chuckle or two from the audience and I felt myself blushing. My eyes found Davy's again and he grinned and winked at me.

"Anyhow, I've met most of you, at the pie supper and through the children. I feel, all in all, we've had a good year, so far, but there are some areas that definitely need improvement. The most pressing need is for more schoolroom supplies. We need books, maps, etc. We had very good support at the pie supper this year, but as you know, we used that money mostly for playground equipment. I've talked to Mr. Hooper, the superintendent of schools, and he has given the go-ahead as far as our raising some money for supplies on our own. How do you feel about that? Does anyone have any comments or suggestions along that line?"

"Like you said, Teacher, it's kinda late in th' year fer that, ain't it?" drawled one man.

"Yes, Mr. Worth, it is, but I was thinking in terms of next year," I answered.

"You plannin' on bein' here next year then, Teacher?"

"I've put in my application, but whether I'm here or not, schoolroom supplies are still badly needed. Any suggestions, anyone?"

"How 'bout another pie supper? Like you said, we done pretty good at that. I seem to remember a certain young feller payin' twenty-thirty dollars just to kiss a certain young gal," Mr. Worth drawled with dry humor and I felt myself blushing again. Davy had been that certain young man, and I had been that young woman.

"I seem to remember something about that, too," I said with a smile, "and another pie supper might be a very good idea. An alternative to that might be a play put on by the students, say toward the end of the school year, and a small admission price charged. Or perhaps an outdoor carnival on the last day of school."

"I think a play put on by the kids would be nice," said Ellen Hilton, now my sister-in-law. Several other mothers were nodding and murmuring their agreement.

"I like that idea best myself," I said, "and it would be a good learning experience for the children. Is there anyone who disagrees?"

No one answered.

"So it's to be a play then, put on by the children, perhaps in May sometime, and I'd like some volunteers to help with that, please."

Ellen volunteered, and Sue, and a young woman by the name of Goldie Sutton. She was not a mother, but she had two brothers in school, so I supposed she was there to represent them. I hadn't met the parents and didn't think they were in the audience.

"Next project is spring cleaning," I said.

There was an audible groan. "It ain't spring yet, Teacher," said a plaintive voice.

"Spring is just around the corner," I said cheerfully. "The yard needs to be raked and cleaned up and the buildings need scraping and painting. The school budget will provide the paint if we provide the labor. I suggest some Saturday when the weather warms up a little more. It would be very nice if it could be a group effort, men, women and children. We could each bring a covered dish and have a picnic lunch and make it an all-day project. How many of you would be willing to help?"

Most of the hands went up.

"Very good. Thank you. Then I'll send a note home with the children to let you know which Saturday to come. The last thing I had in mind to discuss with you is transportation for the children who want to go on to high school next year. As you know, the high school bus only comes to the Owen Miller farm because of bad roads. That's much too far for our children to have to walk, so we need to think of some way that we can provide transportation for them. We only have three eighth graders this year, next year we'll have five. We need something, not just for this next fall, but for every year. Does anyone have any suggestions?"

"Kids don't need no high school, far as I kin see," spoke up one man.

"Actually, Mr. Horton," I said, "a high school education is becoming more and more important all the time. Without it, it's almost impossible to get a decent job these days."

"Don't need no high schoolin' to be a farmer or a carpenter."

"But what if you wanted to be something other than a farmer or a carpenter? What if, say, you wanted to be a lawyer or a doctor or a teacher? Besides, a high school education is very helpful to a farmer or a carpenter, too."

"Your own husband is a purty good carpenter an' he ain't had no high schoolin', has he?"

"One year, Mr. Horton, and he is a very good carpenter, but that's beside the point. The point is, every child should have the opportunity to go on to high school if he or she so desires."

"Girls don't need to go to school to learn how to get married an' have babies."

"There's more to life than getting married and having babies," I said, keeping the lid on my temper with difficulty. "An education can greatly enrich your life, whether you go on to get a job or not. Besides, suppose a girl got married and had babies and her husband died or was disabled? What kind of job could she get to support herself if she didn't have a high school education?"

"What's wrong with A.D.C.?"

"A.D.C. has its limitations, too, you know. The time might come when there are more dependent children than there is aid."

"What about Luther? He quit school an' he's bringin' in a paycheck ever' week, or so I hear."

"Luther is working for his uncle, and I wish him well, but he hasn't proven himself yet. Suppose he finds he hasn't the ability to be a builder? What kind of job would he get then? I hear they're laying men off at the sawmill. What about your sons? What kind of jobs are they going to get? What kind of future are they going to have without a high school education?"

I was beginning to be seriously annoyed, and evidently Davy was aware of it, for he spoke up, calmly and quietly, before Mr. Horton could speak again.

"Th' point is this, Joe," he said. "Th' kids that want to go on to high school oughta have th' chance to, their parents willin', o' course, an' they need a way to get to where th' bus comes. That's th' point we're discussin'."

"Yes, that is the point. In town, everyone just naturally sends their child on to high school. Out here, we just automatically don't, mainly because of the transportation problem. Our children are just as deserving of a high school education as the city children are. It's up to us to see that they get the opportunity. Anybody have any suggestions?"

No one spoke. I felt discouraged. I had known I would run into opposition on this issue, but at least I'd brought it to their attention. Perhaps they would think about it now.

"Let's all think it over and see if we can't come up with something concrete by the end of the school year," I said. "We can talk about it again then. That's basically all I had to talk about. Anyone else have anything they'd like to discuss?"

No answer, but some whispering between some of the mothers.

"All right. We'll call the meeting concluded. Please stay for some refreshments, and if any of you would like to talk to me personally, please feel free to do so. Thank you all so much for coming."

Ellen Hilton dispensed the coffee and Sue Proctor poured out the punch. Little groups of people gathered to talk among themselves. Davy came over and stood in front of me and grinned down at me.

"A glass of punch to cool you off, Teacher?" he asked low-voiced.

"I could choke him," I muttered under my breath.

"Wouldn't try it, if I was you. He's bigger'n you."

He turned as a woman approached us rather hesitantly. "How you doin', Emmy?" he greeted her.

"I'm okay," she said. "I was wantin' to talk to th' teacher."

"Anne, this here is Emmy Palmer."

"Hello, Mrs. Palmer," I said. "Let's go over here and sit down, shall we?"

I had placed two chairs off to themselves to the side of the room. Mrs. Palmer and I sat down and we talked about her children. When she got up to go, another mother took her place. I was kept occupied until the schoolroom was almost empty. Once Davy brought me a cup of coffee, and I was aware of him drifting around, talking to various ones.

The rather buxom young woman named Goldie Sutton always seemed to be in the general vicinity where he was, and she was one of the last ones to go, though she didn't wait around to talk to me.

The Story of Calvin's Birth

I was sitting at the kitchen table with my school work spread out before me. Davy sat in one of the rockers near the stove, reading the newspaper. The older Hiltons had gone to bed and the door into the living room was closed. It was a typical evening scene, and usually I found it peaceful and relaxing, but tonight I was restless, disturbed. I couldn't concentrate on the papers I was trying to correct. I sighed and Davy lowered his newspaper and looked at me.

"Somethin' botherin' you?" he asked.

"As a matter of fact, it is," I answered.

"You visited Granny Eldridge after school today?"

"Yes, I did."

"Well, at least you come home this time on your own two feet," he said with a grin. "Didn't she offer you no blackberry wine this time?"

"No, she didn't," I said a little irritably, "and if she had, I'd have had better sense than to drink it, I hope. You're not ever going to let me live that down, are you?"

"Nope. You was awful cute, staggerin' around, not able to even stand up without leanin' on me. That's when I started fallin' in love with you, I think. I was glad I got to pack you all th' way home. You was so soft an' warm in my arms."

"You may have enjoyed the experience. I didn't. It was so humiliating. I never did understand why she tried to get me drunk that way. But at least she didn't act hostile that time."

"But she did this time?"

"Not — not anything I could really put my finger on, just a feeling I got. She isn't feeling at all well, maybe that's what made her rather — irritable."

"An' maybe it's 'cause you're a Hilton now," Davy said softly. "Come on over here, Honey."

I rose and went around the table toward him, intending to sit in the other rocker, but he took my hand and pulled me onto his lap.

"Come on, stop frownin' an' give me a kiss," he commanded.

I leaned forward and gave him a quick peck.

"Call that a kiss?" he complained.

"It'll have to do for now. Davy, no! I've got other things on my mind right now."

He gave an exaggerated sigh. "Don't tell me th' honeymoon's over already," he said.

"Just because I want to talk? Davy, stop teasing and listen to me. I think since I am a Hilton now I ought to hear the story of Calvin's birth. I know you don't like talking about it, but I am family now, besides being the teacher, and it might help if I knew. It might prevent me making a terrible goof sometime, especially around your father, because I'm determined to make everyone stop treating Calvin as an outcast and accept him as the sweet little boy he really is."

"You can't make nobody do anything, Honey. If their mind is made up they're not going to."

"Perhaps everyone's mind isn't made up to that extent. Perhaps it's only because of the stand your father has taken that the others ignore him as if he isn't even there."

"Not ever'one treats him like that."

"No, but most of your family does. Won't you tell me, Davy?"

"I wasn't but sixteen when it happened," he said slowly, "an' nobody told me that much about it, but Dad was doin' a lot of yellin' an' Mom was doin' a lot of cryin' an' there was lots of talk goin' around. My sister was two years older'n me an' she'd been goin' around with Ben Eldridge for a couple years. They was s'posed to get married, but Ben couldn't find no work around here, so he decided to go to town to see if he could find him a job an' earn some money so they could get married. He couldn't seem to find nothin' here in town so he went on to Kansas City an' got him a job there. Well, it was a couple, three months 'fore he wrote Bertha an' told her that soon he'd have enough money an' he'd be sendin' for her. That was th' last anyone ever heard from him. A few weeks later Granny got a letter sayin' he was found dead in a alley with a bullet in his head. Never did hear who done it or why. Well, Bertha was just wild, went right off her head. I 'member that plain enough. It come out that she was about four months pregnant an' that's when Dad went right off his head. Kicked her outa th' house an' told her never to come back again. Mom tried to reason with him, but it didn't do no good. Bertha went to Granny an' she took her in for a few days, then Bertha went on to town and went to one of them homes for unwed mothers. She was goin' to adopt th' baby out but Granny talked her into givin' th' baby to her cause she said it was all she had left of her only son. Dad tried to stop her gettin' Cal, didn't want him here, but wasn't much he could do. Bertha was eighteen. So that's th' story, an' you can see why Granny ain't too fond of th' Hiltons."

"Yes," I said thoughtfully, "and now I'm a Hilton and she's transferred some of that hostility to me. I hope she doesn't do anything to hinder Calvin coming on to school."

"If she was gonna do that, she'd a done it before now."

"That's true. Thank you for telling me, Davy. At least now I know why she wasn't very friendly toward me today. I can't say I really blame her for it. Has your sister ever come back to see Calvin?"

"Couple times when he was real little. Course she didn't come here, but I think she managed to see Mom. It must be six, seven years since she was here, at least, far as I know."

"That's sad. Poor little Calvin, and your mother too. Too bad your father was so intolerant."

"You think what she done was right?" Davy asked, sounding a little hard.

"No, I don't, but people make mistakes, after all. If we have a daughter some day and she grows up and makes a mistake like that, are you going to cast her off, refuse to see her ever again, refuse to recognize your own grandchild?"

"I'm hopin' no daughter of ours'll ever make a mistake like that," he said.

"Every parent hopes that, but it still happens. It's been eleven years now. Why can't your father just let bygones be bygones? Besides, none of it is Calvin's fault."

Davy gave a little shrug. "Once Dad's made up his mind to somethin', ain't very likely he'll change it."

"Well, I'm not so sure of that," I said. "Anyone can change his mind if given enough reason. As of right now, I'm starting a campaign to make your father acknowledge Calvin as his grandson."

Davy groaned in helpless resignation, and put one hand up to cover his eyes.

"And," I continued, "I'm also starting a campaign to see that these kids out here get a chance to go on to high school. It's downright criminal to condemn them to a life of ignorance and poverty just because their parents didn't get to go to high school."

"You callin' me ignorant?" Davy asked, lowering his hand and looking at me with raised eyebrows.

"Oh, Davy, no! Of course not," I exclaimed quickly, contrite. "But it's different. You've more or less continued your education on your own. You read a lot. You have an inquiring mind, but so many of these kids will never pick up a book again after they leave grade school. And an education is becoming more important every day in our society. Look at Calvin's father. If he'd had a high school education, perhaps he'd been able to get a job closer to home and he and your sister could have been married and Calvin wouldn't have been treated the way he has."

"Course there's no guarantee of that either. A high school diploma wouldn'ta saved Ben from that bullet in th' head," Davy said.

"No, but can't you see what I mean, Davy? The day is past where you can just get by with the basics of education. You're an exception because you have a talent. You have a trade, but not everyone can do what you're doing. There's a wide field of activities, of jobs available out there, but there's more competition, too. Our kids need the ability to compete, or they're going to be left behind."

"Our kids?" he asked with a little grin.

"You know what I mean. The kids in this area, in this school."

"Oh. Thought maybe you was gonna surprise me with a announcement, or something."

"Davy, you know I want to teach at least another year. I have so many projects going, I need at least another year to get them halfway established."

He sighed again. "Ah, well," he said. "Jist remember with all this campaignin' you're talkin' about, you're married to one of these hillbillies now an' you gotta live here with us. Don't get yourself in too much hot water. These people make good friends, but they can make bad enemies, too."

"I know, Davy, and I'll try very hard not to offend anyone, but those two things I've just got to try to do. I feel very strongly about them."

"I was afraid of that. Well, I knew if I married you, life would be excitin', but that ain't exactly th' kind of excitement I had in mind," he said with wry humor.

"Davy, you — are you very much against it?" I asked troubled.

"It's gotta be dealt with sooner or later, I guess. It's jist always seemed easier to put it off. I kinda had a sneakin' suspicion right from th' very first that you was th' kinda teacher that don't put things off. Jist take it kinda easy, will you? I don't wanna have to go around knockin' heads together to defend my wife."

"I'll be careful, Davy. The people in general here have been very kind to me. I'll try to be kind in return, and you'll help me, won't you? You'll back me up?"

"Have I got a choice?" he asked plaintively.

"Thank you, Davy. You're sweet," I said reaching up and drawing his head down.

"A good teacher never stoops to bribery," Davy reminded me with sternness before he pulled me closer.

CHAPTER FOUR

Reminiscences

A few days later the weather turned warmer. March had come in like a lion; perhaps, as my mother-in-law Clemmy was fond of saying, it would go out like a lamb. It was still quite muddy under foot, but a few more days of nice weather would perhaps make it possible to schedule that Saturday clean-up day at school. I was anxious to get that done before the men of the area got too busy with their spring work. Not too many crops were grown here, mostly corn and hay, to provide winter feed for their own livestock, but once the men got busy plowing and planting, they wouldn't want to stop to help at the school clean-up.

When I walked into the kitchen after school that day, the room seemed overpoweringly hot. Clemmy had built up the wood fire and was starting supper. I was a little late. I greeted her and went on into the room Davy and I shared to deposit my books on my desk and hang my coat on the hook in the corner.

"Anything I can do, Clemmy?" I asked going back into the kitchen.

"You can set th' table," she answered. It was the answer I expected. It was about all she would ever allow me to do. Cooking was her job. She'd been doing it all her married life, and it would never have entered her mind to sit back once in a while and let me fix the meal. She wouldn't have known what to do with herself. She was an excellent cook. I sometimes felt a little anxious when I thought about having to compete with her cooking when Davy and I moved into our own house.

"Davy around?" I asked.

"He's off with Lewis somewhere, I think. Cuttin' wood, prob'ly."

"Rabbit or squirrel?" I asked looking at the pieces of meat she was flouring in a large enamel pan.

"Squirrel," she answered. "He got three this mornin'."

My father-in-law was big on hunting. He went almost every day and brought back rabbit or squirrel or sometimes some type of bird. Once he'd brought in a wild turkey and it had been delicious. He only killed enough for the day as there was no good way to keep the meat fresh for long. The cabin did not have electricity, therefore no refrigerator.

Potatoes were boiling on the back of the stove. A half gallon jar each of green beans and peaches sat on the nearby counter, ready to be opened. A large pan of cornbread was ready to go into the oven. Clemmy had things well in hand. She didn't need my help.

I took the tea kettle from the stove and poured hot water into the shallow enamel pan on the washstand. I diluted it with a dipper full of cool water from the bucket beside it and washed and dried my hands. I opened the door to toss the water outside and just missed Davy who was coming up the path.

"You on th' war path or somethin'?" he teased.

"No. I didn't know you were there. Clemmy said you were off cutting wood somewhere."

"I was," he said coming in and closing the door behind him. He bent and kissed me briefly on the lips.

"Fix me some wash water, will you?" he said, removing his jacket. "Supper sure smells good, Mom. I'm starved."

I refilled the wash pan and Davy began to wash his face and hands. As he was drying his face, he peered closely at himself in the mirror that hung from a nail on the wall.

"Whadda you think about me growin' a mustache?" he asked me.

"Depends on the kind of mustache you're talking about," I said amused. "Handlebar or paintbrush?"

He grinned and hung the towel back on its nail. He tossed his wash water out into the yard and went into the living room to sit and read the newspaper until supper was ready.

The sound of the squirrel frying in two big iron skillets filled the air as I took down the heavy plates and began to set the table. My father-in-law, whom I found it impossible to call anything but Mr. Hilton, came in, his pipe clenched between his teeth as usual. He removed his hat and hung it on a nail, nodded to me, ignored his wife, and went to join Davy in the living room. I looked after him and wondered how I was ever going to get better acquainted with him. I'd lived here now for six months, since the beginning of the school year, and we were still virtual strangers. He spent most of his time out hunting; about the only time I saw him was at supper. If I was going to convince him to acknowledge Calvin as his grandson, I was going to have to find some way to bridge the gap between us.

When supper was over and the dishes were done, I went out to the shop to be with my husband. He hadn't worked much in his shop in the evenings since our marriage, but now he was beginning to go out there quite often again. He was making some of the furniture that would go in our cabin. He was bent over smoothing a piece of wood with a hand plane when I came in. I went over to him and he straightened and put his arms around me.

"This is so much nicer than it used to be," he murmured in a little while.

"How do you mean?"

"When you come out here those few times before we was married, you was over there an' I was over here an' I wanted to hold you an' kiss you an' I couldn't. Now I can."

"Yes. It is much nicer."

He held me a few minutes longer, then released me.

"Got a lot more done though than I seem to be gettin' done now," he added, with a little grin.

"You spent so many of your evenings out here then."

"Had to. Had to stay away from you, at least I thought I did."

He picked up the plane and got back to work. I looked at the thin curls of shavings that were falling to the floor. I reached out and picked one up and held it in the palm of my hand.

"Davy, do you remember the time I came out here to talk to you about Luther and you put a little piece of shaving in my hand like this?"

"Um-huh."

"I took it in the house and wrapped it in a tissue, and put it in a drawer. I was very touched by it."

"You still got it?"

"Yes. I'm going to keep it always."

There was a few minutes of companionable silence between us.

"How is Luther doing?" I asked then.

"Okay, I guess. John's got him carryin' hod. So far he's stuck to it pretty good."

"Do you know that several times I used Luther as an excuse just to talk to you?"

"Did you?"

"Um-huh. Calvin, too. Davy, I don't think I've ever properly thanked you for helping me so much when I first came here. I didn't fully realize what a challenge it would be to teach a one-room, eight-grade country school. I couldn't have done it without your help. Thank you for that, Davy."

"You've already thanked me, lotsa times. Not in words maybe, but other ways. An' I'm glad I was here to help. Best thing that's ever happened to me was getting to know you."

"You mean it, Davy?"

He paused and looked up at me, his eyes narrowed. "Course I mean it," he said. "What kind question is that?"

I gave a little shrug and didn't answer, looking down at the curl in my hand.

"What Dad said about city girls botherin' you?" he asked shrewdly.

"It isn't just your dad. Other people seem to feel the same way."

"What other people?"

"Granny Eldridge and — Goldie Sutton."

"Goldie! Where'd you see her?"

"She came to school to pick up her brothers one day this week. She made a smart remark about women from the city not lasting long out here. I don't think I like her very well. I don't know what you ever saw in her."

He turned and grasped my upper arms and grinned down at me.

"Don't tell me I got a jealous wife on my hands," he said.

"I'm not jealous," I retorted. "I just made a simple statement of fact. She's not a very nice person."

"She never was anything to me," he said. "I jist went out with her that one time."

"And came back home with lipstick all over the front of your jacket."

He sighed. "Like I told you then, that was her idea, not mine. I jist walked her up to her door an' she threw herself in my arms. What's a guy s'posed to do? Couldn't help it she had lipstick smeared on half a mile thick. Besides, if we're gonna be talkin' about ol' girlfriends an' ol' boy friends . . . "

"Never mind," I said hastily. "We're getting off the subject."

"What was the subject?"

I looked up at him. He was smiling, his face gentle and a little amused. A reluctant smile tugged at my lips.

"I don't remember," I had to admit.

He laughed and drew me against him.

"Let 'em talk," he said against my hair. "Let 'em say whatever they want to say. You an' me got somethin' not too many people ever have an' they're just jealous. Don't let anything anyone says bother you, Sweetheart. We know better, don't we?"

"Yes, Davy."

"I'm s'posed to be makin' a table an' chairs here," he said releasing me. "You're distractin' me, Woman. Wanta have to eat your meals settin' on th' floor?"

"I wouldn't mind," I answered bemused.

"You in love or somethin'?"

"Must be."

He pushed me over against a table a few feet away.

"Stand over there an' let me get on with my work," he ordered.

I obeyed and he again bent over his work. I watched him in silence for a few minutes.

"Davy?"

"Hum-m?"

"Does Calvin know his mother is a Hilton?" I asked.

"I think you told him."

"I told him?"

"You told him I was his Uncle Davy once or twice."

"Oh, yes. I'd forgotten."

Silence again.

"Davy."

"Hum-m?"

"Do you have any suggestions about how I can get better acquainted with your father?"

"You mean get on his good side?"

"Yes."

"Gettin' ready to start on your campaign?"

"Yes."

"Don't know what to tell you. Dad's always been kind of a loner."

"I don't feel I know him very well at all, even after all this time."

"Felt th' same way myself 'til a few years back."

"How did you go about getting better acquainted with him then?"

"Didn't do nothin'. Jist learned to take him like he is."

"Oh."

I was silent then, digesting that. I was learning that although Davy didn't have much schooling, he had a down-to-earth kind of wisdom that was proving very helpful to me in dealing with these hill people. I found myself wondering sometimes if he wasn't actually much more intelligent than I was.

"You go to see th' Baxters today?" Davy inquired, glancing over at me.

"No," I answered. "I sent a note home with Billy yesterday saying I'd like to come. He brought a note back this morning saying, 'We don't want to talk about no high school for our Billy,' so I didn't go."

"You upset?"

"Not especially. I really didn't expect much else. Billy is not enthusiastic about school. But if I can't talk the other two into sending their children, I am going to be upset. Evelyn especially wants to go very badly."

"Her daddy didn't sound too encouragin' at that meetin'."

"No," I sighed. "I'm hoping I can help change his mind but I'm leaving him until last. I sent a note home with Todd this afternoon asking his parents if I can come after school tomorrow."

"You walkin'?"

27

"I think so. It isn't too far, is it?"

"No. Jist don't stay too long so you have to walk home when it's gettin' dark."

"You've said that before. What's the danger?"

"Jis ain't too smart to be roamin' around in these woods at night by yourself without a gun."

"Then maybe I'll drive to Todd's tomorrow."

"You'll be all right walkin' long as you get home 'fore dark."

CHAPTER FIVE

A Runt in the Bunch

*T*he next day it was sunny with temperatures in the fifties, so after school I walked home with Todd Johnson and his brothers and sisters. It was about a half mile away and I tried to sound Todd out about his parents' attitude toward high school, but he was noncommittal.

Mrs. Johnson met me at the door and was very hospitable, though rather nervous and self-conscious about having me in her home. Her husband rose from a chair to greet me. He was a big hulking man with a serious expression. They were plain, hard-working country people, their home sparsely furnished and unadorned, but clean and neat. Todd was the oldest of seven children. Five of them were my students. Two of them were preschool age. Their mother shooed the young ones off into the kitchen where their older brothers and sisters had naturally gravitated.

"Go have Nonie get you some milk an' cookies," she told them. "You want some coffee and a cookie, Miz Hilton? Seems funny callin' you Miz Hilton."

"I know. I have trouble remembering it myself," I said. "I'll have some coffee and cookies if you're going to have some."

"It's all ready. I'll jist bring it in." She bustled off into the kitchen and presently returned with a tray containing three cups of coffee and cream and sugar. One of her daughters followed her with a plate of cookies. She set the plate down on an end table and scurried back to the kitchen.

"Guess she's bashful 'bout havin' th' teacher here," said her mother with a small embarrassed laugh. "You take cream or sugar?"

"Just a little cream, please."

She poured a small amount of cream into one of the cups of coffee, stirred it, laid the spoon aside and very carefully brought the cup to me. When I took it from her and thanked her, she breathed a small sigh of relief. She presented me with the plate of cookies. I took one and she went over to prepare her husband's cup of coffee and took it to him.

"The cookies are delicious, Mrs. Johnson," I said, "the coffee, too."

She seemed pleased and took her own cup and went to sit down.

Mr. Johnson took a loud swig of coffee, lowered his cup and spoke.

"I want my boy to go on to high school, Miz Hilton," he said earnestly, leaning forward. "Mama tol' me what you said at that meetin' an' her an' me both believe it. We want our boy to have better'n we got. Ain't no kinda livin' to be made out here for so many of our young'uns, that's why they end up goin' off to town, but when they get there, sometimes they can't find jobs 'cause they got no high schoolin'. Me an' Mama made up our minds all our young'uns gonna go on to high school an' get a education."

"That's wonderful, Mr. Johnson. I'm so glad," I said with relief.

"Only how they gonna get there?" Mr. Johnson asked worried. "I work at th' sawmill. Gotta be there too early to have time to drive Todd to where th' bus stops an' Mama here can't be takin' th' little ones out that early an' leavin' th' others to get off to school on their own. Only got one team of mules an' I'll be needin' them myself. Don't see no way for Todd to get there, 'cept to walk an' you can't expect a kid to walk five miles mornin' an night, 'specially in th' wintertime. 'Sides, he ain't got th' time for that. He's got chores to do."

"I know it's a problem, but somehow we'll come up with a solution, Mr. Johnson. I'm just so glad you want to send Todd. We've got five months to figure out how we'll get him there."

"Th' other two plannin' on goin'?"

"Billy's parents have decided against sending him, unless they change their minds. Evelyn Horton wants to go very much, but I haven't been to visit with her parents yet. May I tell them that you're planning on sending Todd?"

"You can tell 'em, doubt it'll make any difference," Mr. Johnson said bluntly. "Joe Horton's 'bout the hardest headed man I ever run up against."

"They ain't got but th' one child, you know," Mrs. Johnson said. She had been silent through the discussion, letting her husband do the talking. I absent-mindedly reached for another cookie as I turned to her.

"Her mother is an invalid, I understand."

"Got a real bad heart," Mrs. Johnson said. "Evelyn does most of th' housekeepin' an' cookin'."

"Maybe that's why Mr. Horton seems so much against Evelyn going on to high school, but it will be a real shame if she doesn't get to."

I stayed about a half hour longer and we talked about the other children and how they were doing in school. Mr. Johnson was just as interested as his wife was, perhaps even a little more so. I was able to give them a good report. Their children were well behaved, in general, and cooperative, but it was just possible that young Andrew might need glasses. He didn't seem to see the blackboard too well and I had moved him to a desk near the front of the room. I recommended that they have his eyes checked when they had the opportunity.

When I rose to go, the plate of cookies was almost empty and I hadn't seen either one of them eat any.

"My goodness," I said. "I seem to have eaten nearly all your cookies."

Mrs. Johnson laughed. She was pleased. They both saw me to the door. I walked home, satisfied with my efforts and more determined than ever to win Mr. Horton over, too.

"Got somethin' to show you," Davy said when I reached home.

"What is it?"

"Jist come on an' you'll see."

He took me by the hand and led me out to the barn. He took me inside to the raised center area and with his finger to his lips, told me to look down into the other side.

A big white sow lay in the straw on her side, with a double row of tiny pink babies attached to her, nursing. I said, "Oh," and she rose with a loud woof and turned toward us as if to charge. I stepped back.

"I'm sorry," I whispered to Davy.

"She'll settle down again in a minute," he said low-voiced. "When she does, I want you to look close at th' babies."

"When were they born?"

"Jist this mornin'."

I peeked over the wall. The sow was settling herself down again with a lot of grunting and huffing.

"See anything different 'bout any of th' pigs?" Davy asked me.

"One of them is so little," I whispered. "It's getting pushed away by the others. It doesn't look very strong."

"In a litter this size there's nearly always a runt in th' bunch."

"How many?"

"Fourteen."

"The little one isn't getting to nurse. Will it die?"

"Probably. It'll get weak an' th' sow'll prob'ly eat it."

"Isn't there anything you can do?"

"Sometimes Mom takes th' runt an' puts it in a box behind th' stove in th' kitchen and gives it a bottle 'til it gets big enough to eat. Trouble is, it gets to be such a pet that way that when it comes time to butcher it or sell it, she gets a little upset."

"I suppose so."

"Stay here an' be quiet," he said, starting toward the feed bin.

"What are you going to do?"

"Give her some feed to distract her an' see if I can get ahold of that runt, 'fore she decides to eat it."

"Be careful."

He mixed water with the feed that he called shorts, and I watched as he poured it into the feeding trough. The sow rose with another grunt and left her babies to go eat. Davy worked his way around the outside of the pen, leaped lightly over, snatched up the small pig, and barely made it back over before the sow charged him woofing loudly. I put my hand to my heart and let out a sigh of relief. The baby pig was squealing and the sow was lunging against the side of the pen.

"Let's get out of here," Davy said. I followed him out of the barn.

Outside the barnyard, he held the baby pig out to me. "Want it?" he asked grinning.

I reached out and took it rather doubtfully and snuggled it against me. It began rooting around and grunting.

"Poor baby, it's hungry," I said.

"Mom'll have some baby bottles around somewhere. Let's go get one an' see if she'll take it."

Clemmy took down a four ounce baby bottle and filled it with milk and warmed it. She handed me an old towel to wrap around the pig, then handed me the bottle. The baby

33

pig took it eagerly, a rim of foam appearing around its mouth. I was seated in one of the rockers, bent over the pig and absorbed in watching it until it finished the bottle. I looked up at Davy.

"Am I supposed to burp it or anything?" I asked half comically. "It ate so fast I'm sure it swallowed a lot of air."

Davy chuckled. "Ask Mom," he said. "She's th' expert."

"I fixed up a box there behind th' stove. Jist lay it in there an' it'll sleep now."

The pig was already asleep, lying across my arm. I rose and put it carefully in the box and knelt there watching it. It slept on. I rose and went to wash up.

"I give it to Anne, Mom," Davy told his mother. "She'll take care of it, nights an' all, if you'll feed it durin' the day while she's gone."

His mother nodded and began to put supper on the table. I felt mixed emotions about having a baby pig in my care, but I made no objection.

CHAPTER SIX

Sue's Announcement

Davy and I were going to the Proctors for supper. They were a young couple about our age with two little girls in first and second grades. They had had a very hard time of it financially for the past few years, but Davy had given Lewis a job working with him, and now they were doing much better. They were a rather lonely couple, having moved to these hills just the summer before. Their home was very small and bare, but Sue kept it clean and made an effort to make it into a home. Coming to the country like this and having to do without modern conveniences had been quite hard on her, but she wasn't a complainer.

Lewis greeted us at the door. He was a smaller man than Davy and very quiet, but both Davy and I liked him very much.

"Hello, Lewis," I said. I reached up and gave him a little kiss on the cheek. He gave me a quick warm smile, then turned to Davy and held out his hand. Davy took it strongly in his own, but gave a mock sigh of melancholy.

"Guess th' honeymoon's over, if she's goin' around kissin' other men already," he said.

I made a face at him and went over to greet Sue with a similar light kiss. She reached out and gave me a quick hug, smiling shyly. She was blond and petite and very pretty. Today she was dressed in a soft blue dress I hadn't seen before.

"You look beautiful, Sue," I said. "New dress?"

"I bought it a few weeks ago," she answered.

I stepped back and looked at her more closely. Her hands went up almost instinctively to cover her stomach.

"Sue," I said uncertainly, "are you — ?"

"Yes," she said, furiously blushing. "Almost five months along already."

"It's easier in winter. I've had a coat on every time you've seen me."

"Davy, Sue's going to have a baby," I said happily, turning to my husband.

"I knew it," he said. He, in turn, bent and kissed Sue on the cheek. It surprised me a little; Davy was not a really demonstrative person in public.

"You knew and you didn't tell me?" I said, sounding a little peevish.

"Couldn't. She wanted to tell you herself."

"Well, I think it's wonderful news. I'm so happy for you. Are you hoping for a boy this time?"

"Yes. Lewis says it doesn't matter to him, but I want a boy."

"I hope you get it."

Lewis was taking my coat from my shoulders. He was a polite, mannerly man. I always thought he should have been an English nobleman.

"You've got a new dress, too," Sue said.

"It's an old one. I just don't have much opportunity to wear it here."

"It's nice. You look so pretty, but then you always do."

"She doesn't look very much like a backwoods country school teacher, does she?" Davy asked proudly.

"Not much," Lewis agreed.

"I don't have to go around looking like a country school teacher all the time, do I? Where are the girls?"

"I put them to bed early," Sue said. "I thought it would be nice if just the four of us could have dinner together."

"The table looks nice."

She had set it with a white tablecloth, a low flower arrangement in the middle, with candles on either side.

"What can I do to help?" I asked.

"It's all ready. Would you like a small glass of wine before we eat?"

Lewis poured out chilled wine and we sat and visited for a few minutes before we went to the table. Lewis pulled out my chair for me, and Davy quickly and rather clumsily pulled out Sue's for her. I lowered my head to suppress a little smile. I unfolded my napkin and put it across my lap and Davy followed my example. Sue set small bowls of salad before us and we ate and made polite conversation. When the salad was finished, she removed the salad bowls and set a filled plate before each of us and filled our coffee cups.

Dinner with Lewis and Sue was quite a contrast to supper at the Hiltons. I thought the change might be very good for Davy, but I didn't know if he was enjoying it or not. He was quieter than usual, being very careful of his manners, manners that were instinctive and effortless with Lewis. I felt very tender toward my husband and I reached under the table once to find and grasp his hand. We held hands then until Sue set dessert before us.

"Thank you, Sue, that was a treat," I said when we were finished. I began to help her clear the table while the men went on into the living room. Neither of them smoked, so they had another glass of wine and sat and talked. Sue wouldn't let me help with the dishes.

"It would be too much of a contrast, washing up in a pan of hot water at the table," she said with wry humor. I laughed.

"It was a lovely meal. I enjoyed it thoroughly."

"Do you think Davy did?" she said anxiously.

"I'm sure he did."

"Lewis thought he might not, but sometimes I miss the nice things so much. Life out here gets so — hum-drum sometimes. I mean, you work on a meal for an hour or two, then you plop it in the middle of a table, and in a matter of minutes, it's demolished. I've been wanting to have you over and serve a decent meal properly for a long time. I hope Davy didn't mind."

"Of course he didn't."

"Don't you miss the — nicer things sometimes?" she asked wistfully.

"Actually, I haven't thought too much about it lately. It bothered me at first that no one sat and conversed at the table at the Hiltons. They just sat down and got at the business of eating and when they were finished, they got up and left. But I guess I've gotten used to it. It doesn't bother me anymore."

"Are you going to do things differently when you get into your own home?"

"Perhaps. I'm hoping we can have a little more leisurely meal with at least some pleasant conversation, at the evening meal anyhow. But actually, I like my husband pretty well as he is. There's not too much about him I'd like to change."

"Oh, I didn't mean to criticize him," Sue said quickly.

"I know you didn't. I didn't mean to imply that you were."

"I like Davy very much. It's no exaggeration to say that he almost literally saved our lives when he gave Lewis that job. I'm so glad you decided to marry him and stay out here. I just — wondered if sometimes you don't get a little homesick for the city."

"Not yet. Perhaps I will when I've been here a few years, but it's still new to me and right now, very exciting. Davy's started on our house, you know, and he's already built some of the furniture. I'm so excited about getting into our own home."

"Yes, I'm sure you are."

I thought she sounded a little depressed.

"You'll soon have something better, Sue," I said. "Davy says Lewis is getting to be quite a good carpenter himself. Maybe some day you'll be able to build a home, too."

"I wish. Shall we go join the men? I'd love to stay here and talk, just the two of us, but this is supposed to be an evening for the four of us to get better acquainted. They'll be wondering what we're doing in here."

We went into the living room. She sat in a chair and I went over and sat beside Davy on the sofa. He reached for my hand.

"Get th' dishes all done?" he asked.

"No," I said. "We were just talking. We decided to save the dishes for Lewis."

"Thanks a lot," Lewis returned mildly. "Want a glass of wine?"

"No thanks."

"She tell you about her baby?" Davy asked Sue.

"Anne! You're not — ?"

"No, I'm not. It's a pig."

"A pig?" she echoed blankly.

"Yes. The sow had pigs and there was a runt in the litter, so Davy gave her to me."

"Oughta see her," Davy drawled. "She wraps th' pig in a towel and sets with it in th' rockin' chair and gives it a bottle. When it's done, she sets there and scratches its ears and rocks it 'til it goes back to sleep."

"It's not an 'it.' She's a girl and her name is Rosy," I said.

"Ever see anyone rock a pig?" Davy continued. "She even tried to burp it once."

Lewis chuckled and Sue looked slightly appalled.

"A pig for a pet?" she asked incredulously.

"A pig is actually a very intelligent animal," I replied.

"And they're clean, too, if you take proper care of them. They'll eat anything, of course, so if you want a clean pig around the house, you have to be selective about its diet."

She didn't know what to say. Her mouth was half open, her face filled with conflicting emotions. I gave a little giggle.

"Well, I've heard of everything now," she said. "A dog or a cat for a house pet, maybe, but a pig? You actually have it in the house?"

"In a box behind the kitchen stove."

"But you're not going to keep it in the house?"

"It'll go back out to the barn when it's old enough to fend for itself," Davy said.

"She's my pig," I said. "You gave her to me. I may decide I don't want her out in the barn with the other pigs."

"You gonna put a ribbon in her hair and put her on a leash and lead her around with you like a dog, I s'pose?" Davy said with lifted brow.

"I might. Pigs are very intelligent. They can be trained, you know."

"I never heard of a house pig," Sue said with awe.

"When you decided to become a country girl, you decided to do it up right, didn't you?" Lewis said humorously.

"Why not? At least maybe I'll be called something else besides 'teacher' around here. Maybe I'll become known as 'the pig lady'."

I giggled again.

"What'd you put in that stew, Sue?" Davy asked. "I think she's a little tipsy."

"I did put a little cooking sherry in it," Sue admitted, looking doubtfully at me.

"I'm not tipsy," I protested indignantly.

"Did you ever hear about th' time she went to visit Granny Eldridge when she first come out here?"

"Davy, don't you dare!" I exclaimed, sitting up very straight.

"Aw, come on, Honey. Jist among friends," he pleaded.

"You promised you wouldn't tell."

"That was 'fore we was married. I can tell now, can't I, since you're a respectable ol' married woman?"

"He'll have to tell us now that he's got us curious," Lewis said with a little smile. "What happened when she went to visit Granny?"

"Can't I tell 'em? They won't tell anyone else," Davy said grinning.

"You won't tell?"

Lewis said he wouldn't and Sue nodded.

"I hope you keep promises better than someone else I know," I said peevishly.

"Well, she went to visit Granny, see," Davy began, enjoying himself. "She was gonna try to get her to send Cal back to school. Granny offered her a little glass of wine an' they talked, an' then Granny filled her glass again an' they talked some more. When Anne got up to leave she couldn't see straight an' she couldn't walk straight. Granny sent Cal to get me an' I had to go get her an' pack her all th' way home. She hung onto me for dear life, almost strangled me a couple times. Think she was tryin' to get her hooks in me even then."

"I was not!" I said hotly, pulling my hand away and moving away from him.

Lewis chuckled. Sue was looking sympathetic.

"That must have been embarrassing," she said.

"It was. I didn't think I'd ever be able to hold my head up again."

"I kinda enjoyed it, though," Davy said.

"He laughed at me," I said. "And he also promised he wouldn't tell."

"We won't tell anyone," Sue promised seriously.

"I know you won't. Well, tell us when you're expecting this baby."

"It will be the end of July. I was wondering if you might be able to keep the girls while I'm in the hospital? You'll be in your own house by then, won't you?"

"We hope to be in it a couple of months, when school is out, and yes, I'll be happy to have the girls. You're going to have it at the hospital then?"

"Yes. I've heard there's a mid-wife out here, but I'm not brave enough for that. I want to be in the hospital where I'll be safe. We can't really afford it, of course, but — " she shrugged.

"We'll afford it," Lewis said quietly.

We stayed until quite late and never ran out of things to talk about. Sue told me about a family that Lewis had discovered living far back in the woods behind them. He had not met the family but had seen several children out in the yard, at least one of them school age. No one seemed to know who they were. Davy called it the old Henderson place and said it had been vacant for years. The family must have just moved in. I would have to check them out.

We talked of the school clean-up program that was scheduled for a week from Saturday and also of our house that Lewis was helping Davy build. The subject of Jim and Sally's rocky marriage was touched and skirted. Davy and Lewis talked a little farming and Sue and I talked about the last day of school program. Then we got up to go. It had been a pleasant, relaxing evening. I was very glad there was at least one young couple that Davy and I could be close to.

CHAPTER SEVEN

Jane Decker

*T*he next Thursday after school I drove the little Proctor girls home and stopped to visit for a few minutes with Sue. She gave me coffee, but I didn't stay long.

"I've come to check on the family you told me about last week, Sue," I said. "Can you tell me how to get there?"

"You go back to the main road and turn right. Then there's a little dirt road that goes off to the right. It'll be the first turn but if you're not careful, you'll miss it. It's pretty well grown up with weeds. I don't know if your car will make it or not."

"How far back is it?"

"Half a mile or more. We wouldn't even have known it was there if Lewis hadn't accidently gone that way looking for the cow one day."

"You say there are several children?"

"Lewis said he saw three, and at least one of them is school age."

"He didn't see the parents?"

"No. Just the children and a dog. It was a big dog, a German shepherd. It might be mean. I'm not sure you should go back there alone, Anne. Maybe you should wait until Davy can go with you."

"I can't expect Davy to fight all my battles for me."

"Then maybe I should go."

I grinned at her. "Five months pregnant and with two

small girls to protect, you'd be able to protect me, too?"
I teased.

"I guess I would be more of a hinderance than a help,"
she admitted regretfully.

"Thanks anyhow, but if I have to get out and walk, it's
better that I be alone. Don't worry about me. I'll be all
right."

"Will you drive by and honk or something when you
come back so I'll know you're okay?"

"You're as bad as Davy. All right, I'll do it. See you later,
Sue."

I got in my car and drove away, turning right on the
main road as Sue had directed. When I saw a break between
the trees on the right, I slowed and stopped. Was this the
road? I got out and went over to have a closer look. I saw
that it was a road of sorts, but it was narrow and overgrown
with weeds. At first I thought no one had traveled over it for
years, but when I looked closer I saw where the weeds had
been crushed down on either side by wheels of some kind.
I got back into the car and turned down the narrow road. If
someone else could do it, so could I.

I drove slowly, peering straight ahead over the steering
wheel. The weeds were tall enough that I wouldn't see a
stump or a log in the middle of the road if there was one.
I had to trust that whoever had gone ahead of me had made
it safely, and hopefully I would, too.

I came to a clearing and saw the house. It was small and
old and weather beaten. There was the usual outhouse and a
shed off to the side. There had once been a picket fence
around the yard but most of it was on the ground now.
Smoke was rising lazily from the chimney. The German
shepherd came bounding out to meet me, barking and
growling and lunging at the car, the hair raised up on the
back of his neck. I was glad I hadn't tried to walk in.

I drove up to the yard and stopped, and a tall, thin

woman came out of the house, the screen door banging behind her. She called sharply to the dog and he subsided and went to her, tail wagging and tongue lolling. The woman came on up to the car and bent down to look inquiringly at me. She was very plain, her face angular, her teeth rather prominent. Her hair was scraped into a bun at the back of her head. I rolled my window down.

"Hello," I said with a smile. "You've got a good watch dog there."

"Don't nobody come around without us knowin' it, at least," she replied. "You lost or somethin'?"

"No. I'm the teacher at Willow Creek Grade School."

"Oh," she said straightening.

"I've been trying to get around to visit everyone," I continued. "Is it all right if I get out? Will your dog let me?"

"He won't bother you. Go lay down, King."

The dog obediently went over and lay down near the fence. I got out and the woman stood looking at me rather uncertainly.

"I'm Anne Hilton," I said holding out my hand.

She took my hand briefly and her own was big and work worn and calloused.

"Jane Decker," she said. "Am I in trouble for not sendin' th' young'uns to school?"

"Not that I know of," I answered quietly. "As I said, I've been trying to get around to visiting everyone. I didn't know you were here until last week."

"Well, come on in, an 'scuse th' place. It ain't much but it's a roof over our heads, at least."

She led the way up to the house and I followed. The dog lay quietly, watching me with disinterest. I decided I was safe from him and focused my attention on the woman ahead of me. She was dressed in a cotton dress over which she wore a loose gray sweater. She wore long stockings and her shoes were broken down and cracked, but she was clean and her carriage was straight and erect. She was different from most of the local people I had met who had a tendency to slouch. There was no slow drawl to her speech either; her manner was blunt and forthright. I was intrigued.

The room she led me into was rather bare, but it too was clean. The furniture was sparse. There was a wood stove, an old sofa and rocker, and that was all. Two small boys were there, the youngest with his thumb in his mouth, both of them staring up at me.

"Set down," said my hostess, indicating the rocker. "Can't offer you anything to drink, 'less you'd want a glass of water."

"I don't want anything, thank you," I said, taking the seat she indicated.

"Johnny an' Jimmie, come on in here," she called, seating herself at the end of the sofa.

Two older boys came into the room, one of them with both hands taped together in front of him with what looked like masking tape. I wonder if they'd been playing cops and robbers.

"Th' oldest there is Johnny, he's eight. That's Jimmie, he's six. This'un here is Jerry, he's four, and th' little one is Josh. He's two."

"Hello, boys," I said. "I'm the school teacher, Mrs. Hilton."

"S'pose you've come about Johnny an' Jimmie not bein' in school," Mrs. Decker said. "I know they oughta be, but the plain truth is I ain't been able to send them 'cause they ain't got no decent clothes."

"I'm sorry to hear that. Has Johnny been to school at all?"

"Went through second grade, but when we moved out here I didn't bother sendin' him. It was too far for him to walk by hisself an' I didn't have any way of takin' him an' like I said he didn't have no decent clothes. Jimmie here shoulda started this year, too, but things was in a mess an'

I decided th' best thing was just to keep them home this year. Don't s'pose you agree with that," she ended bluntly.

"Being a teacher, of course, I feel school is important. You haven't lived here long then?"

"Since last summer. Moved here in July."

"I see. I wish I had known. Perhaps I might have been able to help in some way."

"Ain't nothin' nobody coulda done. There was jist things I had to get worked out. I'll be sendin' them next year. Ain't no point in sendin' them now."

"I suppose not, except it might help prepare them for next year."

"By next year I'm hopin' I'll have some money so I can buy them some decent clothes so's I won't be ashamed for them to be seen by other folks."

I had been watching the second oldest boy. Even though his hands were taped together he seemed to manage to use them. He had picked up a toy animal and was looking at it.

"Is — something wrong with Jimmie's hands?" I asked a bit hesitantly.

"No, nothin' wrong 'cept he can't seem to keep them outa things. You'll have your hands full with that one if you teach here again next year. Jimmie, come here," she commanded.

He went to his mother and stood before her.

"You ready to behave yourself now?" she asked.

He nodded solemnly.

"You gonna keep your hands off your brother's things an' outa th' cookie jar?"

Another solemn nod.

"All right then." She took hold of the end of the tape, unwound it and ripped it off. I couldn't help flinching for him, but he didn't blink an eye. I wanted to protest, but held my tongue as he went off into the next room. His mother wadded the tape up into a ball and set it on the floor beside her.

"He's tough, that one," she said, with simple pride. "You could whip him all day long an' he wouldn't let out a squeak. Jerry there cries if you even look at him cross-eyed. It ain't no small job tryin' to raise these four boys, I'm a tellin' you. Always somethin' goin' on. If one don't think it up, th' other'n does."

"You don't have any girls?" I said for want of something better to say.

"No, an' I don't know if it's a blessin' or a curse. Course I mighta been havin' a girl right now if I hadn't kicked my husband out when I did. Likely it'd be another boy though. You married?"

"Yes," I said. "Just recently, three months ago, in fact."

"You marry someone from around here?" she asked with bright interest.

"Yes. I married the youngest Hilton son. Do you know the Hiltons?"

"No. Heard th' name but don't know them. It workin' out?"

"My marriage, you mean?" She nodded. "It's working out very well," I said, a bit defensively.

"You ain't from these parts, are you?"

"No. I'm from St. Louis. I came out here to teach this school and that's when I met Davy."

"Well, I hope it works out better for you than it did for me. I was a country girl myself an' my husband was from th' city. When I married him I thought I was flyin' high. Wasn't long though 'til I was shot down with my tail feathers a draggin'. My mama tried to tell me country an' city don't mix but I wouldn't listen. Didn't take me long to find out she was right. He couldn't stand th' country and I couldn't stand th' city. Wouldn'ta been so bad in town, though, if he'd been able to keep a job, but seemed like, soon's he got a couple paychecks, he didn't want to work no more, an' in town you can't raise chickens so's your kids can have eggs and have a cow for milk an' a garden for vegetables. Ever'thing you get, you gotta buy an' if there ain't no money, you don't eat. That's why I decided it was time one of us got out 'cause I'd been comin' up with another kid ever' two years, and wasn't nothin' comin' in to feed them. So I kicked Jesse out, an' tried it on my own, but that didn't work 'cause hirin' a babysitter cost more money than I could make workin'. So I found this place an' me an' the' boys moved in. Had to borrey from my Daddy, but I was able to get some garden in an' I got a few chickens an' a goat an' a dog an' looks like we made it through the winter. I'm gonna plant a big garden an' put up enough vegetables for th' winter. I'll get more chickens an' maybe be able to sell some eggs. I'll try to get work choppin' an' pickin' cotton, or pickin' corn or whatever's around to be done. I'm a pretty good farm hand. All I knew when I was growin' up. What I really want to do though is raise hogs."

"Raise hogs?"

"Yes, this is a good place for hogs. If I can get ahold of a good sow or two reasonable an' have a couple litters ready to sell by fall, we'll be eatin' high on th' hog as th' sayin' goes," she ended with a little chuckle at the joke she had made. "I'll be able to get some decent clothes for my boys an' they can go to school, same as th' rest of th' kids. Don't happen to know where I could get ahold of a good sow cheap, do you?"

"I don't, but my husband might. His sow just had babies a week ago."

"Have a good size litter?"

"Fourteen. He gave me the runt and I'm taking care of it until it's a little bigger."

"No kiddin'?" she said, seeming pleased. "You're actually takin' care of a baby pig, a city girl like you?"

"I'm enjoying it. I'm going to have a hard time giving it

up when the time comes." I rose and she rose with me. "I'd better be going," I said. "It was very nice meeting you, and I wish you success in your ventures."

"It was right nice of you to come. Stop in again sometime."

"Thank you. Oh, that reminds me, we're having a get together at the school Saturday to clean up the yard and do some painting. We'll have a picnic lunch at noon, and everyone is invited. Perhaps you and the boys would like to come and get acquainted."

She shook her head regretfully. "I'd like to, but like I said, we ain't got no decent clothes to appear in public."

"Your clothes wouldn't matter. Everyone will be dressed in old work clothes anyhow. If you don't have transportation, perhaps the Proctors could come and pick you up. They live just a mile or so from here."

She shook her head again. "Ain't hardly seen no one all winter, 'cept my brother that comes out to bring us groceries an' things ever' couple weeks. I let myself go, an' I don't want people starin' and feelin' sorry for me. I'll be ready to meet a few people by th' time school starts again maybe. By that time, things oughta be better, but I thank ya anyhow for askin'."

"Well, if you change your mind, you'd be welcome. Good-bye, boys. Perhaps I'll see you again soon."

She went out to the car with me and we said good-bye. Another poverty case, I thought, but somehow this one was not so discouraging. Jane Decker was a fighter. She'd pull herself up by her own bootstraps, if necessary, and lick her four boys into shape at the same time. She intrigued me. I'd have to tell Davy about her and see if he had any suggestions for her about getting started in the hog-raising business.

CHAPTER EIGHT

Tom's Snub

"**A**in't you got any ol' clothes you can wear?" Davy asked eyeing me dressed in blue jeans and a long sleeved red checkered blouse. "You'll ruin them clothes if you do any paintin'."

"Not here I don't," I said looking down at myself. I was remembering what Jane Decker had said about not having any decent clothes to wear in public, and thought perhaps Davy was more concerned about my being overdressed than he was about the possibility of ruining my clothes. I should really be dressed more as he was, in faded and paint splattered jeans and shirt.

"I really haven't had an opportunity to put much wear and tear on these jeans, you know, since your parents don't approve of pants for women," I said a little tartly.

"I got a undershirt here somewhere," he mumbled, pulling open a drawer and rummaging in it. He held up a white undershirt. It was splattered with dried gray paint and was rather rumpled.

"You want me to wear this?" I asked, holding it up rather distastefully.

"Put it on over your clothes," he said. "It'll maybe keep you from gettin' too dirty."

"Okay."

I pulled it on over my head. It hung down halfway to my knees, and the short sleeves came to my elbows. I looked up doubtfully at my husband and he grinned at me.

"Well?" I asked.

"Turn around."

I turned around and he gave a chuckle and swatted me on the rear.

"You look cute," he said.

"I'm sure I do," I said, starting to take it off.

"Leave it on," he said.

"Why?"

"It'll protect your clothes."

"If I'm not concerned about my clothes, why should you be?"

"Man's s'posed to be concerned 'bout protectin' his wife, ain't he?" he asked evasively.

I put my hands on my hips and regarded him silently for a minute.

"You really want me to appear in public like this?"

"You look fine," he said.

"Why, Davy?"

" 'Cause."

" 'Cause why?"

" 'Cause I don't want any of th' men fallin' off ladders 'cause they can't keep their eyes off you," he retorted.

I thought about that for a minute. "I don't know whether to be flattered or insulted," I said. "Do you think I'm immodestly dressed? Are you against women wearing pants, too?"

"No, but nobody's used to you wearin' pants around here, an' most of th' women will be wearin' dresses. Ain't too many of 'em shaped th' way you are either."

I felt half exasperated, half pleased. I gave a little shrug. "If you want me to wear this thing, then so be it," I said.

"I'll go out an' hitch up th' mules," he said.

When he had gone I went over to the mirror and regarded as much of myself as I could see. I had earlier put on lipstick. Now I took a tissue and rubbed it off. A little smile played around my mouth as I took a comb and parted my hair all the way down the back. Quickly I plaited my hair in two short braids and secured them with rubber bands. Then I went out into the kitchen where Clemmy was preparing some food for our picnic lunch. She looked rather startled for a minute, then went placidly on with her work.

"You've gone to a lot of trouble, Clemmy," I said.

"It's 'bout all I could do to help," she returned.

Impulsively, I hugged her. "And it's a big help, too, Clemmy. Everyone will have a good feed. We ought to do this sort of thing more often."

I heard Davy drive up in front of the house with the mules and wagon. I picked up one of the boxes of food Clemmy had prepared and carried it out. I put it in the back of the wagon with the cans of paint Mr. Hooper had supplied, and posed before my husband.

"Well?" I challenged. "Is this the effect you wanted?"

He jumped down to the ground and stood looking at me. "You look like a little kid," he said. His eyes narrowed. "Except — " he qualified.

"Oh, there's no pleasing you," I said, flouncing away.

"You're wrong there," he said softly, catching up with me and putting his arm around my waist.

We took the rest of the food out to the wagon. Clemmy also supplied a large tablecloth and some cleaning rags. Davy had already thrown a couple of ladders in the wagon, along with a rake, sawhorses and boards and several cans and paint brushes. When we had it all loaded, Davy climbed into the wagon and hauled me up after him.

"Wanna drive?" he asked, holding the reins out to me.

"Oh, I don't know, Davy."

"If you're gonna be a country girl you oughta learn how to drive a team of mules hitched to a wagon."

I took the reins from him and he clucked to the mules and we were off.

"Nothin' to it," Davy told me. "Jist hold th' reins loose an' let th' mules follow th' road. Don't pull to th' left or right, less you want them to turn. Now, ain't that easy?"

"I should have had these mules when I went to see Mrs. Decker Thursday."

"There's lotsa times when it's best to use the mules 'stead of a car or truck. You can use them when you need to, they'll be safe. Mules ain't like horses. They won't go chargin' off through th' woods for no good reason. They're plodders, like th' rest of us hillbillies. They're slow but they get you there."

"Have I ever called you a plodder?"

"No. Not to my face, at least."

"Davy are you implying — ?"

"Ain't implyin' nothin'. Jist kiddin'. Pull on the right rein a little bit up here where th' road turns. There! You're doin' fine."

There were already several people in the school yard when we arrived. I swung the mules around and pulled up beside another wagon with something of a flourish. Jim Baker was there and set up a noisy cheer for my efforts. Davy was grinning and I felt myself flush.

"Show off," he hissed in my ear as he swung me down from the wagon.

"You trainin' her right, Davy?" Jim bantered, coming up to greet us. "Got her paintin' shirt on too, I see."

"That's what we're here for, isn't it?" I returned. "Did Sally come?"

His face almost instantly sobered and I was sorry I had mentioned his wife.

"She's cookin' up some food," he said. "She'll be here a little later. Well, Davy, who's in charge of this mess, you or th' teacher here?"

"Don't know that anyone's in charge," Davy said, beginning to unload the wagon. "Where you want th' table set up, Honey?"

"Over there, I think," I answered, pointing.

"No one's in charge, huh?" Jim said, his grin very much in evidence again.

Davy thrust a sawhorse at him. "Make yourself useful," he ordered.

We set up the sawhorses with boards across them for a table for the food the women would be bringing. I spread Clemmy's tablecloths across them while the men began to set up ladders and pour paint into cans.

More people arrived. The table was soon loaded with food, the school yard scattered with children. It took awhile to get things organized, but soon several men were painting, some standing on the ground, some on ladders. I would have preferred to paint but every time I took up a paint brush some man removed it from my grasp and took over. I had to be content to organize the younger children into picking up sticks and raking leaves and pulling weeds in the fence row. Most of the women just stood near the table talking. They had prepared the food, so I supposed they considered that enough.

It was close to lunch time when I noticed a small boy crouched down outside the school yard, peering through the fence. I knew it was Calvin. He was shy around crowds of people. It had only been after weeks of effort that I had finally succeeded in persuading him not to disappear at recess. I went over to where he was.

"Hello, Calvin," I said.

He rose and looked over the fence at me.

"Come in and join us."

He hesitated, his eyes going to Tom and Brad Hilton, two of Davy's brothers who were bent over, one pouring paint into another can, the other holding the can. He seemed to sense that he might not be welcomed by them. His eyes came back to me.

"You can work with me," I said. "I need some help raking the leaves together in piles. Come on, Calvin."

He went around to the gate and came through. We walked back together. I gave him a rake and a few instructions and he set to work, glancing up often to make sure I was still there.

When one of the men called "eatin' time", I took Calvin by the hand and we went to stand in line to wait our turn to wash up at the pump. Tom Hilton was working the pump handle with one hand, the other hand on his hip, joking a little with each person who bent to wash his hand and urged him forward. Just as the man in front of us finished and stepped away, Tom bent and took a drink himself, washing first one hand, then the other.

"Time someone else had a turn at th' pump handle," he said and turned away. It was a deliberate snub. I was suddenly furious. I stepped up to the pump.

"You first, Calvin," I said keeping my voice steady with an effort. "I'll pump for you, then you can pump for me."

He washed his hands then changed places with me. I managed to smile at the next person in line.

"Next," I said. I again took Calvin by the hand and led him over to the table.

Several of the women were behind the table serving, including Tom's wife Ellen. I watched her rather closely as Calvin and I approached. She was a quiet, pretty woman, in her thirties and the mother of five children, four of them my students. My face felt stiff with anger, but I managed to return her smile when I stood before her.

"A big spoon of baked beans or a little one?" she asked me.

"Little," I said.

"Where's Davy?"

"Back there somewhere. Calvin and I were hungry and decided not to wait for him."

"Big dip or little dip, Calvin?" she asked pleasantly.

56

Well, at least she wasn't a hypocrite, I thought. I'd like to get my hands on that husband of hers. I'd wring his neck, or at least give it a good try.

Calvin and I went and sat on the ground in the general vicinity of everyone else and began eating. I looked around for Davy and saw him off to the side talking to Jim. Jim's head was bent and Davy's hand was on his shoulder. Presently Jim walked over to his wagon, got in, and drove away. I looked around; evidently his wife hadn't shown up as he had expected. Perhaps he was going after her. Calvin and I were almost finished eating when Davy joined us. I was bursting to tell him how his brother Tom had acted, but one look at his face made me refrain.

"Something wrong?" I asked him in a low voice.

"'Fraid Jim's got real trouble with Sally," he said with a sigh. "She didn't want to come today an' they had a quarrel. He ordered her to cook up some food an' bring it before noon an' she didn't. He's pretty upset."

"Oh. I'm sorry."

"Tried to talk to him, but don't think it done any good. He's jist in th' mood to tear into her good when he gets home, an' that ain't gonna help matters none."

"No."

"Feel sorry for him. She don't even try to please him. Says she hates it here an' don't see why she should have to do anything she don't wanta do. Actin' like a couple spoiled brats if you ask me, but she's worse'n he is. Least he's willin' to make some effort. She ain't."

"It's too bad," I said.

"Yeah. Well, ain't nothin' much we can do about it," he said. He seemed to make an attempt to shake off his mood and spoke more cheerfully.

"It's lookin' good, ain't it?" he asked, his eyes on the schoolhouse.

"Yes, it is. Very nice."

"Oughta be done in a couple hours. Some of th' people'll probably be leavin' after lunch. Maybe you oughta thank'em for comin' 'fore they all get scattered again."

"Oh yes, I wasn't thinking. Thank you, Davy."

I stood up where I was and raised my voice.

"While we're all here together, I'd like to thank you so much for coming today," I said. "Together we've been able to accomplish a lot in a few hours. It's looking very good. The children and I are very grateful to all of you."

I had a sudden crazy impulse to add some derogatory remark about my brother-in-law, Tom, so I closed my mouth and sat down quickly. There was some clapping and a few yays in response to my little speech.

"I'm proud of you, Honey," Davy said. "Lotsa people been comin' up an' tellin' me what a great little person you are. Some of 'em even said they liked your shirt."

"That is a compliment indeed," I said, but I was touched. I put my hand through his arm and leaned my head against him for a minute.

"Here. None of that, Teacher," one of the men called. " 'Member, you're on school property."

Davy grinned but I felt myself blush and quickly released him.

"How is your grandmother today, Calvin?" I asked to cover my embarrassment.

"She's okay," he answered.

"Is she feeling better, now that the weather is warmer?"

He nodded.

"Does she know you're here, Calvin?"

A negative shake of his head. I worried sometimes about the amount of time he spent wandering around alone. Granny didn't seem to keep a very close watch on him. Perhaps that was all right, but there was always the possibility of accident or injury, and who would be there to help him? I found myself wondering if Tom might have at one time or another frightened or threatened him. Calvin was always on guard, wary when Tom was around, but then he acted the same way around any of the Hiltons, except Davy and Clemmy. I told myself that probably Granny had let some of her own hostility toward the Hiltons spill over and that was what was affecting Calvin.

"Let's fix up a plate for your grandmother," I said getting to my feet and holding out a hand to Calvin. "There's plenty of food left over."

"We're going to fix up a plate for Calvin to take to his grandmother," I told Ellen. "Is there an empty pie plate or something like that?"

"There's this aluminum one."

"Oh, good. That will be fine. Then Granny can just throw it away when she's finished, Calvin. We'll just put a little of everything on it."

Ellen helped me fill the plate. Out of the corner of my eye I saw Tom watching us. When Calvin started off with the plate, Tom's two sons, third and fourth graders, ran out, evidently playing tag or chasing each other. I took a few quick steps and caught up with Calvin.

"I'll just walk along with you part way," I told him. I raised my voice. "Chad and Tommy, go play on the other side of the school house. You might accidentally run into someone over here."

They stopped. They looked at me, then back at their dad.

"Go on," I said firmly but pleasantly.

They obeyed. I was their teacher and they were really pretty well-behaved children. I gave credit to Ellen for that. I walked to the fence with Calvin, opened the gate, and smiled at him as he went through.

"Good-bye, Calvin," I said. "Thank you for helping with the raking. I'll see you Monday morning."

I went back to join the others. Some of them were

drifting back to work. Tom was standing watching me. I would have like to have gone up to him and slapped that face that so much resembled my husband's, but I was a little afraid of Tom. I didn't want to antagonize him too much. Not because he was my brother-in-law now but because I was afraid he might somehow take it out on Calvin. I grabbed a rake and began to rake furiously.

CHAPTER NINE

City Girls

"**T**hought you needed another drivin' lesson," Davy said to me.

I had just dismissed school for the day and when I came out he was there waiting for me with the mules and wagon. I put my books inside the wagon, took his hand, put one foot on the step and he hauled me up. He handed me the reins. I clicked my tongue and the mules started up.

"Hey, it worked," I said, happily surprised.

"You're learnin'," Davy said.

"Soon I'll be tooling all over the countryside in my horse and buggy, just like the heroines in the novels back in the good old days."

"Mules an' wagon, not horse an' buggy. It ain't the same thing," he corrected, but his voice lacked its usual twist of wry humor.

"Something wrong?" I asked glancing quickly at him.

He didn't answer.

"Turn to th' right up here when you get past that clump of trees," he said.

"But there's no road."

"Then we'll make our own road."

I obediently pulled on the right rein and the mules swerved and started down a long incline.

"Are we going to our cabin?" I asked.

"Yes."

"Have you been working on it today?"

"Un-huh, me an' Lewis. Wanted you to see what all we got done."

"Did you run into some trouble?"

"No trouble. Got most of the foundation dug an' th' hole for th' septic tank. Got th' pump house built, too."

"You've been busy then," I said. Probably he was just tired and that accounted for his unusual soberness, I thought.

I could see the cabin site now as we approached. I felt a little stir of excitement as I drove closer and stopped the mules in the shade of a large oak tree.

Davy jumped down and reached up to help me. He lifted me down with a hand at either side of my waist, then stood there holding me and looking intently at me.

"What is it, Davy?" I asked quietly.

"Nothin'."

"Something's bothering you. I wish you'd tell me."

He was silent. I waited.

"Jim was by today. He was pretty upset," he said then.

"Oh."

"Him and Sally's busted up. She's left an' went back to her folks."

"I'm sorry. I had hoped they'd be able to work their problems out."

"He asked me if I wanted to buy his house, furnishin's and all."

"What did you say?"

"Told him we needed to be here close to Mom an' Dad."

"It sounds — terribly final, if he's trying to sell the house."

"Yes."

"I'm sorry, Davy. It's upsetting news, I know, especially for you. You and Jim have been friends for a long time. You say he was pretty upset?"

"Yes. Seemed to think — "

He paused and gave his head a little shake as if to clear it. His hands dropped from my waist to hang loosely at his sides.

"He seemed to think what?"

"Nothin'!"

"It must have been something. Maybe if you told me and we could talk about it, you'd feel better."

His eyes came back to me, somber gray and troubled.

"You haven't even kissed me, Davy," I reminded him quietly. "Are you upset about something?"

"No."

He pulled me into his arms and held me tight, his face against my hair.

"Did he by any chance suggest I might some day contemplate something along the same line as Sally?" I asked.

He seemed to stiffen momentarily, but he made no answer. I had guessed it then.

"Davy, I'm not Sally and you're not Jim," I said gently. "The situation is not the same at all. Just because we're both from the city doesn't mean I feel the same way about the things that she does."

"No, but — "

"But what, Davy?"

"I been thinkin' 'bout how I rushed you into marryin' me. You wanted time to think, time to go back to th' city for a while but I wouldn't let you."

"So?"

"So, I was thinkin' maybe someday you'd resent that. Maybe someday, after th' newness wears off, you'll get lonesome for th' city an' wish you was back there again."

"I'm not going to tell you I won't ever get homesick for the city, but there's nothing says I can't go back once in a while for a visit is there? Davy, I'm not Sally. I like it here. Sally never did. I love you and I love the life we're building together. As for rushing me into marriage, you did, of course. But you should know by now that I definitely have a mind of my own. You couldn't have rushed me into marriage if I hadn't wanted to be rushed."

He drew back and looked at me.

"You mean it?"

"Of course I mean it. I thought we weren't going to let what other people say bother us."

"I know, but I got to thinkin' about what Jim was sayin' an' I guess I got a little scared. You're so sweet an' pretty. Ever'one likes you, th' men 'specially. Even Jim, broke up as he is, is still halfway in love with you, I think. You coulda had any man you wanted."

I had to smile. "You're prejudiced, Davy, but even if that's true, what does it matter? I have the man I wanted."

"You're sure?"

"Davy, for heaven's sake! You know I love you."

"I know you do now, but will you, say ten years from now?"

"Of course I will, unless you become an ogre or some-thing. Davy, do you think I ought to doubt your fidelity just because your brother Tom doesn't know the meaning of the word?"

"No!"

"Then why are you doubting my loyalty to you, just because of what Sally has done and just because we both happen to be from the city?"

"I'm not. I jist — "

"You're just what?"

"Nothin'. I'm sorry."

"Well, I should hope so. The very idea."

I put my hand up to his cheek and smiled at him. He bent and kissed me, holding me close. I slid my arms up around his neck and gripped him tight.

"Davy, I love you," I said.

"I love you, too. Too much, I guess. Sometimes it scares me."

"I know."

"You too?"

"Yes. Sometimes. Other times it just makes me so very happy. Are you happy, too, Davy?"

"Yes. I think I must be th' luckiest person in the whole world."

"And I think maybe I am. Come on, Davy. Show me what you've been doing here today. It seems to me it's moving along really fast. We'll be in our own home before we know it."

He released me and led me over toward the foundation he had been digging.

"Once th' foundation is laid and John an' his crew comes out to help, you'll be surprised at how fast it'll go up," he said with enthusiasm. "Come over here an' see this."

He was enthusiastic and happy again. I thought just possibly we really were the two luckiest people in the world.

A New Home for Rosy

The electricians had been out to run a wire to the cabin. Davy and Lewis were working on the cabin every day and now they were nearly ready for John Hilton and his crew to come in and put the walls up. Davy had already hauled home the logs he and Lewis had felled during the winter months and had taken them to the sawmill to be cut and treated. Once the main structure was up, Davy and Lewis would finish the inside themselves. It was toward the end of April, so it looked as if we'd be able to move in by the time school was out. Davy and I were both looking forward to that and it was just possible the older Hiltons were, too. I got along well with Davy's parents, but our living with them naturally created more work for Clemmy. I tried to help, but there was not a whole lot that she allowed me to do.

Early in April Davy had asked me if I would help his mother with the garden. He usually helped her but he was too busy this spring. Next year we would have our own garden, but there wasn't time to get the new ground in good enough shape for planting this year, and Clemmy had a big enough garden spot for both of us.

Now I stood at the edge of the garden and looked with pleasure at the rows of green that marked the length of the garden. We had planted potatoes, onions, radishes, peas, carrots, beets and spinach. Clemmy identified each row for me and I tried to remember for future purposes what each kind looked like. It was a Saturday morning and the sun was warm, the breeze gentle and fragrant.

"What are we planting today, Clemmy?" I asked.

"Couple rows of beans," she answered, hoe in hand. "It's a little early for them. Beans is delicate, so we'll jist plant a few. We'll plant a few more beets an' some sweet corn an' zucchini an' cucumber. That'll be 'bout all for today."

"All right. Shall I make the rows or plant the seeds?"

"I'll make th' rows. Don't have to do quite so much bendin' at that."

We worked for a couple of hours and it was very pleasant. I enjoyed the contact with the warm earth, and the warmth of the sun on my bare head and arms. Clemmy was patient with me, showing me what to do and answering all my questions. In the distance I could hear the hammering and occasionally the drift of their voices as Lewis and Davy worked. I found myself frequently looking in that direction and dreaming of my life there with Davy.

When we finished planting, Clemmy went in to start lunch and I started doing my laundry on the side porch. I didn't have a lot of it. Clemmy did all the sheets and towels and Davy's work clothes, but it kept me busy until lunch time. Clemmy used lye soap and a washboard, but I used a gentle laundry soap I had bought in town and what rubbing I had to do, I did between my hands. I was hanging the last of the clothes on the line when I saw Davy and Lewis coming in for lunch. I walked a short distance to meet them.

"Hi, Sweet," Davy said, with a quick kiss and an arm around my waist.

"Do you know the first thing we're going to buy when we get in our house?" I returned.

"What?"

"An electric washing machine. Look at these hands," I said, holding them out. "Hello, Lewis."

"Hello," he said with his quiet smile.

"How's Sue?"

"She's well. She wanted me to tell you she made the acquaintance of Jane Decker yesterday."

"Oh really?"

"She and the boys walked over to the house. Stayed a couple hours."

"How did Sue like her?"

"Guess she takes a bit of getting used to, but Sue said by the time she left, they were getting along fine."

"Has she started up her hog business yet?"

"No, but she still intends to, according to what she said."

"I'm tempted to give her Rosy. Davy says I've got to put her back out with the other pigs. She won't stay in her box anymore."

"Blame pig's under foot ever' time you turn around," Davy grumbled. "Shoulda been put back in th' barn couple weeks ago."

"He's jealous," I told Lewis. "He thinks I spend more time with the pig than I do with him."

"She's got th' thing so blasted spoiled, starts squealin' to beat th' band ever' time she walks in th' kitchen."

"I'm afraid she's annoying Clemmy, too," I said, "but I don't like putting her out with all the other pigs. They're all bigger than she is and I'm afraid they'll push her around."

"Then give her to your friend Jane Decker," Davy said in faint exasperation.

"May I?" I asked. "I know pigs are valuable, but I couldn't stand the thought of having her sold or butchered. If I gave her to Jane, she'd keep her to have babies, and I could go and see her sometimes."

Davy snorted and Lewis chuckled. We had reached the house and Davy held the door for me to enter first. The minute I was inside squeals and banging came from the box behind the stove. There was a thump and Rosy came rushing toward me. I bent and picked her up and held her against me, scratching behind her ears and talking to her.

"That pig has gotta go," Davy said in disgust. "Today, if not sooner."

"Can I really take her to Jane?"

"Soon as lunch is over, an' with my blessin'," he answered.

So after lunch I changed my clothes, put Rosy in her box and carried her out to the car. I drove to Jane Decker's house and again was met by the big German shepherd dog. I had a moment's terror thinking of what might happen to Rosy if the dog got hold of her. If I'd remembered about the dog, I might not have been so eager to give Rosy to Mrs. Decker, but I was here and I couldn't turn back now.

The screen door opened and banged shut and Mrs. Decker was coming out to the car as she had done the first time. Rosy was being very noisy and unruly in her box beside me on the front seat.

"Go lay down, King," Mrs. Decker ordered the dog. She stooped to look in the car window.

"My goodness," she said. "What's all th' racket?"

I opened the box and lifted Rosy out. She made little eager grunting sounds and appeared to be trying to kiss me on the chin. I held her off.

"You takin' her around visitin' with you now?" Mrs. Decker asked in awe.

"No. Rosy, for heaven's sake! Will the dog attack us because of all this noise if we get out?"

"King wouldn't attack nothin'! He's all bark, an' no bite," she replied.

I wasn't sure I believed her, but I got out of the car and held Rosy and scratched her ears, so that she quieted in my arms.

"Ain't that somethin' now," Mrs. Decker marveled, reaching out and scratching Rosy's other ear. "You got her plumb spoiled."

"I know I have. That's why Davy says I've got to get rid of her. I refuse to put her out with the other pigs, she's still so little. I wondered if you'd take her."

"She's a fine, healthy lookin' little pig. How much you wantin' for her?"

"Oh, I don't want any money for her. I just want her to have a good home, and I don't want her butchered or taken to market. You said you wanted to raise hogs, so I thought if I brought her to you, you'd keep her to have babies, and I wouldn't have to worry about her getting eaten."

"You wanta give her away?"

"Yes, but you have to promise you won't sell her or eat her if I do."

"Your husband know about this?"

"Yes."

"An' he's willin' you should give her away?"

"She's mine. He gave her to me and I can do with her as I please. As long as I get her out of the house, and today," I added ruefully.

"Well, ain't that somethin'," Mrs. Decker marveled, still rubbing Rosy's ear. Rosy was about to go to sleep. "Sure I'll take her if that's what you're a wantin'."

"Your dog won't bother her?"

"That dog wouldn't bother a flea. 'Course I'd jist as soon you wouldn't spread that around."

"And you'll keep her and let her have babies and not sell her?"

"Sure I'll keep her. She looks like she'll make a fine little mama someday."

I handed Rosy over and she was perfectly content to leave me. I felt a little pang of jealousy.

"I still give her a bottle mornings and evenings, though I don't suppose she really needs it now," I said.

"I got a bottle, if you want her fed that away awhile longer. Will you come in th' house?"

"I'm sorry, I can't today. I have somewhere else I have to go. How are the boys?"

"Fine. They're jist fine," she answered, her attention obviously fully occupied with Rosy.

"Well, good-bye, Mrs. Decker. Thanks for taking her for me."

"Call me Jane."

"All right, Jane. Her name is Rosy."

"Come see her anytime."

"Thanks, I will."

I got in my car and drove away, blinking back tears and feeling like a fool for crying over a pig.

I had decided earlier that if I was going to take Rosy to Jane, I'd go ahead and pay a visit to the Hortons afterward. School would be out in five weeks and I still hadn't talked to Evelyn's parents about sending her on to high school. It was time I did that. Evelyn kept reminding me; she wanted to go so badly. I dreaded it, because I knew from the meeting we'd had at school what Mr. Horton's feelings were. I didn't know what argument I was going to use to try to change his mind. I'd just go and play it by ear and hope for the best. According to Evelyn, her mother was not against it. Maybe between the three of us we could convince him.

When I pulled up before the house, Evelyn came out to meet me. I got out of the car and smiled at her, putting my arm across her shoulders as we walked back up to the house together. She was a sweet, shy girl and a shy student.

"Mama," she said shyly to the woman who sat in a chair just inside the door. "This is the school teacher, Mrs. Hilton."

I leaned forward to take the hand she extended. She was thin and looked very frail.

"It was nice of you to come," she said in a rather stilted voice. "Excuse me for not getting up. Won't you please sit down?"

"Thank you."

"Evelyn, perhaps you could make Mrs. Hilton a cup of coffee."

"Oh, no thanks, Mrs. Horton, that isn't necessary," I said quickly. "I just had lunch a short time ago."

"A glass of lemonade, perhaps?"

"No, thank you. I'm fine. I just wanted to stop by for a few minutes. I had to go by Mrs. Decker's this afternoon, and your home is right on the way."

I paused. I had the feeling I was babbling. I don't know exactly what I had expected, but not this delicate woman with the air about her of a southern belle. It was faintly unreal. Their home, too, was more modern and refined than I was used to seeing in these hills. Somehow I couldn't fit Joe Horton into this scene at all.

"I don't suppose you know Jane Decker?" I asked.

"I don't believe so. The name is not familiar, though of course, I get out very little."

"She hasn't lived in this area long," I said. Better not tell her about Rosy. She wouldn't understand.

"Evelyn tells me she wants to be a teacher just like you, Mrs. Hilton. That's a very fine testimony of your teaching ability. You should be flattered."

"I am." I glanced at Evelyn. She was seated forward on the edge of her chair, her hands clasped together tightly in her lap. I smiled at her.

"Evelyn is a fine student," I added. "I've enjoyed having her in my school. Which brings me to the subject I wanted to discuss with you and your husband, Mrs. Hilton. Is he at home today?"

"He is out and about somewhere. If it's high school you want to discuss with us, I can assure you Evelyn will be going."

I was faintly startled. I knew what Mr. Horton's attitude was and I also knew that Evelyn was very fearful of not being allowed to go.

"I had understood that your husband is against it," I said.

"Nevertheless, Evelyn will go. My mind is quite made up about that, so you need have no fear, Mrs. Hilton."

"But — have arrangements been made to get her to the bus?"

"Something will come up. One way or another it will work out."

"I see," I said slowly. I didn't know quite what to think or what to say. "I'm very glad, of course. Evelyn deserves a high school education. Todd Johnson's parents are planning on sending him, too. Perhaps arrangements can be made between the two families for some kind of transportation."

"Perhaps."

The interview seemed to be over. I tried to make polite conversation for a few more minutes then rose to go. She held out her hand once again and as I took it, bade me a rather formal good-bye. Evelyn came out to the car with me.

"He won't let me go. I know he won't," she said, low-voiced and distressed.

"But your mother seems so confident."

"Sometimes I think Mama isn't living in this world at all. She reads all the time. It's about all she can do, and sometimes . . . well, she sort of becomes the people she reads about. I think she just finished 'Gone With the Wind'."

"I see," I said slowly. "Well, Evelyn, I don't quite know what to do. Have you been able to talk to your father at all?"

"He won't talk about it. Just says no."

"Do you know why he's so much against it?"

"He thinks I belong here, taking care of Mama and doing the housework. I keep telling him I could still do it and go to high school, too. I'm doing it now and high school would only take a couple more hours, but he won't listen."

"Well, Evelyn, all I know to tell you is just keep trying. Don't give up. Perhaps he'll change his mind or perhaps your mother has more influence with him than you realize. If I get a chance, I'll try to talk to him, too. Good-bye, Evelyn. I'll see you Monday."

I got in my car and drove home, still puzzling over the situation.

CHAPTER ELEVEN

A View from the Hill

When I came over the hill one Thursday afternoon on my way home from school and looked down in the valley below, I stopped short with a little exclamation of delight. The log walls of our cabin were up. It was roofless yet, but the walls were up, and it looked so right nestled there in the valley with the scattering of trees to the north and west of it. Davy had been wise when he declared that a log cabin was the only way to build in these hills. There were very few log cabins being built these days and I had had mixed emotions about it, but Davy had been right. It looked like home already.

I started down the hill at a fast walk. There seemed to be about a dozen men swarming around the cabin. One of the men detached himself from the others and came toward me. It was Davy. His long strides ate up the distance between us and soon he was catching me up in his arms in a bear hug.

"Oh, Davy, it's so beautiful," I said. "It's perfect, it looks just right."

"No need to cry about it," he teased gently.

"I can't help it. It looks so — so natural, so much a part of the scenery. You were right about any other kind of house not fitting in here. A modern house would have looked out of place."

"You really like it?" he asked pleased.

"Yes! You should see it from the top of the hill. Come on up."

"Later, Honey. I gotta get back to work, but you come on down an' look around. Then I think you maybe oughta go on to th' house an' help Mom with supper. She insists on feedin' th' whole gang tonight."

"Oh. Of course I will, Davy. I can't believe you've got so much done this week."

We went hand in hand the rest of the way. Davy's brother John met me with a grin and an outstretched hand.

"Well, what do you think?" he asked.

"It's beautiful. I love it."

"Watch where you're walkin'. Don't want you steppin' on any nails."

He pointed out a few things to me then went off about his business. Davy took me inside and showed me around. He introduced me to a couple of the men. Lewis was there and a tall gangling youth I recognized as a former student of mine.

"Hello, Luther," I said with a smile. "How are you?"

"Fine," he said, with an awkward ducking of his head. He scurried away on some errand, evidently embarrassed by my presence.

I stayed a few more minutes then went on up to my in-laws' house to help Clemmy with supper. She was already at the stove taking an enormous peach cobbler from the oven. Her face was red and perspiring from the heat, but she looked calm and unflurried.

"What can I do, Clemmy?" I asked when I had washed my hands.

"Could you peel them taters?" she asked, indicating a large enamel pan filled with potatoes sitting on the table. "Of course," I said. It was more than she usually allowed me to do. I sat down at the table and pulled the pan over toward me.

I talked to Clemmy a little about the cabin as we worked. She let me talk but didn't have a lot to say herself except that the cabin was looking 'right pretty', and that John and Davy were both good builders.

I went down into the cellar and brought up jars of green beans, corn and beets, and Clemmy opened them and put them in pots on the wood stove to be heated and seasoned. She made her delicious biscuits while I set the table and tried to watch her at her task. Clemmy didn't measure or use recipes but she was an excellent cook. She made the most delicious biscuits I'd ever eaten.

"Someday you're going to have to teach me how to make biscuits like you do, Clemmy," I said. "Otherwise I'll have Davy sneaking back here to eat with you instead of eating with me. What else can I do?"

"You might go down to th' crick for a couple jars of milk," she said. "An' you might jist give a wave to th' men if you can catch their eye. This'll be ready time they all wash up."

"All right, Clemmy."

I went out of the house and down to the creek where Clemmy kept her milk and butter in a wooden box that the cold creek water flowed through. It was an ingenious method of refrigeration, and served its purpose quite well, but I would be glad of the electric refrigerator Davy and I would have in our cabin. Also the electric stove, I thought, remembering the heat of Clemmy's kitchen.

I ducked under the branches of a weeping willow and bent to lift the lid of the wooden box resting there at the edge of the creek bed. I took out two gallon jars and closed the lid. The milk was cold with several inches of thick cream at the top. I would have to skim that off to be made later into butter in Clemmy's daisy churn. Which reminded me that I would be needing a daisy churn myself before long. I had determined to do things the country way as much as possible, but not a wood cook stove, a creek box for refrigeration, or a washboard for laundry. Those things were a way of life for Clemmy, the only way of life she had ever known, but I was not prepared to follow in her footsteps to that extent, nor did Davy expect me to. He was prepared to provide me with all the labor-saving devices available, within reason, of course. He was a very satisfactory husband and I a very happy wife.

I stopped on the way back to the house and put one of the jars of milk down on the grass. When I caught one of the men looking my way, I gave a wide beckoning wave. When he waved back I picked up the jar and went on up to the house.

Clemmy was mashing the potatoes. I skimmed the cream off the milk and she used some of it in the potatoes. I glanced out the window and saw the men coming toward the house. Clemmy sent me out with a couple of towels and a bar of soap. The men would wash up outside at the pump since there were so many of them. I counted eight in all, but Lewis excused himself to me and went off toward his wagon. Sue would be expecting him home for supper, he said.

The men sat at the table. Clemmy and I didn't join them but remained standing, attending to their needs. Mr. Hilton didn't come in, he must be off somewhere hunting. The meal was quickly and hungrily eaten, then the men were scraping their chairs back and going off to their various vehicles. John stayed awhile and visited with his mother. Luther and Davy went off somewhere. I supposed out to the shop. I fixed a plate and set it before Clemmy, then fixed myself a plate and sat down at the other end of the table.

"Guess I'd better be on my way, too," John said finally, rising. "Thanks for the supper, Mom. It was delicious, but don't do it again. Th' men are used to goin' to their own homes for supper, an' we all pack a lunch. Couple more days an' we should be through here, an' Davy an' his friend can fix it up. You'll be in your own home 'fore you know it," he ended, looking at me.

"It's wonderful," I said. "I was so surprised when I came over the hill and saw it today."

"Get th' roof on tomorrow. Be seein' you then."

He was gone. Clemmy and I finished our meal and cleared the table. She washed the dishes and I dried and put them away. Shortly before we finished, Davy came in.

"Has Luther gone?" I asked.

"Yep. John was gonna drop him off at home. You 'bout finished?"

"Just about."

"Want to walk up the hill?"

"All right. Just give me a couple of minutes."

He poured himself a cup of coffee and sipped it while he waited. I finished the last of the dishes and hung up the dish cloth. Davy took my hand and we went out of the house and started up the hill together.

We sat at the top of the hill, side by side on the grass looking down at our cabin and talking about our plans. Dusk came, the evening cooled. Davy put his arm around me and hugged me close to warm me. I was filled with warm content.

CHAPTER TWELVE

The Rambler Returns

"**W**hy, hello, Mr. Horton," I said to the big man that filled the doorway. "I believe Evelyn just left."

"She's waitin' in th' wagon. I wanted to talk to you a minute."

"Would you care to sit down?" I asked, indicating the bench.

He shook his head, his hat in his hand. "My wife says you was at th' house Saturday."

"Yes, I was."

"She says she told you Evelyn's goin' on to high school next. Well, she ain't."

"I'm sorry to hear that, Mr. Horton. Evelyn wants very much to go."

"That's your doin'. You put th' idee into her head."

"I've encouraged all the children to consider going on to high school, Mr. Horton, because I feel it's necessary. Anyone growing up today without a high school education is put at a serious disadvantage in the job market."

"Evelyn's got a job, takin' care of her mama an' th' house."

"I know, but she feels she can do both. She is doing both now, and high school will not involve that much more of her time. And what of her future, Mr. Horton?"

"I can take care of her future."

"Can you? What if something should happen to you?

What if Evelyn is left to face the future alone? It does happen sometimes, you know."

"It happens too sometimes when th' young'uns goes off to town to get more schoolin'. They forget about th' folks at home or get to thinkin' they're too good to come around anymore. I seen that happen too, Teacher."

"Perhaps," I said more gently, "but I don't think Evelyn is like that. I know you love her and don't want to lose her, but — "

"She's th' only one we got. Her mamma wasn't well enough to have any more," he said, a bit gruffly.

"She's a fine girl. She's pretty, bright and affectionate. You have reason to be proud of her."

He cleared his throat, looking down at the hat in his hands.

"Will you do me a favor, Mr. Horton?"

He looked up, a frown wrinkling his forehead.

"Before you make a final decision, will you at least discuss it with Evelyn? Let her tell you how she feels, the reason she wants to go on to high school, her hopes, her plans for the future. Then whether you allow her to go or not, at least she'll feel you were interested enough to listen. That's important to a child, Mr. Horton. Evelyn feels very hurt and frustrated because she says you won't even discuss it with her."

"Ain't no point in it," he said shortly.

"Yes, there is. Didn't you ever want something very much when you were a child, and feel very hurt and upset because you were not even allowed to talk about it? The important thing is not your feelings or mine, but Evelyn's. You owe it to her to at least discuss it. Will you do that, Mr. Horton?"

"If I do, will you stay out of it? Will you stop talkin' to her about it?" he asked a bit belligerently.

"Yes, I will, if you'll sit down with her and let her talk

and really listen to her."

He nodded his head and turned to leave, clapping his hat back on his head as he reached the door.

"Good-bye, Mr. Horton," I said.

He didn't answer. I gathered up my books and prepared to leave. I heard Mr. Horton and Evelyn drive away. Just as I reached the outer door, another man was coming up the steps. He was a stranger, obviously not local, dressed in a gray business suit, white shirt and tie. He was tall and thin and good-looking in a rather austere way. He paused on the steps looking up at me.

"You're the school teacher, I presume," he said.

"Yes, I am," I answered.

He held out his hand. "My name is Jesse Decker."

Surprised, I let my hand be taken in a firm clasp. He shook it briefly and released it. This then was Jane Decker's husband. He wasn't at all as I had pictured him.

"I'm Mrs. Hilton," I said.

"I came to inquire about my two young sons, John and James Decker. How are they doing in school, Mrs. Hilton?"

"I'm sorry. There are no children by the name of Decker in my school," I replied.

He looked at me with something like consternation.

"They're not — in this school?" he asked blankly.

"No."

"But I made sure — you're positive there's no John or James Decker enrolled here?"

"Positive," I said a little tartly. "There are only thirty-two children in the whole school, Mr. Decker. I have no trouble remembering their names."

"Then is there another school in this area?"

"No, not for some distance."

"I see. It seems I was misinformed, then."

He gnawed at his lower lip, his expression puzzled. I didn't know what to do. He was obviously looking for his family, but I wasn't sure Jane wanted to be found by him. He reached in his inside jacket pocket and brought out a business card.

"I wonder if I might ask a favor of you," he said. "This is my business card. If you should happen to come in contact with a Mrs. Jane Decker, would you let me know? It's urgent that I talk to her."

I took the card. He gave a little half salute and turned and went down the steps. I watched him walk to the car that was parked at the side of the road. As he got in I turned and padlocked the door. He was driving away as I came down the steps and started toward home.

I looked down at the card in my hand. It had his name in the lower left hand corner with "Sales Representative" under it, and a phone number, and in larger letters in the center above, the name of a local insurance agency. I quickened my step. I hadn't particularly liked the man, though I knew I shouldn't judge on first appearance, but he was looking for Jane and he would be sure to find her sooner or later. Whether she would want to see him or not I didn't know, but I felt she should be warned so she wouldn't be caught completely unaware.

I turned and went down the hill toward our cabin where Davy and Lewis were sure to be. On the outside, the cabin looked complete and I felt a little thrill of delight as I looked at it, but there was still a lot be done on the inside. Lewis and Davy were working on it together every day. In just a few weeks now Davy and I would be able to move in.

"Anyone here?" I called as I stepped through the door. Davy came out of one of the bedrooms in answer to my call. I lifted my face for his kiss.

"Can't stay away from th' place, can you?" he teased.

"No. I wish I could help."

"You can help when it's wall paperin' and curtain hangin' time. Come see th' bathroom."

I went with him and looked into the bathroom. The tub and sink and stool were in.

"Plumber was here today. It's all done, 'cept for th' finishin' touches. Wanna try it?"

I stepped over and turned on the "hot" faucet. Hot water poured into the sink.

"Th' kitchen sink is in, too," Davy said.

"It's wonderful. When do you think we can move in?"

"Couple, three weeks, maybe. Wanta pound a few nails?"

"I'd love to but I think I'd better run over to Jane Decker's for a minute," I said. Lewis came in and we said hello. "Jane's husband is looking for her," I told them both. "He came by just as I was leaving school and asked about the boys. I didn't tell him anything, but someone will, and I think I ought to warn her. He said it was important that he talk to her, but I decided to let her be the judge of that. He gave me his card so I thought I'd just run out there and give it to her. I'll be back in a little while."

I went on up to the Hiltons', told Clemmy I'd be back in an hour and got in the car to drive out to Jane's.

This time the whole family was out in the yard and came to greet me. Even the dog was wagging his tail.

"Bet you come to see Rosy," Jane said.

"Well, no, but how is she?"

"Doin' fine. Come an' see her."

I followed her out to the old shed off to the side of the house. The four boys and the dog came along too.

Rosy was enclosed in a pen in one corner of the shed. She greeted us with eager squeals and grunts of pleasure. I knelt and put my hand on her. She wiggled out from under my hand and went to Jane.

"I been th' one feedin' her lately, ya know," Jane said apologetically, scratching behind Rosy's ear.

"It's all right. I'm glad she likes you."

I straightened and stood looking down at Rosy. Jane rose too, dusting her hands on the sides of her skirt.

"She's grown a lot," I said. "I'm glad I brought her to you. I'm sure she's much happier here than she would have been at home competing with all her brothers and sisters."

"Th' boys an' me been makin' regular fools of ourselves over her. She's a bigger pet than King here."

"I've been wondering how she was doing but that isn't the reason I came out here today. I wonder if I could speak to you alone for a minute?"

"You boys run off an' play now," she ordered. "Take King with you. What is it, Mrs. Hilton? You're not wantin' Rosy back?"

"Oh no, nothing like that. It's just that I had a visitor after school today. He was asking about Johnny and Jimmie. It was your husband, Mrs. Decker."

"Jesse? Here?" Her expression was surprised and incredulous. Her hands went up to her hair and unconsciously smoothed it back. I handed her the card her husband had given me. She stared down at it for a long minute and her hand trembled.

"I didn't know what you wanted me to do, so I didn't tell him anything, except that there were no children by the name of Decker enrolled in school. He gave me that card and asked me to contact him if I should ever run across you. I thought you should know because sooner or later someone is going to tell him where you are."

"Jesse here," she repeated in a bemused way, still looking down at the card, and again touching her hair with an unconsciously smoothing hand.

"I have to go now," I said. "I just wanted to let you know."

"I can't believe it," she said.

"Are you all right, Mrs. Decker?"

"Huh? Oh! Yes, I'm fine, jist fine. It was good of you to come."

"That's all right. If you should need anything, let us know."

"I don't need nothin', but thanks jist th' same."

"I'll be seeing you then."

I went back to the car and got in. She was staring down at the card in her hand again as I drove away.

CHAPTER THIRTEEN

Rain on the Tin Roof

"**Y**ou need a good sized bowl," Clemmy told me. "An' put it about half full of flour. Then make a well in th' middle of th' flour like this."

She demonstrated while I stood at her elbow watching. She was showing me how she made her delicious biscuits.

"Then you fill th' well with buttermilk an' a big glob of butter. Then a pinch of salt an' a good-sized pinch of sody. Now start workin' th' flour into th' liquid with your hands, 'til you got enough worked in so's th' dough is smooth an' thick. Now you take it outa th' flour an' squeeze off chunks to make th' biscuits, tryin' to get them all th' same size. Then you put them in a hot oven an' let them bake a few minutes 'til they're brown, an' that's all there is to it."

"You make it sound easy," I said. "I'll have to try it your way. I'm not a very successful biscuit maker."

Davy came through the door and bent to kiss my cheek.

"Mom givin' you a cookin' lesson?" he asked.

"I'm trying to learn the secret of her delicious biscuits," I answered.

"Maybe you'll get a chance to try it in our own house in a couple weeks time. Figger we can move into th' cabin by then. Rainin' cats an' dogs out there," he added as he began to wash up. "Be good for th' garden."

Mr. Hilton came in from the living room, removing his pipe from his mouth, and we sat down to supper. We were having fried chicken, mashed potatoes, gravy, green beans and biscuits. Both Davy and his father were hearty eaters. Clemmy was an excellent cook but I thought she prepared too many fried foods. I'd see if I could gradually wean Davy away from that when we got into our own home.

"Come help me with th' chores," Davy said to me when Clemmy and I had done the dishes.

"I have a lot of homework," I evaded.

"Can't you do it later?"

"I suppose so, but it's raining."

" 'Fraid you'll melt or somethin'? You got a raincoat. Put it on an' come with me."

I gave a little sigh of resignation and went to get my raincoat. He was standing there in the kitchen, milk bucket in hand, waiting for me.

"You mad at me or somethin'?" he asked as we went hand in hand toward the barn.

"No. Just tired, I guess, or lazy."

Actually I was feeling a little guilty. I had walked home with Calvin after school that day and visited awhile with his granny. Mostly we had talked about the program the children were putting on the last day of school. I had decided against a play because of the difference in the ages of the children. Instead there would be skits, poems, songs, and Calvin was going to read aloud a short story he had written.

I wanted to make sure Granny felt welcome to come and somehow, during the course of the conversation, I made the observation that it was a shame Calvin's mother couldn't be there. Granny began to look cunning.

Had I actually suggested that she invite Calvin's mother or had that been Granny's idea? I wasn't exactly sure but I was feeling a little apprehensive about it now. Had I been disloyal to the Hiltons with whom I was living? Would Davy be upset if he knew?

I couldn't bring myself to tell him. Probably Calvin's mother wouldn't come anyhow. She hadn't been around for years, according to my understanding.

"Chores won't take long," Davy was saying. "Unless you decide you want to do th' milkin'?"

"No thanks. I'll let you do it."

"Thought you was gonna become a country girl."

"Well, with limitations. I've discovered one thing I'll never do, no matter how long I live in the country."

"What's that?"

"Kill a chicken."

"Was Mom tryin' to teach you how to kill a chicken?"

"Yes. I think she decided to take me in hand today, since we'll be moving soon. I helped her run down two chickens and I helped tie their legs together and hang them upside down on the clothes line. She cut one of the heads off to show me how, but when she handed me that bloody knife, expecting me to do the other one, I couldn't do it. I ran."

He chuckled. "Poor little city girl," he said. "Did you help her scald them an' pluck out th' feathers, an' clean the insides out?"

"No. I couldn't. I felt sick."

"I noticed you didn't eat any chicken at supper."

"No. I don't think I'll ever eat chicken again. Not unless I buy it at the store, already cleaned and cut up and dead."

"Ain't near as good or good for you. B'sides, how you gonna find time to run to th' store 'fore supper?"

"Then you'll have to do the killing and plucking and cleaning or we'll just have to become vegetarians. I'm sorry, but I absolutely draw the line at killing anything before I eat it."

We had reached the barn and Davy opened the door and we went inside. Davy hung the milk bucket on a nail, then took my raincoat and hung it on a nail along with his jacket.

"Let's go up in the loft," he said. "You can go first this time since we're a ol' married couple."

I gathered my skirt together at my side and went up the narrow steps. Davy came after me. It was growing dusk early because of the rain. The barn loft was full of shadows and fragrant with the smell of hay.

"Remember what I told you once about comin' out here an' listenin' to th' rain on th' tin roof?" Davy asked, taking my hand.

"Yes. You said you often did it as a boy. Is that why you brought me out here?"

"Um-huh. It's th' most soothin' sound in th' whole world. Stay here long enough an' all your troubles'll jist melt away. Come sit down on th' hay an' listen."

He led me over to a mound of hay and we sat down side by side and listened to the patter of the rain on the roof. It had a soothing effect on me.

"It's nice," I murmured. "It's making me sleepy."

"Then lay back an' go to sleep," he said, putting his arm around me and drawing me back on the hay with him.

"Go to sleep out here?" I protested. "It's not bedtime and besides, who wants to wake up with straw in his hair and clothes?"

"Sh-h-h," Davy whispered, close beside me, his arm under my head. "Jist relax an' forget about bein' a city girl for a while. Bet you never done anything like this before, have you?"

"No," I said drily. "Have you?"

"Sure. Lots of times. Always find a excuse to come up here when it's rainin'."

"With whom?"

"By myself, a' course. First time I ever been up here with a girl."

"I should hope so."

"Romantic, ain't it?" he whispered. "Been thinkin' about gettin' you up here ever since it started rainin'."

He drew me into his arms and kissed me. Presently I began to push against him.

"Davy, let me up," I said.

"What for?"

"You know what for. Davy, for heaven's sake. Somebody might come."

"Who'd come?"

"Your father, for one."

"He's prob'ly in bed by now."

"You don't know that. Davy, act your age. There's a time and a place, you know. And this is not my idea of the time or the place."

"Don't you love me no more?"

"Of course, I love you," I said in exasperation. "Davy honestly. If I'd known you had ulterior motives, I wouldn't have come."

He sighed and released me. I sat up, brushing straw from my hair. He lay back on the hay, his hands clasped behind his head.

"Well, can't blame a guy for tryin'," he said with a touch of humor.

"Yes, I can."

"Come on, little prude. Lay back down here beside me an' jist relax an' listen to th' rain. I'll be good."

"You promise?"

"I promise."

I obeyed and he put his arm under my neck and drew my head to his shoulder.

"Comfortable?" he murmured.

"Yes."

We were silent, listening to the rain. Now and then there were faint rustling sounds and the stamp of an impatient hoof. My eyes were feeling heavy again. I nestled closer to my husband and he turned his face into my hair.

"Sweetheart?" he murmured.

"Hm-m?"

"You happy?"

"Yes, Davy. Very."

"You as anxious to get in our own house as I am?"

"Yes."

"We could prob'ly move in next week. " 'Lectricity an' plumbin' is all in. Th' kitchen an' bathroom an' our bedroom are all done. Me an' Lewis could go ahead an' finish up th' rest after we moved in, if you wouldn't mind th' mess an' th' noise."

"Would you like to do that?"

"Um-huh. If you would."

"I'd love it. I can put up with the mess."

"We could be together more. We ain't had a chance to be alone much as I'd like since we been married."

"I know."

"Then we can do it?"

"Yes, I'd love to."

He drew me closer, his mouth against my cheek. "You're so sweet an' warm an' soft," he murmured. "Can I take back my promise?"

"No, Davy."

I pulled away from him and sat up. He sighed again and sat up too.

"Spoil sport," he grumbled.

"Too bad. Isn't it time you got at your chores? What's your mother going to be thinking, waiting for you to bring the milk in?"

"Prob'ly that you got me up here to take advantage of me," he said, rising and reaching down a hand to help me up.

"I got you up here?" I protested indignantly.

"Ain't that how it was?"

He reached for a long handled fork that was stuck in the hay nearby and began to lift forks full of pungent hay and push them through open holes into the mangers below. I stood and watched him.

When he finished, he went along closing the trap doors over the holes. Then he came back to me and stood before me, looking down into my face. It was almost dark now, his face was deeply shadowed and looked almost stern. Then suddenly he smiled, his teeth showing white in his darkened face.

"I still love you anyhow," he said softly.

CHAPTER FOURTEEN

A Rumor Going 'Round

We moved into our cabin just a week before school was out. Clemmy gave me a beautiful patchwork quilt she made and several rag rugs for the floor. She took me down into the cellar and gave me an extra daisy churn she had and told me I could come over any time and help myself to the fruits and vegetables she had stored there. She was generosity itself and would have given me the dress off her back if I had asked for it. I loved her dearly; I was very glad we were going to be living so close.

It was a very busy time for us, but a happy time. Besides moving and practicing for the school performance and preparing final grade cards, I was going to take the three eighth graders into town for graduation services for all the eighth graders in the school district. Their parents didn't want to go but they didn't object to the children going if I would take them.

Graduation was on Tuesday evening. I drove the three of them into town in my car, Evelyn sitting in the front with me and Todd and Billy in the back seat. We were a little early. I wanted a chance to show them around the school they would possibly be attending next year. They were all three very nervous.

"It's so big," Evelyn said in awe when I found a place and parked.

"Yes, it looks big but it isn't that difficult to find your way around."

I wanted badly to ask if she'd had a chance to talk to her father, but since I had promised him I wouldn't discuss the subject with her anymore, I refrained. She walked beside me as we went up the steps, the two boys close behind.

I went to the office in search of Mr. Hooper and found him there at his desk, the phone to his ear. He acknowledged us and waved us to seats. When he had terminated the conversation he rose and held out his hand to me.

"You've met Mr. Hooper," I said to the children. "He's Superintendent of schools. This is Evelyn Horton, Todd Johnson, and Billy Baxter."

Mr. Hooper shook hands with each of them, then took us on a tour of the building. He was kind and jovial and did his best to lessen the nervousness of the children.

We got through the evening without mishap. On the way out of town I stopped at a drive-in and treated them to hamburgers and malts. Evelyn's tongue loosened and she began to talk about high school, her words tripping over themselves in her excitement.

"Have you had an opportunity to talk to your father?" I asked quietly.

"Yes. He didn't say much, though."

"I promised if he'd listen to what you had to say, I wouldn't discuss it with you anymore. I have to keep that promise, Evelyn. I'm sorry."

"Oh."

She subsided and we were quiet the rest of the way home. I dropped each of them off at their home and went on to the cabin where Davy was waiting up for me. It was 10:30 p.m. He stood and held out his arms. I went into them without a word.

"How'd it go?" he asked.

"All right."

"Miss me?"

"Yes. I always miss you. It's amazing to me. I used to be

95

so independent. Now I can't even be away from you a few hours without feeling empty and alone."

"It's called love, honey, an' it's th' most wonderful feelin' in th' world if it's shared."

"Yes," I said. "We're very fortunate, aren't we, Davy?"

"You bet we are."

He released me and stood smiling down at me. "Want a little snack before we turn in?" he asked.

"We stopped for hamburgers on the way home," I said.

"Oh ho! An' didn't even think of your starvin' husband at home, huh?"

"I fed you before I left."

"Yeah, but that was four hours ago."

"Do you want me to fix you a sandwich?"

"No. I'll jist have some of that potato salad that was left over from supper."

While he went to the refrigerator to help himself to the potato salad, I went around doing a few last minute things in preparation for the next day. Then I went and sat at the table with him.

"Maggie an' Pete an' their kids stopped by for a few minutes," Davy said.

"Oh? I'm sorry I missed them. How are they?"

Maggie was Davy's youngest sister, the only one of the four Hilton girls who had stayed in the hills. Her oldest child, a girl, was one of my first graders.

"They seemed okay. Maggie's in th' family way again."

"Again? My goodness, isn't four children under six enough for awhile? You certainly have a prolific family, Davy."

Davy glanced up at me, then quickly lowered his eyes to his plate. I was immediately contrite. Had it sounded as if I was criticizing his sister?

"I'm sorry. I didn't mean to sound critical," I said. "It's just that she already has her hands full with the four, and little Pete is only a year old. I wouldn't think they could afford another child, time wise or money wise either."

"It's jist th' natural thing that happens when two people get married, I guess."

"It doesn't have to happen," I said a bit defensively. "There's no reason why a woman is obligated to bear a child every year or two. And it's downright criminal if it ruins her health so that she's not able to care for the other children properly."

He didn't answer. He finished his snack and went to the sink to rinse his plate.

"Does it bother you that I don't want a child right away, Davy?" I asked when he turned back to me.

"Not 'specially. I'm enjoyin' jist havin' you to myself for awhile, but I do want kids someday."

"I want children too, but I don't want so many that it makes me an old woman before my time," I said rather crisply, rising and pushing my chair under the table. "Also I want time for other things in my life beside children. I don't think a woman is fair to herself when her whole life is consumed by her house and her husband and children. And I don't think she's fair to her husband and children either. There are so many more — "

"Okay, okay," Davy interrupted, raising his hand in mock surrender. "I heard all that before, remember?"

"You also heard it before we were married, remember?" I reminded him.

"I remember."

"And you decided you wanted to marry me in spite of it, so no complaining about it now."

"Was I complainin'?"

"No, but — "

"Are we gettin' ready to have our first fight?" he asked with quizzically raised eyebrows.

"I hope not," I said, a little troubled.

97

"Come on, let's get to bed. I think we're both a little tired an' we got some busy days ahead of us. An' I ain't mad at you if you ain't mad at me. Okay?"

"Okay."

"An' I wouldn't trade you for any other woman in th' whole world, kids or no kids. Okay?"

"Okay, Davy. I'm sorry I got on the bandwagon. I won't say any more."

"Live an' let live is what I say. Ever'body's got to live their own life. If Maggie an' Pete end up with a dozen kids, that's their business, an' if we end up with jist two or three, that's our business. Right?"

"Right. I didn't mean to criticize her, I just meant — oh never mind. I guess I'm a little on the defensive. Everybody keeps hinting and speculating on when we're going to have a baby. I've heard there's a rumor going around that I'm 'barren' simply because I'm not pregnant after five months of marriage."

"Sounds like you been talkin' to Granny Eldridge again."

"I did go see her for awhile last week."

"You don't wanta believe half of what Granny says. What she don't know, she makes up herself. Nobody takes Granny serious."

"But Davy, she said — " I paused and bit my lip, looking up at him a bit apprehensively.

"She said what?"

"She said — some people are saying I'm — I'm denying you your husbandly rights — "

He threw back his head and gave a little shout of a laugh.

"Now how would they know anything like that?" he asked.

"I don't know."

"Come to think about it, you did deny me my husbandly rights up in the hay loft th' other day," he said, a whimsical smile around his mouth. "Shame on you, Teacher."

"Davy, I'm serious."

"Then don't be. I told you, Granny makes things up. Ain't nobody who takes a good look at me gonna think I'm a man deprived of his wife's love. Granny's got her own little private war goin' on with th' Hiltons. If she can stir up a little trouble, she'll do it an' enjoy doin' it. You need to let what she says go in one ear an' out th' other. That's what th' rest of us do. Now come on, woman. Let's go to bed. I'm bushed an' I got to where I can't go to sleep without you there."

"All right, Davy. You go ahead. I'll be there in just a minute."

I went into the bathroom to cream my face. Davy's words about Granny kept going around and around in my head.

"She's got her own little private war going on with the Hiltons. If she can stir up a little trouble, she'll do it and enjoy doing it. If she can stir up a little trouble — "

CHAPTER FIFTEEN

Last Day of School

I had decided, instead of charging a set fee at the school performance, to put a small box with a slit in the top at the entrance, so that each person could just drop in the amount he or she wanted to. That way everyone could come, even if they couldn't afford to pay, and those that could afford it and wanted to could contribute more. Since the proceeds were to be used for school supplies for their children, I was sure some of the more prosperous families would be generous.

It was a quarter to eleven. The program was scheduled to begin at eleven and several families had already arrived. It looked as if we were going to have a full house.

The northwest corner of the schoolroom had been curtained off. The children were gathered behind it, some of them in the cloak room. Shuffles and murmuring and giggles could be heard coming from behind the curtain, and now and then a sibilant "sh-h-h" as Ellen Hilton or Goldie Sutton, who were helping with the program, tried to quiet the children. I stood just inside the door to greet the arrivals and direct them where to put their money.

At eleven the schoolroom was full to overflowing. I was about to leave my post when there was the flurry of a last minute arrival.

Granny Eldridge came puffing in, leaning rather heavily on a cane. Behind her was a tall thin woman, well dressed and rather heavily made up. A sudden hush went over the audience.

"Well, we made it," Granny said to me rather loudly. "This here is Calvin's mama, Bertha. Well, she's your sister-in-law too now, I reckon," she ended with a hearty laugh.

"Hello, Bertha," I said quietly. "I'm glad you could come. We're rather full. Perhaps we can find you a seat over here at the side."

I led them to the side of the room where extra seats had been set up. People shuffled, a couple of mothers took their child on their lap to make room.

"Well, well, looks like 'most th' whole Hilton clan is here," Granny said loudly. "You could 'most have a family reunion, huh?"

A man rose. It was Tom Hilton. His face was set, his jaw clamped. He had his youngest child by the hand. He began to push his way to the front. He jerked the curtain aside and said loudly to his wife, "Get th' kids. We're leavin'."

There was a bewildered protest from Ellen.

"You heard what I said," he barked. "We're gettin' out of here."

He took hold of his children and began to push them toward the door. Ellen cut me an anguished look, threw up her hands and followed them out. I stood helpless for a minute, then I took a deep breath and went over to pull the curtain back in place. I turned to face the audience, my hands gripped together in front of me.

"Thank you for coming," I said. "I hope you are all comfortable. If you will just give us a few more minutes, we'll be ready to begin."

I went behind the curtain. Goldie and the children were all staring at me in a stupefied way.

"We'll go ahead as planned," I said quickly, nervously. "Andrew, I'd like for you to take Tommy's place. Just read what you have to say off the back of the card. You come right after Darrell."

I lined them up. The opening scene was to be a short skit

by the first and second graders. The loss of the four Hilton children was going to be a problem, as three of them had been in group projects. Goldie wasn't going to be much help either. Ellen had been the one that was going to be of real help. Sue hadn't been able to come; she wasn't feeling well. I would manage though. I was so angry I felt at the moment I was capable of anything.

It went off pretty well. A couple of the children forgot their lines and had to be prompted. Once the curtain caught and one side came tumbling down and had to be put back up. Ruthie Hilton had been going to sing a song with two other girls. Since hers had been the most dominant voice, the other girls were nervous and were afraid they couldn't go through with it, so I sang with them, concealed from the audience by the curtain. Calvin, very serious, stood and read aloud the story he had written. There was polite applause after each performance and much louder clapping when I announced the end of the program. I was limp with exhaustion but still seething with anger.

We dispersed to the yard where everyone was bringing out the food they had brought. Davy had set up the tables made of sawhorses and long boards under the shade tree. I didn't eat much; I couldn't. I felt the smile was glued to my face. Granny Eldridge and her guest had evidently gone. I didn't see Calvin around either. Once when I caught Davy's eyes on me, I looked quickly away. I didn't even want to talk to my own husband just then.

I invited the children inside to give them their final report cards. I unthawed enough to bid them a warm good-bye and express the hope that I'd see them all again next year. When I went back outside people were waiting to take their children home. I looked around for Davy and didn't find him. I went back inside, gathered up my purse and the four report cards still lying on my desk, took the padlock from my desk drawer, locked the door and got into my car. Almost in a trance, I headed the car in the direction of Tom Hilton's home.

Three dogs came running out barking and growling. Normally apprehensive about dogs, I got out of the car, slammed the door and marched up to the house, not thinking twice about them. Ellen came to the door and held it open for me. Her face was sober, a little apprehensive. I felt a moment's compunction but not enough to stop me. I stepped inside.

Tom was sitting there in a rocker. He lowered the newspaper he had been reading and looked at me.

"I brought the children's report cards," I said in a rather frozen voice, handing them to Ellen. I opened my purse and took out my billfold. I extracted several bills, advanced on Tom and fairly threw them at him.

"I don't know how much you put in the box but there's your refund," I said, coldly. "And I hope you enjoyed ruining the school performance."

"Was it ruined?" Ellen asked hesitantly.

"If it wasn't, it's no thanks to your husband. Husband! Ha!"

Tom rose slowly from his chair and stood towering over me. I was not intimidated.

"That you, of all people, should be the one to make a scene," I said furiously. "Just because your sister, your own sister, comes to hear her son in a school performance. So she made a mistake. She had an illegitimate child. She would have corrected that mistake if her future husband hadn't been killed. What's your excuse?"

His jaw was clamped tight but I gave him no chance to speak.

"You like to think you're a respectable man, a fine family man. Well, I happen to know better. I happen to know that your wife is not your wife at all because you never had the decency to marry her. Your children are just as illegitimate as Calvin is, and you have five of them. The only difference is, everyone knows about Calvin and nobody knows about your children. Well, maybe Granny Eldridge ought to know and maybe I'll be the one to tell her. There'd soon be an equalizing of things around here then."

Tom's fist clenched. He came toward me. Ellen stepped between us.

"No, Tom," she said quietly. "She's right, you know."

"I'm sorry, Ellen," I said. I turned and left the house, feeling drained and very tired. I got in my car and drove away.

As I neared home, I began to feel a little sick. I felt very guilty about Ellen, and I was afraid of what Davy was going to say when I told him what I had done. After all, he had told me of Tom and Ellen's marital status in strict confidence. Very few people knew, not even Tom's own children. It was a good thing they hadn't been there either.

CHAPTER SIXTEEN

What to Do with Calvin

Where was Davy? It was mid-afternoon and I hadn't seen him since noon. I began to be a little worried. It wasn't like him to be gone and not tell me where he was going. Of course, I had left the school and gone to Tom's without letting him know, but I had expected him to be there when I got back. He wasn't at the school and he wasn't at home. I had no idea where he was.

I went over and looked out the window for about the tenth time. There was no sign of Davy, but there was a small figure flying down the hill toward our cabin. I recognized Calvin and went to stand in the doorway. He came straight on without stopping up the three steps and into my arms with such force that he almost knocked the breath out of me.

His breath was coming in short gasps. He buried his face against me and clung with all his strength. I drew him inside and closed the door. I held him close and felt his thin body trembling.

"Calvin, what is it?" I asked. "What has happened?"

"She — she said she was my mama," he gasped.

"She is, Calvin. She's your mother and she loves you. That's why she came to see you in the play."

"She — she said I gotta go back with her."

"Go back with her?" I asked, my heart standing still.

"She said she come to get me, 'cause Granny's gettin' too old an' I can't stay with her no more."

"Oh, Calvin," I said helplessly.

"So I run away cause I ain't goin' back with her. I want to stay here with you."

I continued to hold him, at a loss for words.

He lifted his face to me. It was streaked with tears and dirt.

"Can I stay here with you?" he asked.

"Calvin, I don't know what to tell you. There's so much involved. You stay here with me until Davy comes home. Then we'll talk to him about it. Will that be okay?"

He nodded. I loosened my hold on him and led him into the kitchen and pulled out a chair for him to sit on. I pulled out another chair for myself. His eyes on me were big and anxious.

"Don't worry, Calvin," I said putting my hand over his. "It will be all right. Would you like some milk and cookies?"

He didn't answer so I rose and poured a glass of milk and set it before him. I set a plate of cookies on the table and busied myself making a pot of coffee. Why didn't Davy come? Had something happened to him?

He came about a half hour later. He stood in the doorway of the kitchen and looked down at Calvin. His face was set in sober lines. He didn't look at me.

"Davy, where have you been?" I burst out. "I've been worried."

His eyes lifted to mine then and they were cold and angry. My heart seemed to stop. I swallowed rather convulsively. He knew then. I wanted to go to him, explain, to make him understand, but Calvin's needs would have to be taken care of first.

"Davy," I said, my voice sounding thick and unnatural. "Calvin is here because his mother has decided she wants him to go home with her and he doesn't want to go. We — wanted to talk to you about it."

Davy pulled out a chair and sat down rather heavily and looked at Calvin. I put a cup of coffee before him and absently he reached for it and lifted it to his lips. Calvin was looking at Davy, his eyes big and apprehensive.

"Want to tell me about it, Cal?" Davy invited.

Calvin's eyes left Davy and turned to me. He didn't answer.

"He told me that his mother doesn't feel Granny is able to take proper care of him anymore, because she is getting old and is not in very good health," I explained.

Davy continued to look at Calvin, he was purposefully avoiding looking at me. That hurt dreadfully, but I bit my lip to keep it steady and clung desperately to my control.

"How do you feel about that, Cal?" Davy asked quietly.

"I ain't goin'," Calvin burst out. "Want to stay here with her."

He left his chair and came over and buried his head against my shoulder. I put my arm around him.

"Davy," I said. "This is his home. He's never known any other. To take him away from here to live in the city and with someone who's a complete stranger — "

"She's his mama."

"Yes, but — "

"You said yourself that Granny's gettin' old. You've been worried that he's not bein' taken care of good enough."

"I know, but to uproot him this way, just when he's beginning to make friends, beginning to feel a part of things."

"Thought he was bein' mistreated, discriminated against, accordin' to you. Funny you want him to stay here for some more of th' same kind of treatment. Funny you not wantin' him to get away an' go somewhere where he'll be treated more fair."

It was said in a quiet, non-accusing voice but the sting, the accusation was there. I bit my lip. There was nothing I could say.

Davy rose and refilled his coffee cup. Calvin still leaned

against me. I lifted my eyes and watched Davy as he came back to the table, but he still didn't look at me. He sat down again and gave a deep sigh and rested his head on his hand.

I wanted to go to him, to have him hold me and comfort me, tell me that it was all right, but I couldn't. I knew he was very upset with me and was not going to easily forgive me for what I had done. I felt a surge of rebellion. Maybe Calvin and I would just go off somewhere alone together since it seemed quite obvious that we were both unwanted.

Suddenly Davy lifted his head, listening. I heard the sound of a car drive up and stop and the slam of a car door. Davy rose and went into the living room.

"Hello, Bertha," I heard him say a moment later. "Come on in."

"Well, Davy, it's been a long time, hasn't it? And now you're married and in your own home. So many changes since I left."

"Yes. I s'pose so."

"Is Calvin here?"

"Yes. Come on in th' kitchen. We ain't got much done to th' living room yet."

They came into the kitchen. Calvin was pressing close to me. She stood looking at the two of us for a long moment.

"You met my wife," Davy said.

"Yes, just briefly. Granny said I'd find Calvin here."

"Have a seat," Davy said, pulling out a chair for her. "Would you like some coffee?"

"Yes, I would," she said, seating herself across from me. "Nothing in it."

While Davy went for the coffee, Bertha and I sat and studied each other. Even though she was tall and slender and rather heavily made up, she somehow reminded me very much of Clemmy. It was something about her eyes, her expression.

Her eyes left me and went to her son, still clinging to me. I took hold of Calvin's arms and loosened his grip on me.

"Calvin, go sit in the other chair for awhile. Okay?" I said pushing him gently away.

"I'm not going to force you to do anything you don't want to do, Calvin," his mother said quietly.

Reluctantly he left me and went to sit in the other chair. His head was lowered so that his eyes barely peeked over the top of the table. They were big and anxious, first on me, then on his mother.

"Thank you," Bertha said when Davy set the cup of coffee before her.

He resumed his seat and the four of us sat silent while she took her first sip of coffee.

"Have you seen Mom?" Davy asked her.

"Yes, earlier this afternoon. I had Calvin watch until Daddy left, then I met her out beside the road." She took another sip of coffee. "I suppose you're wondering why I'm here."

"Calvin's told us you want to take him to th' city to live with you," Davy said.

"I've kept in contact with Granny all along," Bertha said. "During the winter when she was feeling so bad, she began to get worried about Calvin. She has a daughter who lives just this side of town who has invited her to come and stay with her. Granny doesn't want to go, but she can see that it might become necessary someday. The daughter is a widow and has no children of her own. She's willing to have Granny, but she doesn't see how she can take Calvin too. She works and is gone all day and Granny would still be responsible for looking after Calvin. Mary doesn't feel that should be her responsibility. I have to agree with her."

I looked at Calvin. His eyes, still barely visible above the table, were on his mother. I wasn't sure it was good for him to be hearing all this, but perhaps it was better than sending him off somewhere to worry and fret about what was going to happen to him.

"So — the only alternative seemed to be for me to take him home with me," Bertha continued, "but he reacted quite violently to that. I don't blame him. He hardly knows me. He's known I was some kind of relative, but he didn't know I was his mother until today."

"He hasn't seen you for several years, has he?" I ventured.

"Two years. I was here a few hours a couple of summers ago. No one knew about it except Granny and Calvin."

"You didn't see Mom?" Davy asked.

"No. I tried to but Daddy didn't leave and I couldn't stay any longer. I asked Granny to tell Mom I'd been here and that was fine, but whether she did or not I don't know."

"But to get back to the story, I've been sending Granny money for Calvin all along. I can afford to now. Four years ago I married. He's forty years older than I am, and quite wealthy. I married him for money and security. He married me so he would have someone of his own to take care of him. Perhaps that shocks you, but it's been a satisfactory arrangement for us. I was working as an aide in a nursing home and he was a patient. I hated the place and so did he. We both wanted out, but I was not qualified for any other kind of work. He had a lovely home but he couldn't live in it because he had no one to take care of him. He's a diabetic and has both legs amputated below the knee. Anyhow, we got our heads together and worked out a mutually satisfactory plan. I've never regretted it. He's very good to me. He's well educated and has taught me a lot. The only thing is, he requires a lot of care, and I'm not sure how Calvin would fit into such a household."

We all looked at Calvin. His eyes flew anxiously to me.

"He's used to freedom," Bertha said. "He's used to the hills and the woods and coming and going pretty well as he pleases. I'm not sure I approve of that, but that's neither here nor there. The point is, there's no way he could be allowed that kind of freedom in the city. It wouldn't be safe. So — where to go from here?"

No one spoke. I looked at Davy. He was looking down at his coffee cup, running his finger along the top of it.

"Granny has written often about your interest in Calvin," Bertha said to me, "and I can see for myself that he loves you. Perhaps, had things been different, I would have been the one to receive that kind of love from him, but as it is, I'm a stranger to him, someone he's not even sure he likes. So when Granny wrote and said you had suggested I be invited to see Calvin in the school play, I decided to come and check things out."

At her final words, my eyes had flown to Davy. He met my eyes at last, but there was a blaze of anger there. I hastily looked away.

"Granny seems to think that Davy too has some interest in Calvin, though to a lesser degree."

Brother and sister looked at each other, a somber rather challenging look. There was a tense moment of silence. Bertha shrugged.

"At least, you've been much more tolerant than the rest of the family," she conceded. "So I wondered if it might be possible, should Granny have to go to her daughter's, for the two of you to take Calvin. I'd pay his way. Granny says he's a good boy. He wouldn't give you a lot of trouble and I know he'd be happy with you. It's what he wants."

Davy was looking at me again. I said nothing, though. I felt my eyes were pleading.

"I know you're just newly married," Bertha said, "but Granny will be all right through the summer, perhaps even for several years yet. By that time perhaps you'll have children of your own and it won't seem such an invasion of your privacy."

"Could we?" I asked Davy.

"Would you like that, Calvin?" Davy asked him.

He nodded vigorously.

"All right then," Davy told Bertha.

"Thank you. I'm — grateful. I haven't been much of a mother, I know, but I've always tried to do what's best for Calvin, and I think this is the best solution for him. I hope it will work out well for you too."

She pushed her chair back and rose. Davy and I rose too.

"Will you ride back to Granny's with me, Calvin?" she asked him. "I might even let you steer when we get out on the road."

Calvin looked at me for guidance.

"Go ahead, Calvin," I said gently. "It's all right. There's nothing for you to worry about anymore and Granny will be wondering about you. Come back over any time you like."

Bertha said good-bye to us and she and Calvin went out the door. The car started up and drove away. Davy and I stood in the living room a few feet apart and looked at one another.

CHAPTER SEVENTEEN

First Quarrel

"**Y**ou — you've seen Tom?" I asked with difficulty.

"I was there right after you was."

"Oh."

His eyes were hard, cold. My hand went up to my throat.

"Then I — guess you know what happened?"

He nodded.

"I'm afraid I rather lost my temper. What he did was so petty, so small — "

"What about what you did? I thought you liked Ellen."

"I do. I like her very much. I didn't mean to say what I did, at least not in front of her."

"What about in front of Ruthie?"

"Of course not. Davy, you know I wouldn't do anything like that."

"Then you didn't know Ruthie was right in th' next room?"

"Oh no! She didn't — "

He nodded grimly. "She did. Ever' word. She's a pretty tore up little girl right now."

"Oh, Davy, I'm sorry! I wouldn't for the world — . I didn't know she was there, I swear I didn't. I'll — I'll go out and apologize."

"You'll do no such thing. You'll stay away from them, do you hear me? I done what I could, but if you go out there now, no tellin' what might happen."

"But Davy — "

"You heard me. Jist leave them alone. They don't want your apology."

I stood there biting my lip, trying desperately to keep back the tears that crowded up behind my eyes. Davy sighed and passed his hand wearily over his face.

"Davy, I'm sorry," I said in a small constricted voice.

"It was you that put it in Granny's head to invite Bertha here, was it?"

"I just said it was a shame Calvin's mother couldn't be here and I guess she . . . I didn't tell her to do it and I certainly didn't expect her to . . . to make such a production of it."

He turned to the door. "I'm goin' out to th' shop," he said. "Don't fix me any supper. I'm not hungry."

I stood mute, looking after him. He paused with his hand on the doorknob but didn't look around.

"Don't wait up for me. I may be late," he said.

He went out and closed the door quietly behind him. I sat in the rocker, my knuckles pressed against my mouth. Presently I rose and washed the few dishes that were in the sink, then went back into the living room to sit and wait. When 10:30 rolled around and Davy had not come in, I decided he was not going to. I went and looked out the window. The lights were still on in the shop.

I turned out all the lights, except the one over the kitchen sink, and went to bed. It seemed hours that I lay there and still Davy didn't come. I must have finally fallen asleep, for the next thing I knew it was morning and the bed beside me was still empty.

I got up, gathered some clean clothes, and started for the bathroom. I felt very calm, almost detached from all the turmoil of the day before. The house was silent. Davy evidently hadn't come in at all.

After I had bathed and dressed I went into the kitchen and made coffee. I was sitting at the table, a cup in my hand when I heard the front door open.

Davy appeared in the kitchen doorway for a minute but I didn't look up. He went on into the bedroom and a few minutes later I heard the sound of running water. When he reappeared at the kitchen door, he was freshly bathed and shaved. He helped himself to a cup of coffee, pulled out a chair and sat down. I couldn't bear to sit there facing him. I got up abruptly and refilled my own coffee cup.

"What would you like for breakfast?" I asked coolly.

"I don't care," he said, sounding weary. "Anything."

I took a skillet from the oven and put it on a burner. I got eggs and bacon from the refrigerator and started his breakfast.

"Aren't you havin' any?" he asked when I set the plate before him.

"No."

While he ate I busied myself wiping off the stove. I poured him a fresh cup of coffee but I didn't sit down at the table with him or look directly at him.

"I been thinkin'," he said slowly, when he had finished his breakfast and pushed the plate away. "It might be a good idea for you to go to St. Louis to visit your folks for a week or two, while me an' Lewis finish up th' house. Ain't much of anything you can do here an' we'll be making a lot of racket an' dust an' all. Figgered if you was gonna spend some time with your folks this summer, this'd be th' best time. Later on there'll be cannin' an' all, an' you promised Sue you'd watch her girls when she has th' baby. You don't want to wait around too long an' end up not havin' th' time to go."

Wait around too long, I thought. It was only the first day of my three month summer vacation. However, I said nothing. I couldn't. There seemed to be an obstructing lump in my throat that I couldn't swallow. I had been looking forward to this time so much, to be home all day and help with the finishing up of our house, and to be with Davy. We had talked and planned and dreamed, and now suddenly everything seemed to be crashing down around my shoulders.

He no longer wanted me there; he wanted to send me away.

"If you was to go tomorrow, me an' Lewis could get a early start on Monday an' it wouldn't take us too long, maybe a week or two, if we didn't have to worry about th' racket an' th' mess we'd be makin'. I could call you when we was done an' you could come home then."

My back was turned to him. I was scrubbing industriously at the sink now and I still couldn't answer.

"Well, what do you think?" he asked.

I swallowed and managed to speak in a fairly normal voice. "If that's what you want," I said.

"I think it might be th' best thing."

His chair scraped back but it was a minute or two before I heard him move away with slow, heavy steps. When the door closed behind him, my hands stilled, my shoulders slumped, hot tears filled my eyes and rolled down my cheeks. Angrily I wiped them away.

I was not going to cry. If he wanted me to go, I'd go, but oh, the awful loneliness that was closing in on me, the longing for the comfort of my husband's arms. But I couldn't go to him. He quite simply didn't want me.

I went into the bedroom and took my large suitcase out of the closet and put it on the bed. I opened it and began to take clothes from the dresser drawer and fill it. If Davy wanted me away so urgently, I wouldn't wait until tomorrow. I'd go today.

There was the sound of a vehicle arriving and a quick tapping on a horn. I peeked out the window and saw Jim Baker getting out of a small truck. Quickly I glanced in the dresser mirror to make sure I was presentable before I went through the house and to the front door.

"Come see what I jist bought," Jim said proudly. "Ain't she a beaut?"

"It's very nice," I said, stepping out into the yard.

"She'll go anywhere too. Mud, snow, water, anything. You name it, she'll go through it. She's got four-wheel drive, ya see, an' these big mud grip tires. I got me this new job in town, so I had to have a vehicle that would get me out of here, whatever th' weather was like. What I thought was, I could drive th' kids, Todd, ya know, an' Evelyn, in to meet th' bus ever' mornin'. I'll be leaving here about 6:30. Someone else will have to pick them up though. I won't be gettin' home 'til 6 or 7. Think that might work?"

"That would be wonderful, Jim," I said. Unfortunately, my voice broke in the middle of the sentence. He looked more closely at me.

"What's wrong?" he asked.

"Nothing," I said, choked.

"You look like you lost your best friend."

"I think I have."

"You an ol' Davy have a fight?"

I nodded, biting my lower lip, surreptitiously wiping the tears from my cheeks.

"Your first one?"

I nodded again.

"Well, that ain't such a bad average. You been married, how long now, 'bout four or five months? Me an' Sally was fightin' a week after we was married. That ain't such a good comparison to be makin' right now, though, is it?"

I tried to stem the tears, but they kept flowing faster than I could wipe them away.

"What did ol' Davy do?" Jim asked gently.

"It w-wasn't what Davy did," I sobbed. "It's what I did."

"Come on now, Teacher. You can't tell me you done anything that was so awful bad."

"I d-did though. I did s-something awful and Davy is s-so angry he's sending me away."

"Sendin' you away? Now I can't b'lieve that. Ol' Davy's crazy about you. Everyone knows that."

He reached in his hip pocket and pulled out a clean white handkerchief and handed it to me. I mopped at the tears, my breath coming in little shaken sobs. Jim put his hand on my shoulder.

"Come on, Honey," he chided. "Whatever you done, he'll forgive you. Jist give him a little more time, he'll come around."

"I'm afraid he won't though. Oh, Jim, we were such good friends and n-now he doesn't even want to be around me. H-he stayed out all night last night."

Jim's arm was around me now, his other hand came over and drew my head against him.

"Davy stayed out all night?" he asked, shocked.

"I-in his shop. H-he was so angry and this morning he said he wanted me to go s-spend a week or two with my parents. And he wants me to leave tomorrow."

"Listen, Honey, I don't know what you done, but — "

"Take your hands off my wife."

Davy's voice was quiet but menacing. Jim and I sprang apart. Davy stood a few feet away, his face grim, his hands clenched into fists at his sides.

"Davy, it w-wasn't the way it looked. Jim was just — "

Davy didn't even glance at me. His eyes were unwavering on Jim.

"Git goin'," he said with a little nod in the direction of Jim's new truck.

Jim stood facing Davy, his legs wide apart as if bracing himself. For a minute I was sure he was going to defy Davy, but he gave a little shrug then and turned away.

"It's your property," he said. "Bye, Teacher. Don't forget what I said. Th' offer still stands."

"Thank you, Jim."

He drove away. Davy watched him go, and I watched Davy. Then his eyes came back to me.

"He's got a nerve. You both got a nerve," he said coldly. "I s'pose I can guess what kinda offer he was makin',

standin' here in broad daylight with his arms around you an'
you lettin' him."

"It wasn't that way at all," I said. "He — he came to
show me his truck and to offer to take Todd and Evelyn in to
meet the high school bus in the mornings. I — I started
crying and — and he just — was trying to comfort me."

"You expect me to b'lieve that?"

"Yes, I expect you to believe that!" I cried hotly. "Just
because I've made one mistake you want to make me out
some kind of monster. Well, go ahead. I don't care! Believe
what you want to believe! I don't care, do you hear?"

I turned and ran into the house and slammed the door. I
stormed into the bedroom and began jerking dresses from
their hangers and throwing them any which way in the
suitcase.

"Anne."

Davy was standing in the doorway. I ignored him.

"Anne, I'm sorry."

"Well, I'm sorry too, but that isn't good enough for you,
is it?" I said furiously. "The first mistake I make, you're
ready to condemn me for life. You wanted me to go away.
Well, I'm going and I'm not coming back!"

He came around the bed and took hold of my arms in a
vicelike grip. I dropped the dress I was holding.

"Let go of me," I cried.

"Anne, listen to me."

"Why should I? Would you listen to me yesterday, when
I tried to explain?"

"I'm sorry. I was upset. We both was, but that's no
reason for you to go off half-cocked liked this."

"Oh no? Well, maybe I happen to think it is. Let me go.
I have some packing to do."

"Honey, I don't want you to go like this. I guess I hurt
you, tellin' you I wanted you to go spend some time with

your folks like that. It wasn't 'cause I wanted to get rid of you. It was 'cause I was worried about you. I was afraid you might try to go out to Tom's or he might come here an' something might happen. Tom was awful mad. I thought if you went to your folks, we'd all have time to cool off an' then maybe ever'thing would be okay. I'm sorry I made you feel bad."

I felt my face pucker. My body went limp, and I was crying in my husband's arms and clinging to him and he was kissing me all over my face.

CHAPTER EIGHTEEN

A Traveling Companion

"**Y**ou still want me to go?"
I asked Davy later that day.

"I think it might be a good idea," he said slowly. "I think maybe you need th' break an' it'll give me an' Lewis a chance to get things done in here, an' it'll give me a chance to talk to Tom again."

"I really am so very sorry about that, Davy."

"I know you are, Honey, but it's done now an' we can't change that. I jist want to give Tom a little time. He's hot-headed but he ain't unreasonable an' he did more or less bring it on hisself."

"That doesn't excuse what I did though."

"No, but then you're a little hot-headed too, aren't you?" he asked affectionately.

"Davy, I wanted to die last night when you didn't come in, and again today when — "

"I know."

"Were — were you in your shop all night?"

"Yes, except when I was settin' on th' front step feelin' miserable."

"I was so afraid I had permanently lost your friendship. You know, I think being friends is almost more important in marriage than being lovers, don't you?"

"No," he said bluntly.

"You don't?"

"No, jist as important maybe, but not more important."

"Oh. Well, it's a matter of opinion, I guess. Anyhow, I'm glad we have both."

"Me too."

"Davy?"

"Hm-m?"

"I'm going to be terribly lonely without you in St. Louis."

"You'll have lots to do, places to go an' old friends to visit. I want you to relax an' enjoy yourself an' not worry about anything here 'cause this visit's gonna have to last you awhile."

"I was wondering, would you mind if I ask if Calvin can go with me?"

"Cal?"

"Yes. I think he might enjoy it and he'd be company for me and — I'm a little concerned about him as far as Tom is concerned too."

"Might not be a bad idea," he said thoughtfully. "But I don't think Tom's as interested in Cal as you seem to think. I think it was more — other things."

"What do you mean?"

"Not sure. I'll let you know if I ever get it figgered out myself, but I don't think it was so much Bertha bein' at th' school as it was Granny tryin' to rub our noses in it. Hafta admit, that rubbed me th' wrong way a little too."

"Yes, I suppose so. I wish I hadn't let what Tom did bother me so much. I feel terrible about Ruth. She's such a sweet little girl."

"Ellen's close to all her kids. She'll help her."

"I still think I ought to go out and apologize."

"Not now. Wait'll you get back from St. Louis, then I'll go with you."

"Then you want me to go tomorrow?"

"If it's all right with your folks."

"I'd better drive to Miller's and call them then, but first I'll go by and ask Granny if Calvin can go with me."

"You won't try to go out to Tom's?"

"Not if you don't want me to. I'll be back in a couple of hours. You'll be here?"

"I'll be here."

I got in my car and drove to Granny Eldridge's house. She was sitting in a rocker on her front porch.

"Hear you been havin' some fireworks over to your place," she said by way of greeting.

"Where did you hear that?" I asked as I stepped up on the porch.

She shrugged. "News gets around," she answered.

"Everything is fine at my house," I returned firmly. "I'm going to take a week or two to visit my folks in St. Louis while Davy and Lewis finish up our house. I wondered if you would let Calvin go with me."

She stopped rocking and looked at me over her glasses.

"Now why would you be wantin' a 'leven year old boy to go with you to th' city?"

"I just thought he might enjoy it and it would be a chance for us to get better acquainted. That might be a good idea, don't you think, since there's a possibility he might be coming to live with us someday?"

"Hm-m," she murmured thoughtfully. "You sure it ain't Bertha's idea?"

"She lives in St. Louis, ya know."

"Yes, but — "

"Did you an' her get your heads together and decide this might be a way of gettin' him to her place without his knowin' where he was goin'?"

"No! It was my idea entirely. Bertha knows nothing about it and I would be taking him to my mother's house, not his mother's. Forget I even mentioned it. Perhaps it wasn't such a good idea after all."

I turned and started to go down the steps. Her words stopped me.

"No jist wait a minute," she said placatingly, her hand

raised. "I ain't sayin' he can't go. I was thinking of goin' to my daughter's for a few days soon to see how I like it. Might be a good time to go, if you're wantin' to take Calvin with you. When was you goin'?"

"About noon tomorrow, I think."

"His mama brought him some new clothes when she was here. He ain't wore them yet. They'd be all right for takin' on a trip."

"Then he can go?"

"I'll have him ready at noon tomorrow."

"Thank you. I'll see you then."

"You ain't afraid to leave your man here all by hisself that long?" she asked innocently as I reached the bottom step.

"Of course not. Why should I be?" I asked turning.

"Jist wondered. They say Goldie Sutton's sayin' you won't last long out here an' she'll be standin' by to pick up th' pieces when you go."

"I'm not going anywhere, except to visit my folks for a week or so," I said shortly.

"Guess you know she was after Davy a long time 'fore you come out here."

"But I got him," I snapped. "I'm not afraid of Goldie Sutton, or anyone like her. Good-bye, Granny. You'll tell Calvin?"

"I'll tell him."

I got in my car and drove away. Granny was without a doubt the most aggravating person I had ever met. Afraid to leave Davy alone for a week because of Goldie Sutton? How ridiculous. It was too ridiculous even to think about.

Nevertheless, I did think about it as I drove to the Millers'. Davy and I had had our first quarrel. Was it wise to be going away so soon afterward?

My mother seemed happy that I was coming. I hadn't

been home since my marriage. I asked about bringing Calvin along and she had no objection, so I told her to expect us late the next afternoon.

Davy and I spent the rest of the afternoon together and we were very close. He said nothing more about Tom's family, and though it lay heavily on my conscience, I said nothing either. Tom was his brother. I would have to be guided by his wishes, at least for now.

Calvin and I left right at noon the next day. He sat very still in the seat beside me. He was dressed in the rather worn jeans I was used to seeing him in. I supposed Granny had packed all the new clothes his mother had given him so he would have them to wear when he got to the city.

"Do you know what I think would be a good idea, Calvin?" I asked. "I think it might be fun if you kept a kind of daily log while we're on this trip. You've never been to a big city before, have you?"

He shook his head.

"We'll have to get you a notebook then and you can write down what you do each day, what your thoughts and impressions are. It will be fun and it might be very useful to you later on, especially if you're going to be a writer."

He didn't answer but his small face took on an eager, animated look.

"We'll stop at a store along the way and get you a notebook," I said. "Are you hungry? Did you have lunch?"

He nodded.

"Then maybe we can just get something to drink. We have a fairly long drive ahead of us, about four hours and there isn't a lot to see, but there will be plenty to see and do when we get there. We'll go to the zoo and to a museum or two and to the park. I think you'll really enjoy yourself, Calvin. I'm glad you could come with me."

A short time later I pulled up at a combination gas

station and country store. When the attendant came out, Calvin and I got out and went into the store while he filled the gas tank and checked the oil.

I bought the notebook and since Calvin was gazing wide-eyed at the candy and gum display, I let him pick out a few suckers and some bubble gum, bought two bottles of pop, and we were on our way again. I noticed while we were in the store that Calvin was barefoot. That was quite a common sight in the country. Even at school about half the children came without shoes in the summer. But of course, in town Calvin would have to wear shoes most of the time. I supposed Granny had packed his shoes away in his suitcase. I hoped they were presentable. The condition and style of one's shoes was not a matter of much importance in the hills.

As we were nearing St. Louis, I broached a subject to Calvin that had been in the back of my mind all the way.

"Calvin," I said, "when your mother was at our house Friday, did you understand the arrangements we were making for you?"

He nodded but there was a look of uncertainty on his face. After all, he was only eleven years old. He drew just slightly closer to me on the seat.

"Your mother loves you, Calvin," I continued. "But she was not able to take care of you when you were born. She was very young and she had no job and no home. That's why she left you with Granny. Now Granny is getting old and she isn't well, so different arrangements have to be made for you. The arrangement is that you'll stay with Granny, at least for now, and then when Granny has to go live with her daughter in town, you'll come and live with me and Davy. Do you understand that?"

He nodded again.

"I just wanted you to understand that we want you, Davy and I. We'll enjoy having you as part of our family. That doesn't mean that your mother doesn't want you. It's just that she feels this will be the best arrangement for you. You've lived in the country all your life and the city would be quite a change for you, so she's trying to take into consideration your feelings and what you want. She wouldn't do that if she didn't love you, so don't ever feel that she doesn't want you or love you, Calvin."

There was a minute or two of silence. His hand slid across the seat toward me and I took my hand from the wheel and put it over his.

"Do you know that your mother lives in St. Louis, where we're going?" I asked gently.

I felt the jerk of his body and my hand tightened.

"I'm not taking you there to leave you with her, Calvin," I assured him quickly. "We're going to my mother's house, not your mother's. I brought you with me because I wanted us to get better acquainted and because I thought I'd enjoy taking you to the zoo and the museum and different places. But I also thought we might go and visit your mother. Granny gave me her address. It's not too far from where my parents live. Can we do that, do you think? I'm sure it would make her very happy, and we wouldn't have to stay more than an hour or two."

"You won't leave me?" he asked anxiously.

"I'll be right there with you the whole time. I liked your mother, Calvin. I think we ought to get better acquainted with her. Have you ever been to a movie, Calvin?"

A negative shake of his head.

"We'll go then, and you'll love it. There's a million things to do in a big city. Perhaps we'll go for a ride on a big bus and do some shopping in the stores, and go out to eat. And we'll go and visit your mother before we go back home. A week or two may not be long enough after all."

CHAPTER NINETEEN

Tying the Knot

"*C*alvin," I said in faint exasperation, "where are your shoes now?"

"Back there."

"Back where? Go and get them, please. I'll wait here."

I sat down on a bench and watched as he turned and went slowly back along the path we had been following. He bent down beside a trash barrel and retrieved the hated shoes. Slowly he came back toward me. If I hadn't been so tired and exasperated I would have laughed at the woeful expression on his face.

This was our fifth day in St. Louis and we were spending it at the city zoo. It had been an enjoyable day for me and a fascinating one for Calvin. The only thing that had marred it so far was this penchant Calvin had for trying to lose his shoes.

When we had first arrived in St. Louis and I was helping him unpack his suitcase, I discovered his grandmother had included everything except shoes. I took him to the store and bought him a pair of what I thought were comfortable canvas shoes, but he hated them. I'd make him put them on and then the next thing I knew, he was barefoot again.

"Come sit down for a minute, Calvin," I said as he stopped before me, holding out the shoes. I took them and he sat beside me, hanging his head.

"I know you're not used to wearing shoes at home, Calvin," I said, "but it's necessary here in town. Stores require you to wear them while you're shopping, movie theaters and museums require them. It isn't considered sanitary to go without shoes in town and it's bad for your feet to walk so much on concrete. Besides that, it's dangerous. Look over there at that broken glass. If you were to step on that with bare feet you'd be seriously injured. I know shoes feel uncomfortable on your feet, Calvin, but it's better to be uncomfortable than injured. Put them on again, please."

I handed him a shoe and obediently he took it and lifted his foot to the bench and put it on. It seemed to take an inordinately long time. When the laces were finally tied, I handed him the other shoe and he repeated the process.

"Let's sit and rest a few minutes," I said then. "My feet hurt too. We seem to have walked miles, but it's been fun, hasn't it? Have you enjoyed it?"

He nodded and I gave a little sigh. I thought he must be feeling very much as I was. Our visit had not been an unqualified success. I missed Davy, the run-in with Tom was still preying on my mind, and the rush and noise of the city bothered me. I hadn't been able to sleep very well and everything seemed a little flat.

Calvin was filled with wonder and excitement over some of the new things he was seeing, but he was uncomfortable because of the confinement and the bustle and the crowds of strangers. My bringing him along had been very much a mixed blessing.

"I'm tired," I said aloud. "I'll be glad to get home. Will you, Calvin?"

He looked uncertainly at me, then nodded. I smiled and tousled his hair.

"Then let's go and visit your mother tomorrow and Sunday morning we'll start home. And I'll be as glad to get away from all this as you are."

We followed through on this plan and arrived back in the

hills about three o'clock on Sunday afternoon. I dropped Calvin off at Granny's and drove on to the cabin.

I was excited about being home and very anxious to see my husband, but the cabin had an almost deserted look about it. I got out of the car and went inside. The living room walls were finished, but no one was there. I called and went through the rest of the house, but it was empty. I went back out to the car to get my suitcases and the things I had bought. I noticed Davy's truck was gone. It was not in his parents' yard either.

I sorted out my clothes and put things away. I went through the house again. Lewis and Davy had accomplished a lot in the week I'd been away. The house was finished except for the wallpaper I wanted in the living room. It was ready to be decorated and furnished. I was very pleased with its appearance, but where was my husband? I hadn't told him definitely that I was coming home today. Nevertheless I had expected him to be there and I was disappointed. The house had an almost unlived in look.

After an hour or so I decided to walk to my in-laws' cabin and ask Clemmy if she knew where Davy was. I took along the gift I had bought, a box of chocolates. She hugged me in welcome and I returned the hug with warmth.

"Clemmy, do you know where Davy is?" I asked when we had talked a few minutes.

"I ain't seen him since yesterday mornin'," she answered. "He come over an' said would Dad see to th' chores an' for me not to cook him any meals 'til he got back, an' he didn't know when that would be."

"He didn't say where he was going?"

"No. Thought maybe he was goin' after you."

"No, he wouldn't do that. He knew I had my car. I can't imagine — . Well, he'll be home soon, I'm sure," I said, trying to sound cheerful. "Did I tell you we went to see Bertha while we were in St. Louis?"

I told her about Bertha's home and her husband. She listened eagerly and asked a lot of questions. I was there an hour and still there was no sign of Davy. I was definitely getting worried and upset by that time, so I decided to leave before Clemmy noticed. A picture of Goldie Sutton kept popping into my mind and I kept resolutely pushing it back. Surely I had more faith in my husband than to suspect him of something like that.

It was six o'clock when I heard the truck drive up. I was sitting at the kitchen table feeling almost numb by that time. I didn't go out to meet him but I rose from my chair when he came into the kitchen. I was slightly reassured by the way he almost leaped at me and took me in his arms. For the fraction of a minute I didn't respond, then my arms crept up around his neck and I raised my lips to his.

"I wasn't expectin' you back for a few days," he said, holding me away from him and looking down at me. "You been here long?"

"Since three o'clock," I said almost accusingly. "Where were you?"

"Had to go into town."

"On Sunday? But nothing is open, is it?"

"Might be surprised what's open on Sunday," he said with a little quirk of a grin. "You have a good trip?"

"Yes, but before we discuss my trip, I want to hear about yours," I said shortly, pulling away from him. "Your mother says you've been gone since yesterday morning. Where have you been all that time? Did you spend the night with your brother John?"

"Nope. Ain't seen John this week, but I don't want to talk about my relatives right now, do you? I'm glad you're home. Been awful lonesome around here without you."

He tried to pull me back into his arms but I evaded him.

"You don't appear to have been pining away for me," I said dryly, looking at his handsome, smiling face. "As a

131

matter of fact, you look as if you've been enjoying yourself hugely."

"Have been, sorta, th' last couple days."

"And what have you been doing the past couple of days?"

"Ain't tellin' 'less you come over here an' kiss me proper like a wife ought to when she's been gone for a whole week."

"And I'm not going to kiss you until you tell me what you've been up to."

"No? What do you think I been up to anyhow?" he asked, his eyes slightly narrowed though he still smiled.

"I — don't know," I said slowly. "I guess — I just expected you to be here when I got home and when you weren't, it upset me."

"You miss me then?"

"Of course I did. Very much."

"Then come here."

I went and stood before him, looking up at him. He was no longer smiling, his eyes were warm and intent on mine.

"Sweetheart," he said softly, and drew me to him. I found myself clinging to him, returning his kisses, thrilling to his whispered words.

"Come set on my lap an' I'll tell you what I been doing this weekend," he said in a few minutes. "That is, if you still want to know. If you'd jist as soon wait — ?"

"I'd like to know, Davy. You have such an air of mystery about you," I said, allowing him to draw me down on his lap.

"That why you're wantin' to know? Thought for a minute there you was a little jealous."

"Of course I'm not jealous," I said, not meeting his eyes. "Naturally, I'm just a little — curious."

"Okay, I'll tell you. I been to a weddin'."

"A wedding? Who got married? Anyone I know?"

"Yep."

"Who?"

132

"Guess."

"I don't know of anyone who — not Goldie?"

"Goldie? Nope, not Goldie. Didn't even know she had a boyfriend."

"She doesn't. She's after you," I wanted to retort, but I didn't. "I can't imagine," I said aloud. "Not Jim? Of course it couldn't be Jim, his divorce isn't final yet. I don't have any idea, Davy. Tell me."

"Tom an' Ellen."

I almost fell off his lap. "Tom and Ellen?" I exclaimed.

"Yep. Got married at noon yesterday. Me an' Ruthie stood up with them," he said proudly.

"Tom and Ellen!" I said again in disbelief. "You mean they actually got married after all this time?"

"Yep, sure did. Guess Ruthie ain't give her dad a minute's peace since — well, since you was out there a week or so ago."

"I can't believe it," I said, beginning to feel excited. "They're really married? You were there?"

"Yep. Tom come by here Friday an' asked me to come along. Seemed to think that was the only way he could be sure you'd b'lieve it. Said Ruthie'd been after him night an' day for a week to do th' right thing by her mother, so he finally give in. Wanted me to be sure you knew, soon as possible. Seemed to think you might be tellin' Granny otherwise."

My eyes fell. "I did threaten to tell her, more or less," I admitted, reluctantly, "but I didn't mean it."

"You sure put th' fear in him though. B'tween you an' Ruthie, guess th' poor devil ain't had a good night's sleep since you was out there."

"Well, if it forced him to do the right thing," I began but at his look, I hurriedly went on. "Tell me about it. Was it a nice wedding?"

"Wasn't much to it. Jist went to a justice of th' peace,

but Ellen was fixed up real pretty an' Tom was nervous as a cat. After th' weddin', th' three of them out for dinner, Ruthie an' Tom an' Ellen, and I went to that hotel you an' me stayed at on our honeymoon an' got them a room for th' night. Not th' same room you an' me had though."

"They spent the night in town?"

"Yep. Me an' Ruthie got our heads together an' arranged it. She packed a suitcase for her mom an' dad an' we hid it in th' back of my truck. I drove them into town an' after th' weddin' an' th' dinner, me an' Ruthie drove them to th' hotel an' left them there. I took Ruthie home an' spent th' night with th' kids. Then we all went into town at noon today an' picked them up an' went out to dinner again an' to a show, one of them matinees, then I took them home an' come home myself. An' that's what I been doin' for th' past two days."

"Oh Davy, it's wonderful! How did they look? Did they look happy?"

"Ellen did. She was jist kinda glowin'. Tom jist looked stunned, like he'd been run over by a truck or somethin'."

"And Ruth?" I asked a bit hesitantly.

"She's doin' okay. She's a good girl. Been doin' a lot of growin' up in th' last week."

"Do you think she'll ever be able to forgive me?"

"We had a long talk last night after th' younger kids was in bed. She don't blame you for what happened. She might feel a little uncomfortable around you for awhile, but she'll get over it."

"Oh, Davy, I'm so glad things have worked out this way and I didn't inadvertently destroy a family. Do you think the marriage will work out?"

"It will if Ellen has her way about it. Shoulda seen th' proud way she was holdin' up her head after th' weddin'."

"I wish I could have seen it. Did the younger children know?"

"No. Don't none of them know anything about any of it. We jist told them their mama and daddy wanted to have a little time to theirselves. Ain't no reason why they should ever have to know."

"I'm not going to tell them," I said defensively. "Just because I lost my temper with Tom — "

"I wasn't thinkin' you would. Get down off your high horse, Woman. I was jist explainin'."

"I'm sorry. I still feel terribly guilty about what I did, but it seems to have turned out well. I hope Ellen and I can be friends again, and Ruth too. Do you think I could go out and talk to them?"

"Better wait for a week or two. Give Tom a chance to get used to th' idea that he's a married man now."

"After what? Thirteen or fourteen years living with the same woman? And with five children to show for it?"

"Well, yeah, but — "

I knew what he meant but I thought perhaps we'd better not go into the subject of Tom's infidelities. I wondered if marriage would change that. Only time would tell of course.

"Know what else I done while I was at that hotel?" Davy asked.

" 'Did', not 'done'," I corrected without thinking. "What did you do?"

"I reserved a room for us, room 104, th' same one we was in on our honeymoon, an' I reserved it for th' night of December 20th. That all right?"

"December 20, our first wedding anniversary," I said, touched. "That's not just all right. That's wonderful. Thank you, Davy."

"Got a present for you but can't give it to you 'til tomorrow," he said, his mouth against my hair, his arms holding me close. "Sure glad you're home. Never been so lonesome in my whole life."

"I'm glad to be home too, Davy," I said.

He gave me my present the next day. He drove off in the truck for a short time and came back with a small brown puppy of mixed breed in his arms. When he gave it to me, it wiggled and squirmed in my arms and licked my face. I was delighted.

"It's darling," I said. "It looks just like Brownie."

"That's why I got him for you. He's a relative of Brownie. Come from th' same people," Davy told me.

"Then is it all right if I name him Brownie?"

"Name him anything you want to. He's yours."

"Thank you, Davy."

"Only one thing. I don't like a dog in th' house. That's why I waited 'til he was big enough to stay outside before I got him."

"But don't you think — ?"

"Nope. I'm gonna build him a dog house an' a pen today. It's plenty warm. He'll be okay an' he's used to it."

"All right. Your Brownie was never a house dog either, was he?"

"No. It spoils a dog to keep him inside th' house, I think. Gonna have to get myself a couple huntin' dogs one of these days, too, but this'n is yours. Which reminds me, it's about time you learned to use a gun."

"Use a gun? But why should I need to know how to use a gun? I hate the things."

"It's necessary out here. Remember th' snake that got Brownie? An' remember that bobcat that got into Granny's pig pen?

"Supposin' I was gone some night an' th' pup here was outside an' there was a bobcat in th' trees there an' you knew he was after th' pup? An' when we get a chicken house built an' get some chickens, there's always foxes that get in, or hawks that swoop down an' get th' baby chickens. What you gonna do about them things if I'm not here an' you don't know how to shoot a gun?"

"You really think it's necessary?"

"I know it is. Give you a shootin' lesson tomorrow. Right now I better get at that pen for th' pup. Why don't you bring a paper an' pencil an' come out with me? We can decide what all we need to get for th' house when we go into town an' you can write it down so we don't forget anything."

"All right, I will. Did I tell you I made arrangements to have my piano and hope chest shipped out later this week?"

"Yes, you did. When do you think they'll get here?"

"He said Thursday or Friday."

"Then we better go on in to town tomorrow, so we'll be sure an' be here. You like th' house since we finished it up?"

"Very much, Davy. I'm anxious to finish decorating and furnishing it. It's going to be beautiful."

"You don't mind th' logs showin' on the outside walls?"

"I like it. It's unique and homey. You've done a wonderful job building it. You just wait until I finish decorating it. I bought some things in St. Louis that I want to use, and I have some things in my hope chest too. I can't wait to get started."

"Well, come on out an' make your list. Maybe you can let th' pup down to run around before he licks you to death, too."

"Good idea," I laughed. "I'll just give him a little something to eat so he'll know we're friends, then I'll join you."

I gave the puppy some ground beef and he gulped it down as if starving. Then I gathered up a pencil and a tablet and carried the puppy out into the back yard where Davy was driving stakes into the ground for the pen. I petted the pup and fussed over him for a few minutes, then I put him down on the ground. He didn't try to run away, but stayed close to me, still wanting to play. I divided my attention between him and the list I was making.

CHAPTER TWENTY

The Flirt

I was at the piano when the front door opened and Jim Baker came in and quietly seated himself in one of the rockers. I was aware of him but I didn't stop playing or look up from the music before me until I had finished the piece. Then I sat back and looked over at him.

"Sorry to jist walk in like that," he said. "I knocked but guess you didn't hear me. Thought I better come on in 'cause from th' sound of things, figgered someone was either dyin' or at least in terrible pain."

I laughed. "The music, you mean? It's a piece by a very famous composer."

"Sounded like someone dyin' to me," he said. "So — how are things goin' for you now?"

"Just fine, Jim. Everything is wonderful."

He nodded. "You look like it," he said. "Get prettier ever' time I see you. You an' Davy worked out that little problem you had, I guess."

"Yes. It was nothing."

"Nothin', she says. Almost got my head knocked off 'cause of it and you say it was nothin'?"

"I'm sorry, Jim. I shouldn't have involved you. I was upset and you just happened along at the wrong time."

" 'S' all right. You sure got a pretty little place here. Too bad. I was hopin', if you wasn't happy with it, I could talk you an' Davy into buyin' mine."

"You're definitely selling it then?"

"Yep. Got to. It's part of th' divorce settlement. Got to sell th' house an' divide th' profit equal between us."

"Is the divorce final then?"

"Yep."

"I'm sorry, Jim."

"I'm 'fraid Sally an' me was a mistake from th' start to th' finish. Jist wish I could get th' house sold an' get it all behind me an' forget it. Don't know if anybody wants to a buy a house, do you?"

"I'll tell you who I'd like to see buy it, and that's Lewis and Sue Proctor. They need a better place, but they're expecting a baby next month, and I don't suppose they could afford it."

"Bank might be willin' to give them a loan, if their credit's good."

"I don't know," I said.

"Might mention it to them when you see them. Lewis still works for Davy, don't he? Can't hurt anything to ask."

"No."

"So, how was your visit back home?"

"Fine. I had a nice time."

"You got any sisters like you left at home?"

"I have two sisters, one older, one younger. The older one is married, the younger one is not, but — "

"But what? You don't think she'd like th' likes of me, huh?"

"She's strictly a city girl, I'm afraid."

"So? You was a city girl once yourself, wasn't you?"

"Yes, but I've always liked the idea of living in the country. Liz says the thought makes her shudder."

"Her name is Liz? Is she as pretty as you?"

"Some people think she's prettier, but I'm afraid she's a little spoiled. She's the youngest, you know."

"She ever gonna come visit you?"

"I don't know."

"Well, if she does, you let me know. I'd like to take a look at her."

"All right, I will, but I'm not sure it's a good idea. I don't think the two of you would be good for each other."

"Tell you one thing for sure, if I wasn't a married man when you first come here, I'd a give ol' Davy a run for his money."

"Jim — "

I heard the truck drive up in the yard and stop. We were sitting silently when Davy came in.

"I hid all your guns," Jim quipped, with a little crooked grin at Davy.

Davy looked from him to me, eyebrows raised. He came over and kissed me on the cheek, then his hand went to Jim's shoulder and gripped it for a moment.

"Why don't you stay and have lunch with us, Jim?" I said rising. "It's just a cold lunch, but we'd love to have you. It's all ready."

"You talked me into it," he said.

"She show you around th' place since we got it all fixed up?" Davy asked.

"Nope. Jist got here. She was playin' some gosh-awful mournful thing on th' piany here an' I thought I better come in an' cheer her up a little."

I laughed. "You show him around, Davy. I'll put lunch on the table."

I set the table for three and made coffee. Then I put out the cold lunch I had prepared earlier. I'd made potato salad and a fruit salad and tuna salad sandwiches, and there were radishes and green onions from the garden, and carrot sticks. I was able to prepare such things ahead of time and plentifully, to last a few days, because of the refrigerator. I saved the preparing of a hot meal for evening. Davy seemed to enjoy the cold lunch, but I sometimes wondered if he missed the hot meals his mother always prepared.

I heard the men washing up and was pouring the coffee when they came in to the kitchen.

"You've fixed it up real nice," Jim told me, "but it don't look much like a city girl's doin's. It's a real country home."

"Well, why not? This is the country, isn't it?"

"You got a real sweetheart here, Davy ol' boy. Hope you appreciate her. If you don't, I can think of someone else who'd be glad to take over."

"Hands off my wife, Jim," Davy said drawing out his chair. "I appreciate her plenty, don't I, Sweetheart?"

"You do. Sit down, Jim."

I drew out my own chair and sat down and we began the meal. Jim broached the subject of selling his house to Sue and Lewis and we discussed the pros and cons of that. Jim told us about his new job and his new truck and we talked about the arrangements that could be made for him to drive Todd and possibly Evelyn in to meet the high school bus. It was a pleasant meal and the men ate heartily. When they left the table and went into the living room to sit and talk some more, I cleared off the table, and then went to join them.

"Davy and I have been talking about having open house," I said to Jim when there was a lull in the conversation. "We'd like to set a day and invite all the neighbors to drop in for coffee and cookies, and to see our new house. Do you think that might be a good idea, or do you think some people might think we're boasting, trying to show off?"

"What's wrong with showin' off a little when you got somethin' like this to show off? I think it's a good idea an' I think you oughta invite that sister of yours to come. Make it on a Saturday so I can come too."

At Davy's inquiring look, I explained that Jim thought he'd like to meet my sister Liz.

"I asked her if there's any more at home like her, an' she

says there's one, so I wanta meet her," Jim said calmly.

"Do you think Liz is anything like me, Davy?" I asked with a little smile.

"I only met her that once, at th' weddin'," he answered, "an' I s'pose there is some resemblance, but not much. She seemed a little — young."

"Actually in some ways she's a lot like you, Jim. She's a flirt," I said.

He looked pained. "Me, a flirt?"

"In a nice sort of way, of course. Can we go ahead and have the open house, Davy? I'm so proud of the house and I'd like to show it off and I'll try not to sound boastful about it. It would be an opportunity for me to get better acquainted with everyone, too."

"Okay by me, if you want to do it."

"Would next Saturday be all right? Say between ten and four o'clock?"

"Sounds okay."

I jumped up and clasped my hands in delight. "I'll bake cookies and make gallons of punch. I'll have to run into town before then, Davy. And Jim, you'll pass the word around, won't you? Next Saturday, between ten and four. Everyone in the neighborhood is invited."

"Ever'one?"

"Yes. Everyone."

"An' are you gonna invite your sister?"

"I'll invite my sister, but I don't know if she'll be able to come. She works, you know."

"She have a boyfriend?"

"Dozens," I said.

"Tell her there's a feller out here would like to meet her, an' you might tell her what a great guy I am, too."

"I won't tell her any such thing. I'll let her make up her own mind. If she comes."

CHAPTER TWENTY-ONE

The Apology

On Thursday evening after supper, Davy and I went to Tom's house. I was nervous, uncertain of the kind of reception I would receive. Davy was quiet and I thought he was a little apprehensive too.

The younger children were playing in the yard. They came running to meet us and followed us up to the house. Davy knocked and Tom came to the door. He looked straight at me and he didn't smile or speak or make a move to invite us in. I saw Ellen come up behind him.

"Who is it, Tom?" she asked.

Tom stepped aside, with a little wave of his hand in our direction. Ellen stepped forward.

"Hello, Anne, Davy," she said quietly. She pushed open the screen and held it. "Come on in. You kids go back and play. It'll be gettin' bedtime soon."

I stepped inside and Davy followed me. Tom was standing to one side, watching me with hard, unfriendly eyes. From the kitchen came the sound of dishes being washed and I caught a glimpse of Ruth, their oldest daughter, through the open door. Ellen pulled a couple of chairs forward.

"Sit down," she said. "Would you like a cup of coffee?"

"No thanks," I said, taking the chair she offered.

"You, Davy?"

"No thanks, Ellen, we jist got through eatin'."

Davy sat down and Tom and Ellen did likewise. There was a tense silence.

"I guess," I said rather hesitantly, "this is up to me, isn't it? I don't quite know what to say, except that I'm sorry about — what I said the last time I was here. I was angry and I — but I'm not trying to make excuses for myself. What I did was very wrong. I had no right to say what I did and I certainly didn't mean for any of the children to hear. I'm very sorry and I hope you'll both forgive me."

"Did you tell anyone?" Tom demanded in a hard, clipped voice.

"You mean — ?"

"You said you was gonna tell Granny."

"Oh. No, I didn't tell anyone. I wouldn't have. I was just angry and — " I paused, my eyes locked with his and some of the old unease began to stir in me again. I tossed my head a little. I was not going to crawl. "I guess I was trying to scare you to get even with you for ruining the school performance, and for your attitude toward Calvin. I happen to be very fond of Calvin, and I resent your attitude toward him very much."

I paused. He said nothing but his eyes were still hard on me.

"Anyhow, I do apologize for my behavior and I assure you, I haven't told anyone else, and I won't."

I turned to Ellen. "Ellen, I'm sorry. Please forgive me," I said more quietly.

She nodded and reached over and briefly touched my hand. I took a deep breath.

"Davy and I are having an open house Saturday, between the hours of ten and four. Our cabin is finished and we're inviting everyone over to visit a little and have some refreshments. I hope you'll all come, the whole family. We'd love to have you."

Tom spoke. "Ever since you come out here," he said, "you made it plain I ain't good enough for th' likes of you.

Ever' time I come near you, you run like a scared rabbit. I could count on one hand th' times you lowered yourself to even speak to me. You sure you're wantin th' likes of me to dirty that new house of yours with my presence?"

I sat stunned, staring at him almost open-mouthed. I tried to speak but no words came out. I moistened my lips and tried again.

"I'm sorry. I didn't realize. I thought you were — " I floundered and stopped. I glanced at Davy but he was silent, looking at me. Ellen was sitting quietly in her chair, her hands clasped together, her eyes lowered. I was on my own.

"If I've given you the impression that I think I'm better than you, Tom, I'm sorry. It was unintentional."

"Was it? You seem to have time for ever'body else. Jim can joke around with you an' you're might chummy with Lewis an' you can go an' set an' visit with the Hortons an' the Johnsons an' spend a lot of time with Granny Eldridge, but have you ever took th' time to come out here an' visit with us? Even since you married Davy an' we was part of th' same family, you ain't been near us. You think we got th' plague, or somethin'? Or was it 'cause — "

"No! No, Tom. It wasn't that at all," I interrupted. I swallowed rather convulsively. I seemed to have done a pretty thorough job of misjudging him. I didn't know what to say. "I'm sorry," I said slowly. "The honest truth is that I thought you were trying to flirt with me and — and I didn't quite know how to handle the situation. I knew you were a married man. At least, I thought — I mean, I like Ellen very much and I — "

His hard eyes flickered and lowered. He looked a little shame-faced.

"Jist cause a man tries to be friendly — " he said and left the sentence unfinished.

"If I misjudged you, Tom, I'm sorry. As a teacher, I have to be very careful, you know."

"Maybe you oughta be a little more careful about th'

amount of time you spend with Jim Baker, then," he said shortly.

"Jim is my friend," Davy spoke quietly for the first time. "If he comes to visit me an' I ain't there an' he stays an' visits a little with my wife, that ain't nobody's business but ours."

Tom didn't answer. His eyes came back to me. I rose and took a few steps toward him and held out my hand. He sat looking at me for a minute, then slowly his hand came out and took mine, he stood up and towered over me.

"I'm sorry, Tom," I said looking up at him. In that moment, he reminded me very much of Davy. I felt a slight shivery feeling go through me; not at all sure even now that my original instincts about him had been wrong. "I hope we can put all these misunderstandings behind us and be friends, the whole family, I mean, and I hope you'll come to our open house Saturday. We'd be very glad to have you."

He nodded and I drew my hand away, still feeling a little uncertain and confused.

"May I go into the kitchen and talk to Ruth a minute?" I asked, turning to Ellen.

She nodded, and I went into the kitchen, thankful to escape the charged atmosphere there in the living room. Ruth had her back to me. She was putting dishes away in the cupboard.

"Ruth," I said quietly.

Her body stiffened. She finished putting the plates on the shelf, closed the cabinet door and turned slowly to face me.

"Ruth, I came to ask you to forgive me for what I did a couple of weeks ago. I know it was very upsetting to you and I don't blame you if you don't like me very much right now, but I hope that, in time — "

Tears welled up in her eyes, her lower lip quivered. I reached out and touched her shoulder and a moment later she was in my arms sobbing.

"Ruth," I said, holding her close. "I'm sorry. Don't feel badly, please. None of it was your fault. I wouldn't have had you hear what I said for anything in the world."

She pulled away and wiped her eyes with her hands.

"I'm glad I was here," she whispered fiercely. "I'm glad you said it an' I'm glad I heard it. I made Daddy marry Mama. I told him I'd run away if he didn't an' I'd never come back again. He didn't want to do it, but I made him, an' you wasn't wrong about him tryin' to flirt with you either. I saw him myself, lots of times, when — "

"Sh-h-h, Ruthie. Don't — don't say that," I whispered back.

"Perhaps we were wrong, perhaps he didn't intend it to be . . . anyhow he married your mother and perhaps things will be different now."

"They better be or I'll threaten to run away again."

"Ruth, your mother loves him and he loves her too, and he loves you and your brothers and sisters. Things are not always what they appear to be. Anyhow, I want you to know that I'll never, never tell anyone about — what I said last time I was here. No one else need ever know and you can hold your head up and be proud, Ruth. You have nothing to be ashamed of."

Ellen came into the room then and we both turned and looked at her.

"Is — everything all right in here?" she asked.

"Ever'thing's fine, Mama," Ruth said briskly. "Are we goin' to their house Saturday?"

"Would you like to?"

"Yes, Mama, I would. Th' house is real pretty on th' outside an' I'd like to see what it's like inside."

"Then we'll go. Is there anything I can bring?"

"No, just yourselves. Thank you, Ellen."

Impulsively, I went over and gave her a quick hug. She stiffened and flushed, but she didn't draw away.

"I suppose Davy will be wanting to get back," I said. "He still has the chores to do. I'm glad you can come Saturday."

They went into the living room with me and the men rose from their chairs.

"How you doin', Ruthie?" Davy asked gently.

"Fine," she answered.

"You ready to go?" he asked me.

"Yes."

"We'll be seein' you on Saturday then."

They saw us to the door and in silence Davy and I got in the car. He was driving. I sat thoughtful for a long moment.

"How did it go with Ruthie?" Davy asked then.

"Good. She was very sweet. I got off easy, I guess. Thank you for paving the way."

"Ellen acted all right, I thought."

"Yes. Davy, do you think I misjudged Tom?"

"No."

"You don't? He had me almost believing I had for awhile. I felt terrible."

Silence again.

"I could have handled it differently, I suppose," I mused almost to myself. "After all, Jim is a flirt too and I didn't refuse to be friendly with him. Somehow it was different though. Jim does it in such a lighthearted, teasing way and Tom always seemed — so serious."

"You want to be careful about gettin' too friendly with Tom now that you two seem to have decided to bury th' hatchet. It might cause problems."

"I know. He reminds me of you quite a lot at times. Did you know that?"

He glanced quickly at me.

"Not too much, I hope."

"No, just occasionally, a look or an expression. I'm wondering now if he really does have that much animosity toward Calvin. I'm wondering if it wasn't just his way of getting back at me for being ... rather aloof with him."

"I been thinkin' that for quite awhile now. He didn't pay no attention to Calvin that I know of before you came here."

"Hm-m. Strange. I've made an awful lot of mistakes in my relationships with people since I came here. I'm beginning to think I'm not as perceptive as I thought I was."

"Bound to make a few mistakes," Davy said. "Don't s'pose you've made near as many as I'd a made if things had been th' other way around."

I moved closer to him and he put his arm around me. I leaned my head against his shoulder.

"Davy, Tom loves Ellen and his children, doesn't he?"

"Yep."

"Then why?"

He shrugged. "Don't know for sure, but sometimes I think it might have somethin' to do with him bein' married before."

I lifted my head. "I didn't know he was married before," I said.

"Not many people do. She was a beauty an' Tom was crazy about her but she run off with another man before they was married even a year. After that Tom changed. It was like he had to keep provin' he was as good as anyone else, 'specially with th' women."

"And Ellen?"

"She lived jist over th' hill from where th' Proctors live now. Her ol' man was pretty mean to her from what I heard. One day when he was mistreatin' her, Tom stepped in an' took her away an' took her to his house. He wasn't in love with her but she didn't have nowhere else to go. She started cookin' and housekeepin' for him an' things jist sorta drifted on from there. He told her they'd get married someday, but guess it was jist easier to keep puttin' it off. I figger Tom was afraid of marriage because of what happened th' first time. He's always been good to Ellen an' th' kids, an' Ellen's crazy about him. Didn't take him too long to start lovin' Ellen too, but I don't know if he realizes it hisself, even now."

"He loves her but he still has to prove he's attractive to other women?"

"Guess so."

"Maybe now that they're legally married, he'll feel differently. He wasn't officially committed before so he was free to — well, to flirt with other women. Perhaps that will change now."

"Don't know," he said doubtfully. "Maybe."

"Let's hope so anyhow. I'd like to see every married couple as happy as we are, Davy. Wouldn't it be wonderful if things worked out that way for Tom and Ellen?"

"Sure would," he said.

CHAPTER TWENTY-TWO

Open House

"**W**ell, at least you'll get a chance to get better acquainted with one member of my family," I said to Davy, arranging paper cups on the kitchen table.

"She's gonna be here a week?"

"Not necessarily. She said she has a week's vacation and would like to spend part of it with us. What's wrong, Davy? Don't you like my sister?"

"It ain't that. It's jist that I ain't so sure this idea of her an' Jim is such a good one."

"I know what you mean. Jim's very vulnerable right now, isn't he?"

"An' your sister is ... "

"Is what?"

"Well, I don't know how to say it, but she might give him th' come on an' not mean it."

"Do it just for a lark, you mean?"

"Yes, guess that is what I mean."

"She might," I said slowly, "or it's just possible that Jim will give her the come on and not mean it. He's just as capable of that as she is, you know."

"S'pose so. Crazy idea he had, havin' you write her an' tell her to come 'cause he wanted to meet her."

"It's just the sort of thing that would intrigue her though. It isn't going to do any good for us to fret about it, Davy. They're both adults and responsible for themselves."

"An speakin' of th' devil," Davy said looking out the window. I heard a car door slam.

"Which one?" I asked.

"Jim. He's nearly a hour early. You don't s'pose he's really serious 'bout all this, do you?"

"I don't know. I hope not."

Davy went to the door to let Jim in. They both came into the kitchen where I was. Davy and I exchanged a quick glance. Jim was dressed in the usual blue jeans but they were new and so was his blue plaid shirt. His sandy hair was slicked down, his freckled face clean shaven and liberally doused with after shave, from the smell that wafted across to me.

"Hello, Jim," I said with a smile. "You're out and about early."

"It's th' early bird get's th' worm," he quipped. I was arranging cookies on a platter and he reached out and helped himself to one.

"Coffee?" I asked.

"Sounds good."

I poured a cup and handed it to him.

"Your sister not here yet?"

"No. She just said sometime this morning."

He nodded and helped himself to another cookie.

"Didn't you have any breakfast?" I asked, faintly exasperated.

"Nope. Too excited, I guess."

I stopped arranging the cookies, my hands resting on the edge of the table, and looked at him with a frown.

"Jim."

"Huh?"

"I'm afraid you're . . . well, putting too much importance on all this."

"How do you mean?"

"I mean my sister may not like you or you may not like

her. She may not be coming because of you at all. Maybe she's coming to visit me."

"But I can look, can't I, an' at least meet her?"

"Of course you can but ... "

"Are you worryin' about me?"

"Yes, Jim, I am. Davy and I both are. We don't want you to get hurt. My sister is young and rather flighty and ... and not too serious about anything. She may lead you on and then drop you like a hot potato."

"Sounds like my kinda girl." He came over to me and bent to kiss me on the cheek. "You're awful sweet, but don't worry 'bout me, Honey. I can take care of myself," he said.

"I hope so. I don't want my sister to be hurt either."

"Gotcha," he said. "Well, this looks like enough cookies for me. Where's ever'one else's?"

I rapped his knuckles as he took another one. "Davy, please, take him away," I said, "before he eats them all."

"Come in th' livin' room," Davy said, taking his friend by the arm. "I'm s'posed to show ever'body around, but since you done seen th' place, maybe I'll jist let you do it. You'd be better at it than me."

"Don't you dare run off, Davy," I called after them.

The punch was ready, the coffee made, and there were more cookies in the cupboard. The table looked nice. I had spread it with a white tablecloth and put out paper cups and napkins. I was keeping it simple. With only coffee, punch and cookies to serve, there was no need for plates and forks. I looked around me with satisfaction. The kitchen was clean and bright and full of sunshine. It was a big country kitchen and I loved it.

There was nothing more to do so I went to join Jim and Davy in the living room. They were idly talking so I wandered through the rest of the house to make sure I had left nothing undone. Everything was in order. Davy was very good at helping me to keep things neat.

Sue and Lewis and their girls were the next to arrive. They drove up in their wagon and I saw that Jane Decker and her boys were with them. I'd asked Sue to be sure and tell Jane. I thought she needed to get out among people more and I wanted Davy to meet her. I greeted them at the door.

"I'm so glad you and the boys could come too, Jane," I told her when they were all inside and the first greetings were over. "I want you to meet my husband. Davy, this is Jane Decker. Jane, my husband, Davy."

While she and Davy shook hands, she subjected him to a close scrutiny. "My, my," she murmured with an arched glance at me. "Ain't you th' lucky one?"

Davy flushed and looked embarrassed. I laughed a little.

"I am, actually," I said. "And this is Jim Baker." She turned away from studying Davy and shook hands with Jim. She was dressed a little better than I'd seen her dressed before and she looked a little less angular, probably because her hair was not drawn back from her face quite so tight. She still wore it in a bun at the back, but it was looser and a little fluffed out about her face. I wondered if her husband had ever located her. I hadn't seen her since the day I'd gone out to warn her that he was searching for her.

The boys were standing silent and solemn behind their mother. I introduced them by name, then took them all on a tour of the house. Lewis and Sue hadn't seen it since we had finished furnishing and decorating it. I was so proud of our home but I suddenly wondered if this had been such a good idea after all. Jane Decker had so little and Sue and Lewis didn't have much more. I was afraid they might feel deprived and depressed. Sue was rather quiet but Jane was liberal and rather loud in her admiration of the beauty and coziness of the cabin. There didn't seem to be an envious bone in her body.

We ended up in the kitchen and as I poured the drinks, Jane told me she and her husband were back together again.

He had to work on Saturdays, otherwise he would have come too.

"I'm so glad for you," I said. "Would you like coffee or punch?"

"I'll try th' punch," she said. "Coffee sure smells good but I'm a itchin' to see if that punch tastes as good as it looks. My land, look at all them cookies. Better keep a eye on my Jimmie. He's a great one for always havin' his hand in th' cookie jar. How many kinds you got?"

"Four. I've fixed a bench over there in the corner for the children, if you don't mind their kneeling on the floor."

"Land sakes, why not? Floor looks clean enough to eat off of. Jist hope them boys of mine don't make a mess."

"Don't worry about that. We'll just put a plate of cookies on the bench and they can all help themselves. Would you like to take them their drinks?"

When the children were served, Jane and Sue and I seated ourselves at the table, Sue and I with coffee, Jane with a glass of punch. Lewis had taken his coffee and joined Jim and Davy in the living room.

"So how are you feeling, Sue?" I asked. She was in the last weeks of her pregnancy and she looked tired and rather miserable.

"I'm all right. The heat is starting to get to me a little, but other than that, I'm doing pretty well. I brought you a book to read."

She reached in her purse and brought out a paperback. I took it and looked at the title. It was *Secrets to a Successful Home Delivery.*

"Good grief, Sue," I exclaimed. "I promised to baby-sit with the girls, not to deliver the baby."

"I know, but there's always the possibility that something unexpected could happen. I want to be prepared. I've read the book and I made Lewis read it and I want you to read it too, just in case."

"Sue, I've never even seen a baby born. Puppies once, but never a baby. I wouldn't know what to do. In the movies, you always boil water, but I don't know why."

"The book explains all that. I'm not planning on having it at home but it's so far into town, you just never know what might happen."

"Sue, you're one of my best friends. I'd do almost anything for you. I'll baby-sit your kids, I'll put my car at your disposal, gassed up and ready to go at a moment's notice, I'll drive you in to the hospital if Lewis isn't home, but I won't deliver your baby. I'd be so scared I'd be useless."

"I helped deliver a baby once," Jane said. "I could maybe help if you needed someone."

"Thank you, Jane," Sue said quietly. "If I need you, I'll call on you. But, if something happens and I have to have it at home, I want Anne there too."

"I'll send Davy. He's been around a farm all his life, he knows more ... "

"Davy!" Sue exclaimed, shocked. "I wouldn't let a man help me have a baby, not even Lewis, if I could help it. I'd have it by myself first."

"But your doctor is a man, isn't he?"

"That's different. He's a doctor. Promise me you'll come if I need you, Anne."

"All right, I'll come, but don't expect me to be any help to you. I'll probably faint or something."

"No, you won't. You always stay so calm and collected."

I looked at her in something like awe. Was that the impression I gave?

"Guess who's here?" Davy said dryly from the doorway. "An' guess who went out to welcome her?"

"Not Liz?" I asked, rising.

Davy nodded. I went and looked out the window. My sister was standing by her car and Jim was standing beside her. They seemed to be holding hands.

"Excuse me," I said. "My sister is here. I want to go out to see her for a minute. I'll be right back."

"Come with me?" I said to Davy as I passed him. "Lewis, excuse us for a minute, will you?"

My sister and Jim were no longer hand-locked, but they were standing a few feet apart talking. Liz had worn a dress as I suggested, a cool sleeveless cotton dress, white with small pink flowers. She looked delicate and dainty and very pretty. She turned as Davy and I came toward her and called out to us in a happy voice.

"Hello, you two lovebirds. I hope you don't mind my crashing your party."

I hugged her. "I'm glad you could come. You remember Davy?"

"Of course. How could I ever forget such a good-looking man? Is it all right if I hug him?"

She didn't wait for my permission but reached up and gave Davy a tight hug around the neck and a peck on the cheek. Davy didn't hug her but he returned the kiss almost solemnly.

"Is this the fella you wanted me to meet?" Liz asked me with a nod in Jim's direction.

"It was his idea, not mine," I answered. "Come on in the house, you two. We have other guests waiting."

"Did they come in that?" she asked in awe, indicating the wagon and the mules that were drowsing under a shade tree.

"Yes, they did."

"Mom told me people still used them here, but I don't think I believed her. And your house. It's beautiful, but logs?"

"Yes, logs. Come see the inside, I think you'll like it. Coming, Jim?"

Jim gave a little start. He had been staring at Liz in a rather bemused way and it was obvious to me that she was aware of it and not averse to it, but she wasn't letting on.

"Can I bring in your things?" Davy asked.

"Thank you, that would be very nice. They're in the trunk."

She opened the trunk. She had two large suitcases and several bags and parcels. We all took something and went up to the house. I led the way to the spare bedroom. Liz was looking around in wonder, but she said nothing.

"Come meet our guests, then I'll show you around the house," I said. I introduced her to Sue and Jane and their children. She was polite and smiling, but her eyes kept darting back to Jane and the children who were frankly staring at the picture she made. I felt a surge of pride in her. She was five years younger than I and I hadn't seen much of her for several years, but she had grown into a beautiful young woman and she was very dear to me.

"I'll show you around the cabin," I said when she had had a cookie and a glass of punch, "then perhaps you'd like to freshen up and unpack."

"I'll be glad to show her around for you, since you got other guests," Jim said from the doorway.

"Thank you," I said dryly.

She went with alacrity. I sat down with Jane and Sue.

They left soon afterward, but Jim stayed on. He and Liz certainly seemed to be hitting it off well. They had gone into the back yard to see the pup. Their voices and Liz's laughter floated in through the open window. Davy and I exchanged looks and Davy shook his head.

Several more people arrived and I didn't keep track of Liz and Jim after that. Calvin crept in and said that Granny would like to come but she didn't have any way to get there since it was too far to walk. I told him one of us would come after her later in the afternoon. I gave him a glass of punch and a handful of cookies and he was on his way. At twelve o'clock we had a short respite from our company and I brought out the sandwiches I had made earlier and put in the refrigerator. I stuck my head out the the back door and called to Jim and Liz.

"I thought you might like a little light lunch," I said when they came in. "I have some sandwiches ready."

"Oh goody," said Liz. "I'm hungry. I didn't have any breakfast."

"Me neither," Jim said, reaching for a sandwich. "You as good a cook as she is?" he asked Liz.

"No," she said, wrinkling her nose at him. "I'm good at sitting around and looking helpless so that people want to wait on me. Could I have a glass of milk, Anne?"

I got her the glass of milk. Jim handed her the plate of sandwiches.

"Thank you," she said sweetly. "Will you please pass me a napkin, Davy?"

Davy handed her a napkin and she thanked him prettily.

"See?" she said, looking up wide-eyed at Jim.

"I see," he said dryly. "You all mind if I take her off your hands this afternoon? You got lots more people comin' prob'ly an she kinda wants to see some of th' countryside. Thought I might show her my place too."

"Which one? Old or new?" I asked.

"Both."

"I see. Well, it's up to her, of course."

"You don't mind, do you?" she asked me. "We won't be able to do any visiting today, anyway, because of all your company."

"I don't mind. How is everyone at home?"

"Fine. Mom sent all kinds of messages, can't remember them all, but everyone is fine."

"Another sandwich?"

"No thanks, that was plenty. Is there anything you need me to help you with before we go?"

"There is one thing. That is, if it's convenient." I looked up at Jim. "Granny Eldridge would like to come but she has no transportation. Would it be possible for you to go by, say about three, and get her and bring her here?"

"Think she'll fit in my truck?" Jim bantered. "May have to put your sister in th' back."

"Why is that?" Liz asked.

"Jist wait'll you see her. Might oughta take your car."

"We can take mine," Liz said.

"Okay. We'll do it."

"May I see you for a minute before you go, Liz?" I asked, rising, avoiding Jim's eyes.

"Oh, oh. Big sister talk?"

"Precisely. Come along, Child. Excuse us, please."

I took her into the spare bedroom and closed the door. She stood looking at me, eyebrows raised inquiringly.

"Do you like him?" I asked bluntly.

"Jim? Yes. Why?"

"Has he told you anything about himself?"

"Not much. Why?"

"I'm not trying to interfere, Liz, but you're young ... "

"I'm twenty. I've lived away from home nearly a year now. I choose my own friends."

"I know. Don't be angry, please, but I thought you ought to know that Jim is just recently divorced. He has been pretty upset about it. He seems to be doing fine now but he's, well, susceptible I guess would be the word. I just don't want to see either one of you get hurt."

"He's a special friend of yours?"

"He and Davy have been friends for a long time and yes, Jim is a friend of mine, too. You two seem to be getting along so well and that's fine, but I just wanted you to know all the facts before ... well, before things develop any further."

"Are you in love with him?"

"No! Of course not! Liz, what an awful thing to say."

"Is he in love with you?"

I opened my mouth to deny it but I found my eyes faltering before hers. Was Jim a little in love with me? It was a question that had been bothering me for some time.

"Of course not," I said then.

"In other words, he is. Does Davy know?"

"There's nothing to know. There's nothing between Jim and me but friendship. Liz, please don't misunderstand. I just wanted you to know the facts because I don't want either of you to get hurt. I suppose I feel responsible because of inviting you here today. I'm sorry if I'm interfering where I'm not wanted."

"He talks about you a lot. I think he is in love with you but he knows he can't have you so he's hoping I'll make a suitable substitute."

"And I think you've been reading too many trashy novels," I said shortly. "Really, Liz, what you're saying is preposterous."

"Is it? Are you sure?"

"Of course I'm sure. There is nothing between Jim and me but friendship. Look, just forget I said anything at all, will you? We'd better get back. Sounds like someone else is here."

"After you."

Davy was opening the door to Goldie Sutton. I groaned inwardly. Just what I need at this exact moment, I thought. Liz looked at Goldie and back at me with raised brows and a little grin.

"Hello, Goldie," I said. "How nice of you to come. I'd like you to meet my sister, Liz Davis. Liz, this is Goldie Sutton."

"Hello. Nice to meet you. Will you excuse me, please?

I was just . . . going out," Liz said, edging her way into the kitchen.

"You'll remember to pick up Granny at three?" I called after her.

"I'll remember. See you later."

CHAPTER TWENTY-THREE

Ellen Takes a Stand

*R*ight after Goldie came Tom and Ellen and their family, so after I had greeted them I took them all through the house together. It was not an ideal situation. Goldie was dressed in a very tight blue dress with a low neckline and Tom couldn't keep his eyes off her, but there was nothing I could do about it. I felt depressed. Nothing was turning out as I had planned. I was beginning to regret my idea of having open house. Davy seemed to have disappeared. Ellen was very quiet. Goldie was babbling. I could have strangled her.

When I took them to the kitchen Davy was there with Joe Horton. They were having coffee and cookies.

"Joe come by to talk to you," Davy said to me.

"Didn't know you was havin' people over today," Mr. Horton said, shifting his feet in embarrassment.

"You didn't know we were having open house? I'm sorry. We tried to make sure everyone was informed. We would have enjoyed having your wife and Evelyn come too."

"My wife don't go out an' one of us has to stay with her. Guess I could come back later."

"That isn't necessary. We can go in the living room and talk, or perhaps you'd like me to show you through the house?"

"That'd be real nice. Quite a house your husband's built."

"Yes, he did a wonderful job. Davy, will you see that

everyone gets refreshments while I show Mr. Horton around?"

I took him around as I had the others, not saying much, just letting him look. He paid more attention to detail than most of the others had. When we got to the utility room, we paused for the talk he had come for.

"Guess I'll be lettin' Evelyn go on to high school," he said. "She's got her heart set on it. Ain't had no peace from her or her mama either since school was out. Can't let her mama get too excited, so I had to give in. Jist wanted to know if you come up with anything for gettin' th' kids to th' bus."

"Yes, I'm glad to be able to say I have. At least, I didn't come up with the idea, Jim Baker did. He has a job in town now, working from eight to five Monday through Friday. He'll be leaving for town every morning at about six-thirty and he's volunteered to take the kids with him to catch the bus. We haven't figured out exactly who will pick them up to bring them home yet, but one of us will. I'm so glad you've decided to let Evelyn go, Mr. Horton."

"Like I said, a man don't have much of a chance when his woman folks gang up on him. You'll let us know when you figger out who's gonna bring them home?"

"I will."

"Guess I'll be goin' then. Real nice place you got here."

"Thank you. Will you have some more coffee and cookies?"

"Had three or four a'ready."

"Have another one, and I'd like to send some home for your wife and Evelyn."

I wrapped several cookies in waxed paper and gave them to him. I saw him to the door then turned, puzzled to look for our other guests. The house was very quiet. There didn't seem to be anyone here.

"Davy?" I called.

"I'm in here," he called from the bedroom. His voice sounded odd. I went to find him. He was sitting on the edge of the bed, his head in his hands.

"What's wrong?" I asked.

"Nothin'."

"Where is everyone?"

"Gone."

"Already? I thought Tom and Ellen might stay and visit for awhile."

"Nope. Had to leave."

His voice sounded thick, almost choked. I felt a flash of panic.

"Where's Goldie?" I asked sharply.

"She's gone too."

"Davy, what's the matter with you? Look at me. Did something happen?"

"Um-huh," he said and raised his head.

"Well, what?"

He gave a little sputter and began to laugh, holding his sides.

"Davy, what on earth?" I exclaimed.

"Think my sides are gonna bust," he said, wiping his eyes. "Had to come in here so's you an' Joe wouldn't hear me."

"For heaven's sake, will you please tell me what's going on?"

"Think maybe you better stay away from Tom for awhile. He may be gunnin' for you again."

"But why? What did I do?"

"Ain't what you did. It's what Ellen done."

I sat down on the bed beside him. "What did Ellen do?" I asked puzzled.

"Well, we was there in th' kitchen where you left us. Me an' Ellen an' Tom was on one side of th' table an' Goldie was on th' other side. Well, she leans over to get herself a cookie. Seemed like she was havin' a hard time decidin' which one she wanted. Her dress was . . . Well, you know, kinda low in th' front."

"I noticed," I said dryly.

"Well, when she was leanin' over th' table like that — "

"All right. I get the picture. Go on."

"Tom's standin' there with his eyes sorta poppin' out of his head. Ellen, she reaches out with her left hand like she's reachin' for th' coffee pot. She's standin' beside Tom, to his right an' I'm to th' right of her."

"Yes?"

"Ellen pretends to burn her fingers on th' coffee pot an' she jerks her arm back an' her elbow goes wham! Right in Tom's belly. Tom gives a grunt an' kinda doubles over, holdin' his stomach."

He started to laugh again and I sat silent, a little awed at what Ellen had done.

"Well," Davy continued, "Ellen pretends she's so sorry an' she starts pattin' him an' makin' a fuss over him. Then while Tom is still doubled over, she looks up at Goldie an' says, 'I think you better leave, don't you?' "

"And she went?"

"She did. When Tom finally straightens up, you can tell by th' look on his face he knows what's goin' on, but he don't let on he knows. An' Ellen knows he knows but she don't let on either. Th' kids are standin' around wonderin' what in th' world is goin' on, 'cept Ruthie. She knows an' she joins her mama in pettin' an' sympathizin' with her daddy. They decide they better get him on home so he can lay down, so they help him out to th' wagon an' help him in an' Ellen takes up th' reins and they drive off."

"I wish I could have seen it. I'd give anything if I could have seen it," I said wistfully.

"Wish you could've too. Poor ol' Tom. Hope she didn't really hurt him. Bet it'll be a cold day in August 'fore he looks at another woman like that, at least while Ellen's around."

"Good for her. More power to her. I hope she can keep it up."

"Boy, I tell you, jist put a ring on a woman's finger an' a marriage license in her hand an' she turns into a reg'lar tiger. Couldn't hardly b'lieve my own eyes. Ellen's always been so quiet an' sorta timid, couldn't b'lieve she'd do somethin' like that. If it'd been you now ... "

"You better believe it," I said. "Just remember that when Goldie starts trying those tricks on you."

"You don't think maybe part of it mighta been for me today?" he asked with an air of innocence.

"Probably most of it," I answered shortly. "You just keep your eyes to yourself or you might find you're worse off than Tom."

"How does a fella keep his eyes to hisself in a situation like that?" he asked plaintively. "We're jist human, you know. Ain't no harm in lookin', is there?"

"I'll make you think 'ain't no harm in lookin'," I mocked, hitting him on the arm with my fist. He grabbed me, laughing, and pulled me down on top of him. I pummeled him on the shoulders and chest with both fists but he just laughed harder. He gave a sudden lithe twist of his body and I was pinned beneath him, unable to move.

"Say uncle," he said.

"Davy, let me up," I gasped. "You're squashing me."

"Not 'til you say uncle," he said, but he eased his weight a little so that I could at least breathe. He lowered his head and began giving me little teasing kisses on my face and neck. There was no point in struggling, I couldn't even move, so I lay quietly and when he paused to look down at me, I smiled dreamily up at him.

"I love you," I said softly.

"That ain't what you're s'posed to say if you want up."

"Do you love me, Davy?"

"You know I do, more'n anything else in th' world."

"Even though I've made mistakes, caused problems with Tom?"

"Nobody's perfect, an' I wasn't thinkin' I deserved a perfect wife. Figger I come 'bout as close as it's possible gettin' one though."

"Thank you, Davy. You're sweet."

I lifted my lips and he leaned down to kiss me. Suddenly I became aware of someone knocking at the door.

"Davy, someone's here," I gasped.

He raised his head and listened. The knock came again, louder this time.

"Davy, please," I said in a panic. "Get up and go to the door or they'll be coming on in."

"What a perdicament for a respectable teacher to find herself in," he teased, rising leisurely from the bed.

"Davy, hurry! Take them to the kitchen for refreshments first. Don't let them see me coming from the bedroom looking like this."

"Why not?"

"In the middle of the day and when we're having open house?" I whispered horrified. "Why, it would be all over the countryside in a matter of hours and I'd never be able to hold my head up again."

He laughed, but left the room, tucking his shirttail in as he went. I flew up off the bed and smoothed the covers down with unsteady hands. I was running a comb through my hair when I heard Davy greeting the visitors. Thank goodness they hadn't just opened the door and walked in as so often happened around here.

CHAPTER TWENTY-FOUR

Granny's News

*P*eople came and went for the rest of the afternoon. It was pleasant but very tiring. It was three-thirty when Liz and Jim arrived with Granny Eldridge in the back seat of Liz's car. When they got out I saw that Calvin had come with them. Jim was helping Granny, holding on to her arm while she leaned rather heavily on her cane on the other side. Liz and Calvin were walking ahead and she was talking to him. They had gotten acquainted on our visit to St. Louis.

I greeted Calvin again with a smile and a hand on his head. I glanced at Liz.

"Have a good time?" I asked lightly.

"Yes, a very good time," she said a bit defiantly.

"Hello, Granny. How are you today?" I asked.

"Not so good but wanted to come an' see this new house ever'one's been talkin' about," she answered, breathing heavily.

"I'm glad you did. Let me get on this other side and help you up on the steps. There's three of them."

"Where's that husband of yours?"

"He's out in the back yard at the moment. We'll manage without him."

It was a real effort, but between the two of us, Jim and I got her up the steps and into the house. She was panting with the effort. I led her to the sofa so she could sit and rest for awhile before I took her through the house. She was so large she took up half the sofa. I thought her color was not good, she was rather pasty-faced. Perhaps the effort to get here had been too much for her.

"Can I get you something?" I asked. "I have coffee or punch and cookies."

"Jist a glass of water would be good."

I went for the water. Jim and Liz were in the kitchen helping themselves to refreshments again. Calvin was standing rather wistfully at the side of the room.

"Have some more cookies and punch, Calvin," I said. "Then maybe you'd like to go out to the back yard and see the puppy Davy gave me. Just help yourself to whatever you want."

I put ice in the glass of water and took it in to Granny. She was looking about the room with bright, curious eyes. She took the glass from me and sipped at it.

"You got it fixed up real pretty," she said. "You like them logs showin' through like that?"

"Yes, very much. It adds character to the room, don't you think?"

"Hummph. Don't exactly know what you mean by that, but th' room looks real homey. Had many people here today?"

"Yes. Quite a lot."

"That Jane Decker an' her man show up?"

"Jane and the boys came but her husband had to work today and didn't come."

"Good thing, if you ask me. Wouldn't trust him far as I could throw him. Got shifty eyes, sticky fingers, too, prob'ly. Apt to carry off anything that ain't fastened down."

I didn't comment, though I hadn't been impressed with Jane's husband, either, the one time I'd seen him.

"Reckon I'm ready to take that look aroun' now if you give me a hand gettin' up."

I helped her up and we made our way slowly through the house. Her eyes darted from one thing to another; there wasn't a thing she missed. I was glad the house was spotless.

"What you call this here room again?" she asked as we neared the end of our little tour.

"The utility room. It's where all the leftovers and extras are kept. That's the water heater and, of course, the washer and tubs." I opened one of the closet doors. "I have plenty of shelf room for sheets and towels and other things I need to store. My iron and ironing board I keep here at this end."

"My goodness, you got about ever'thing a body could need, ain't you?"

"Yes, and it's all very handy. I may move the washer and tubs out on the side porch later in the summer. It will be less messy. Well, this is it except for the kitchen."

"What I'm wantin' to know is where you gonna put Calvin when he comes to you?"

"In the spare bedroom, I suppose, except perhaps when we have overnight company. We've been thinking of getting a rollaway bed to put here in the utility room in case that happens. Later, of course, we can always build on extra rooms if it becomes necessary."

"You ain't in th' family way yet then?"

"No. We're going to wait awhile. I'm going to teach school another year."

"Wouldn't wait too long if I was you. You an' Davy ain't gettin' no younger."

"We have plenty of time. Come see the kitchen."

When she was seated on the sofa again in a little while, she asked me to call Davy in. I went to the back door and called him. He and Calvin were playing with the pup. He rose and came striding toward me.

"What is it?"

"Granny wants to talk to you."

He lifted his brows inquiringly, but followed me into the living room. He shook hands with Granny and we both sat down.

"Your sister an' that Jim Baker still around?" she asked.

"I don't know where they are."

"They went for a walk," Davy said.

"She's a fast worker, jist got here today, didn't she?"

"Yes. What did you want to talk to us about, Granny?" I asked, cutting her short.

"Well, when you took Calvin with you to visit your mama, I told you I might go to visit my daughter in town. I did go, but th' reason I went is 'cause she wanted me to see th' doctor an' have some tests done. I done it an' found my trouble ain't all rheumatism. Seems I have a bad heart, too."

"I'm sorry, Granny. Is it bad?"

"Bad enough, but th' doc says ain't no reason why I can't have a few good years yet it I take proper care of myself. I ain't s'posed to do any liftin' or packin' anything, so I decided 'fore winter gets here, I'll go ahead an' move to my daughter's. Won't be much for me to do there an' I figger Calvin'll be needin' more care'n I'll likely be able to give him this winter. So guess you can plan on gettin' him 'bout th' time school's startin'."

"I . . . see."

Davy and I exchanged looks and didn't know what to say.

"You're still willin' to take him, ain't you?" she asked sharply.

"Of course, we just didn't expect it to be this soon," I said then. "However, it's all right. I hope you'll be happy at your daughter's, and we'll do our best to see that Calvin is happy."

"He'll be happy. He's crazy 'bout you, talks 'bout you all th' time. Teacher says this an' teacher says that. Ain't nobody knows as much as teacher does, accordin' to him.

172

What's your thinkin' on it?" she asked, turning suddenly to Davy.

"I agree with him 'bout th' teacher," Davy said with a touch of humor. "He'll be okay here. We'll look after him."

"That's all I wanted to know. Well, s'pect I better be goin'. Who's gonna drive me home?"

"I will," Davy said. "All right if I take th' car?"

"Of course. Thanks for coming, Granny. I'll call Calvin."

"By th' way, his name's Hilton, not Eldridge. It says so right on th' birth certificate, Calvin Benjamin Hilton. Ever'body jist got in th' habit of callin' him Eldridge 'cause he was livin' with me, I guess. Might be handier for ever'body to be called by th' same name since he'll be livin' with you."

"Perhaps," I said. "I'll call him."

After they were gone I went through the house straightening things and ended up in the kitchen. I was cleaning off the table when Davy came back. I looked thoughtfully at him.

"Are you upset about Calvin coming to us so soon?" I asked.

"Not exactly," he said slowly. "I was kinda hopin' we could be alone a little while longer, but guess maybe it's a good thing he's comin' when he is. Don't think Granny's exactly a good influence on anyone. Never seen anyone so full of gossip."

"I know, but I suppose she's lonely and doesn't have much else to do but speculate about people."

"You happy about Cal comin'?"

"Yes. He's a dear little boy and he's good. He won't get in our way that much, Davy, and just think, when we decide to have our own baby, we'll have our own built-in baby sitter."

"Think so? When's this gonna be?"

"Granny says we'd better not wait too long. Our age, you know."

He snorted. "Wish Granny'd mind her own business jist once in awhile. All she wanted to talk about on th' way home was your sister an' Jim."

"That doesn't surprise me. Where are they, by the way?"

"Don't know. Said they was goin' for a walk."

"I suppose I ought to think about starting supper. Are you very hungry?"

"Nope. Ate too many cookies."

"There are some sandwiches left and some salad. Do you think that will be enough?"

"Suits me."

"I wonder if Liz and Jim will be here for supper."

They came in a short time later, hand in hand like two happy children.

"Jim wants to take me to a drive-in movie," Liz said. "It's a triple feature, so it will be late. Do you think I ought to go?"

"It's entirely up to you," I said.

"We thought you two might like to come along with us," Jim said.

"I don't know about Davy," I said, "but I'm bushed. I'm not going anywhere, but thank you, just the same."

"You don't mind if I go?"

"Not at all."

"It will be late. Will you leave the door unlocked?"

"We never lock it. I'll leave the porch light on. Are you two going to be here for supper? We're only having sandwiches again and salad. I'm too tired to cook."

"Got enough?" Jim asked.

"Plenty."

"We might jist have a sandwich with you then, if it's all right with Liz."

"Fine with me," she said. "I ought to unpack my bags,

I suppose, but I think I'll wait until tomorrow. Did your open house go okay?"

"Pretty well. More people came than I actually expected. All in all, it's been an eventful day." I caught Davy's eye over the open newspaper and laughed.

"What's funny?" Liz asked.

"Nothing really. Just something that happened. Well, shall we eat? You two kids will be wanting to start for town soon, I suppose."

"Kids?" Jim asked, eyebrows raised. "I can give you a few years, young'un."

"I know, but let's just say some of us mature earlier than others."

He reached over and gave my hair a little tweak and grinned at me. I caught Liz's eye on us and quickly turned away.

"Are you ready to eat, Davy? Anyone want coffee?"

"No coffee for me. I drunk enough today that I prob'ly won't sleep for a week. How about some milk?"

"How about the rest of you?"

Everyone chose milk and I poured it and set it before them, along with the sandwiches and salad.

"Know what?" Jim said to me as he reached for a sandwich. "I kinda like this sister of yours."

"Do you?"

"Yep. She's jist as pretty as you . . . "

"You told me I was prettier," Liz spoke up with a little pout.

"Shush now," Jim told her. "You don't tell no woman someone else is prettier. You'll hurt her feelin's."

"My feelings are not hurt," I said dryly. "It's a matter of opinion. Davy thinks I'm prettier, so there."

"That doesn't count. Husbands have to say things like that," Liz said pertly.

"Ladies, ladies," Jim chided. "Let's don't fight about it.

You're both mighty pretty an' cute, but what I was startin' to say was, what I like most about your sister is she actually laughs at my jokes."

"That really is something," I said.

"Yeah, sure is. I think I'm in love," he ended on a sigh.

"Already?"

"Happens like that sometimes, you know."

I looked at Liz. She was making a little face at Jim. They both seemed to be teasing, but I wondered if Jim might be a little more serious about it than appeared on the surface. I wasn't going to say another word about it, though.

They left soon after that and Davy went out to do the chores. I sat down at the piano. I was troubled and music had always been a solace.

When Davy came back I was still at the piano. He washed up and sat down in his rocker and took up the paper again. I stopped playing, but I sat on, my head lowered, my hands in my lap.

"Somethin' botherin' you?" Davy asked.

I hesitated then shook my head. I didn't think it was anything I wanted to talk to him about.

"Just tired, I guess," I said.

"Me, too. Ain't done a thing but I'm plumb wore out. Let's go to bed."

"In a minute."

I got up from the piano bench and when I turned, Davy was looking at me. I hesitated, then went to him. He pulled me on to his lap and held me. I put my head down on his shoulder and we sat silent for a long time. What Liz had said earlier about my relationship with Jim bothered me, not just for Jim's sake but for Davy's sake, too. Jim had been his friend for a long time and I didn't want him to have to worry about us. I'd had a small taste of the green-eyed monster myself on a few occasions and it was no pleasant experience. I wanted Davy to feel secure and confident in my love, but I was afraid if I tried to talk about it I'd just make matters worse. So I remained mute and just snuggled closer to him. Drat that sister of mine anyhow.

"You asleep?" Davy asked.

"Just about."

"I'm gonna put you to bed. Whatever you think you got to do can wait 'til tomorrow."

"If you say so."

He rose with me in his arms. "I do say so," he said. "I'm sure glad you didn't want to go into town with your sister an' Jim."

"So am I," I murmured sleepily.

CHAPTER TWENTY-FIVE

Talk of Marriage

"**W**hat in the world are you cooking?" asked Liz, looking into the pan on the back of the stove.

"Cottage cheese."

"Cottage cheese? You mean people actually make cottage cheese? I thought it was just something you dipped out of a carton."

"Silly. Someone has to make it."

"You've really taken all this country business to heart, haven't you? I mean, you make your own butter, you say you're learning to milk a cow and drive mules and shoot a gun. You're gardening and canning, and now cottage cheese?"

"Well, why not? I'm in the country to stay, so I'd better learn country ways, don't you think?"

"Doesn't that bother you?"

"Doesn't what bother me?"

"Knowing you're here to stay. I mean, don't you miss the city and all that goes with it? Don't you get tired of the silence, the lack of anything to do, the . . . the backwardness of the people? I mean, you're living in something like the eighteenth century out here."

I laughed. "You're exaggerating. Actually, I like it here very much. I like the peace and quiet. Frankly, the noise of the city nearly drove me batty when I was there last time. As for nothing to do, why there's a million things to do. An ordinary lifetime isn't going to be long enough to do all the things I want to do, and as for the backwardness of the people, I can do something about that, at least for the future generation."

"But won't you get tired of it someday? Just think of it, to live out here for years and years and years with no prospect of ever going home to the city."

"The city is not my home anymore. Home is here now. I love my husband and I love my home and I'm very happy."

"You are, aren't you? I'm glad. I like Davy. He's a swell person, but I can't see . . . "

"You can't see what?"

"I can't see sacrificing my whole life for a man."

I laughed again. "I'm not sacrificing my life. I'm living it. I'm doing what I want to do. You have no reason to feel sorry for me."

"Well, I'm happy for you, but as for me, I'm getting out of here before I find myself facing a lifetime sentence, too. I'm afraid I don't feel the same way you do about the country."

"I didn't at first, but it grows on you. Has something happened, Liz?"

"Jim asked me to marry him last night. Can you believe it? Five days and already he's asking me to marry him. The worst part about it is, I almost said yes."

She was looking upset and appalled and slightly watery eyed. I didn't know what to say.

"So," she said, "I'm getting out of here before he comes home from work and asks me again. Excuse me while I pack my bags."

She went off to the bedroom and I slowly followed. She lifted one of her suitcases on to the bed and began to fill it with frilly underclothes from the dresser drawer.

"You're going without telling him good-bye?" I asked.

"I more or less told him that last night."

"I see."

"Well, you don't think I ought to marry him, do you?"

"After five days? Certainly not, but it might not be a bad idea for the two of you to allow yourselves time to get better acquainted."

Her hands stilled, she stood staring off into space. "I do like him so much," she said wistfully. "He's so much fun to be with, but I don't want to spend the rest of my life way out here in the country like this. It's all right for you, but I don't think I'd be able to take it."

"Jim's wife divorced him because she couldn't stand the country. At least, that was supposed to be the reason."

"He told me. All the more reason for me to get out of here before things go any further." She closed the bag and replaced it with the other one. "You'll tell him I had to go?"

"If that's what you want."

"And Davy, too. Tell him I'm sorry to rush off like this."

"All right, but don't you want to stay for lunch?"

"I'll get something on the way. I'm not hungry right now. I hope I've got everything. Want to help me carry this stuff out?"

"Yes, but this is so sudden, Liz. We didn't get to do much visiting at all."

"That was my fault or Jim's fault, but I do have to go now. I'm sorry. You do understand?"

"I suppose so."

"Thanks, Sis. I'm sorry if I've been a brat."

"You haven't been. We've enjoyed having you and I hope you'll come back again soon."

"I'll come back sometime but probably not very soon."

We were putting her suitcases in the trunk of her car when we both heard the sound of an automobile coming fast down the road. When it came around the bend at my in-law's house I saw that it was Jim's new truck. Liz put her head down against the side of the car and groaned. She was still in

that position when the truck pulled up and stopped and Jim
got out. I looked from him to Liz and back again.

"Hi, Teacher," he said, sounding subdued.

"Hello, Jim."

"Mind if I talk to your sister by myself?"

I turned and started back to the house. Liz lifted her
head and looked at Jim.

"What are you doing here?" she asked.

"I come to see you. I think we need to talk."

I didn't hear any more but went on up to the house and
went inside. I was straining the cottage cheese when they
came in, each carrying a suitcase.

"Do you mind if I stay another day or two?" Liz asked.
She was very subdued and Jim was quiet, too.

"Of course I don't mind," I said. "You can stay as long
as you like."

"I'll put these back in my room then. I think maybe I
could use some of that big sisterly advice."

They came back and drew out chairs at the kitchen table
and sat down. I sat down, too, and looked from one to the
other of them. "I don't know about this advice business,"
I said slowly. "I always seem to get myself in trouble when I
start trying to give advice, but one thing I do know for sure.
You two are going into this thing much too fast. You've
known each other five days, and you're already talking of
marriage?"

They were both silent. It was such a rare thing for Jim
that I was seriously disturbed.

"Look," I said. "What's the big rush? You hardly know
each other. Take some time to get acquainted, relax and
enjoy yourselves. After all, St. Louis is not the other side of
the world."

"It might as well be. This is not just the other side of the
world. It's another world altogether," Liz said with a touch
of bitterness.

"There is such a thing as compromise, you know. There is an in-between."

"There wasn't for you."

"Because I didn't want it. Davy told me before we were married that he couldn't live anywhere else and I accepted that. Perhaps Jim doesn't feel that strongly about it. Anyhow, it's too soon to be worrying about that now. Perhaps when you get better acquainted, you'll find you don't like each other at all."

They exchanged a glance and a small secretive smile. Liz's hand crept across the table and Jim quickly covered it with his.

"I been thinkin'," he said. "Maybe I ought to get me a place closer in to town. I mean with this new job an' all, it'd be lots easier goin' an' comin' from work. It could still be in the country, jist not so far out."

"But Jim, you promised — " I stopped and bit my lip. Liz was looking oddly at me.

"I know I promised you I'd drive th' kids in to meet th' bus," he said, troubled, "but maybe I could still work somethin' out, or maybe Davy'll be gettin' hisself a truck like mine one of these days soon. He's been talkin' 'bout it some. Anyhow, I ain't gonna be movin' for awhile yet. Got to sell th' other house first. Lewis an' Sue say anything more 'bout buyin' it?"

"With the baby coming, they don't feel like they can afford it."

"Too bad. I'd like to see them get it. Maybe we could work somethin' out."

"You have to sell it?"

"Have to an' want to. Want to get that part of my life behind me an' start all over again. You knew she was married again?"

"Who? Sally?"

"Yep. Married again jist a week or two after th' divorce went through."

"Forgive me for asking this, Jim, but does this have anything to do with your wanting to marry my sister so soon?"

"No."

I looked at Liz. Her eyes were lowered, she was tracing a pattern on the table with a forefinger.

"I still say you're rushing in too soon," I said. "You can write to each other, visit each other, get to know one another better. Friendship in marriage is very important, you know. As a matter of fact, I think it's just as important as being in love. It's what makes a marriage last."

"She ain't said she'll marry me yet," Jim said glumly.

"Good for her. I hope she doesn't for a while. Now let's stop being so gloomy and smile a little, for goodness sake. Love is supposed to make you happy and if it doesn't, there's something wrong."

"Maybe you're right. Maybe I am tryin' to rush her into this too fast," Jim admitted slowly.

"Maybe? Five days, Jim? Mom and Dad would have a fit."

"They might anyhow," Liz said. "Dad wasn't too thrilled about your marriage to Davy, you know."

"I know, but Davy and I were friends, we knew each other. You think you and Jim know each other but you don't. Nobody knows another person in five days, so if you want my advice, it's this. Cool it and give yourselves time to get better acquainted, then you can talk of marriage."

"Thanks, Teacher. Guess maybe you're right. Well, I got th' rest of th' day off, what are we gonna do with it?" Jim asked Liz.

"Why don't you go out in the back yard and talk a few minutes while I get lunch on? Davy will be coming in soon and he'll be hungry so I'd better get busy. I'll call you when it's ready."

They rose and linked hands and left through the back door. I looked after them, concerned and very disturbed.

CHAPTER TWENTY-SIX

In the Family Way

"**W**hat's th' matter with you?" Davy asked, looking at me with concern.

"Do you know what I've been doing?" I asked, sitting limply in a chair, my hands hanging down at my sides. "All morning long I've been helping your mother shell peas and we only got ten quarts done."

"Did you get them canned?"

"Your mother is doing them now. I had to get out of there, it was too hot. I tried to get her to come over here and can them but she wouldn't. This afternoon she's coming over here to help me can some for us."

"Quite th' little farm wife you're turnin' into," he said, bending to kiss my cheek.

"I don't know. I sometimes wonder if Liz wasn't right. It is a lot easier just to open a can."

"Cost money that way an' it ain't near as good. By th' way, I saw Jim an' he says Liz has invited him to come to St. Louis next weekend. Guess he's planning on goin'."

"They must be writing each other then."

"Guess so. My lunch ready?"

"It's in the refrigerator."

I took out cold chicken and potato salad, sliced some whole wheat bread I had baked the day before, opened the butter dish, set two places on the table and lunch was served. Davy filled his plate and began to eat.

"Davy?"

"Hum-m?"

"Do you mind a cold lunch like this?"

"Mind? It's real good. Why?"

"Your mom was fixing fried squirrel and mashed pota-toes and gravy and peas and biscuits for your dad. I know you're used to eating like that and I just wondered if . . . "

"Sounds good, too."

"Well, I don't think your mother should have to fix a big lunch like that when she's spent the whole morning canning. I know she doesn't have a refrigerator to keep things cold, but she could just fix him a sandwich or something or let him fix his own. Your father is spoiled. She waits on him too much."

"An' you don't b'lieve in spoilin' a man, huh?"

"No, I don't. There's nothing wrong with a man fixing a meal for himself once in awhile. You'll have to do it when school starts."

"You don't think I could jist go to mom's an' eat?" he asked wistfully.

"No, I don't, at least not on a regular basis. Your mother has enough to do without waiting on you, too."

"Yes, ma'am. You mad at me for some reason?"

"No, but I get a little aggravated with your father sometimes. Your mother works so hard and then she has to wait on him."

"She wouldn't want it no other way. Far as she is concerned, that's her job. Got any more of them cookies?"

I rose and got the cookie jar and put it on the table. I poured him another glass of milk and sat back down.

"What are you grinning at?" I asked suspiciously.

"You," he answered. "Thought you didn't b'lieve in waitin' on a man."

"I don't. Oh well, I don't mind a few little things like that, but . . . "

"Face it. Women like waitin' on their men. It makes them feel important."

"Oh, it does, does it? Well, for your information ... "

"Am I in for a lecture, Teacher? Sorry, I ain't got th' time. Gotta get back to work, make hay while th' sun shines, as th' saying goes. Got a kiss for me 'fore I go?"

"I'm not sure that I do."

He grinned and reached out for me and hugged me close. He smelled of hay and sweat and horses, but I didn't find it offensive. I lifted up my lips and kissed him.

"Don't get too hot," I said.

"An' you don't work too hard," he said. "See you at supper."

Clemmy helped me shell and can seven pints of peas that afternoon. When she had gone home and I was cleaning up the kitchen, there was a knock at the door. I saw through the screen that it was Jane Decker. She was breathing fast and her face was red and perspiring and deeply troubled. I went to let her in.

"Why, Jane," I exclaimed. "Is something wrong?"

"Ever'thing," she said, her breath coming short. I looked beyond her. There was no sign of her boys or of any kind of conveyance.

"Come and sit down. Did you walk all that way in this heat?"

"Had to talk to you," she panted.

"All right, but you sit and relax for a minute first. I'll get you a glass of water."

I ran the water until it was cold, then took it in to her. She drank it thirstily. I took the glass back to the kitchen and wet a washcloth and took it to her. She mopped her face with it, then held it pressed tightly against a suddenly trembling mouth. Slow difficult tears began to course down her cheeks. I sat beside her and put my hand on her arm.

"What is it, Jane?" I asked gently. "Is it one of the boys?"

She shook her head vigorously and a little sob broke from

her. She mopped at the tears with the washcloth and made a valiant attempt to calm herself.

"Well, then, if the boys are all right and you're all right, it can't be so terribly bad, can it?" I said in what I hoped was a bracing tone.

"He sold . . . Rosy," she gasped, the tears flowing faster.

I was silent a minute, letting that soak in. I hadn't thought much about Rosy lately. I had the pup now and I had been so busy with other things.

"Your husband?" I asked then. She nodded, still mopping at the tears.

"Don't worry about it, Jane," I said. "I haven't really thought much about Rosy lately. My husband gave me a puppy, you see, and he's more or less replaced Rosy for me."

"But you give her to me on th' understandin' that I wouldn't sell her, an' I promised."

"Well, you didn't sell her, did you? Your husband did. You're not responsible for that. Don't cry about it anymore, Jane. I'm not angry."

"Well, I am," she cried, the washcloth clenched in her hands. The tears seemed to have stopped, replaced by righteous indignation. "I'm so mad I could jist literally wring his neck with these bare hands. He better not try comin' 'round me no more, or I jist might do it, too."

"Has he left you, Jane?"

She nodded. "Been gone all week, didn't know where he was, jist didn't come home one night. Then this noon, him an' this other man comes in this pickup truck an' backed up to Rosy's pen an' jist loaded her up an' drove away. I run out when I seen what they was doin' but this other man was bigger'n me an' he jist kept shovin' me back. Jesse didn't say nothin', wouldn't answer me or even look at me. This other man says Jesse sold him th' pig an' he was jist takin' what b'longed to him. Wasn't nothin' I could say or do to stop him."

Fresh tears started to her eyes. Furiously she wiped them away.

"I ain't a cryin' woman," she said, "but right now I feel like jist standin' up and bawlin' out loud like a baby. I jist feel so awful bad about Rosy an' lettin' you down like that."

"You haven't let me down, Jane. I'm sorry it happened, too, but it wasn't your fault. Don't cry anymore now, please. It's over and done with and there's nothing you can do about it. I tell you what. Why don't you go into the bathroom there and wash your face, then come into the kitchen and I'll make us some coffee. Where did you leave the boys?"

"Left them at Miz Proctor's place," she said, rising. " 'Spect I best be gettin' back soon. She ain't well enough to be lookin' after four extry young'uns right now."

"I'll drive you home. You'll feel better after a cup of coffee."

She went into the bathroom and I went into the kitchen to make coffee. When she reappeared a few minutes later, her eyes were puffy and red, but her face was calm.

"This is real nice of you, Miz Hilton, givin' me coffee after what I done," she said.

"Stop blaming yourself, Jane. You couldn't have stopped them any more than I could have. Sit down. The coffee will be ready in a minute."

She pulled out a chair and sat down. I sat across from her.

"How are things going for you otherwise, Jane?" I asked.

She shook her head. "Bad," she said. "Ain't nothin' like I planned this summer, 'cept th' garden an' th' chickens. Guess them two things'll have to get us through th' winter."

Her voice broke, her lower lip trembled. She put up a hand to cover it and swallowed convulsively. I reached out and touched her hand.

"Worse thing is," she said, her voice shaky, "I'm near certain I'm in th' family way again."

"Oh no," I said.

She nodded. " 'Fraid so. There's a sayin', 'Ain't no fool like a old fool!' What I say is, 'Ain't no fool like a lonely fool!' You'd think, knowin' him like I did, I'da had more sense than to let him sweet talk me into takin' him back again, but I didn't. Fell for it hard as I ever did when I was still jist a girl, but I learned my lesson this time for sure. Ain't no men ever gonna take me for a fool again. From now on it's jist me an' my boys. An' whatever this new little 'un is," she ended uncertainly.

She looked over at me, her expression woebegone. "If it's a sin not to want th' young'un you're a carryin' inside you, then I'm a sinner of the worst kind, 'cause goodness knows, I don't want this one. Ain't no use cryin' over spilt milk, though. What's done's done, an' I can't do nothin' about it now."

"I'm sorry, Jane. If there's anything I can do to help . . . "

"Bless your heart, ain't that jist like you, but there ain't nothin' I know of you can do. We'll jist have to get along th' best way we can. At least we got a roof over our heads. What's worryin' me now is I promised you I'd send them boys to school next year an' I don't know how I'm gonna do that now. What little money I had he took an' they still ain't got no clothes an' no way to get there."

"They have to go, Jane. They need an education and besides, it's the law."

"You wouldn't turn me in?" she asked fearfully.

"I'm afraid I'd have to. It would be my responsibility. Don't think in terms of not sending them, Jane. Just think that they have to go and together we'll work something out."

"But what? I ain't one to take charity an' I ain't in no position to go out an' get me a job of any kind right now."

"No, of course not, but there are organizations that are set up to help people in your position."

"I always swore I'd never go to none of them, that I'd always provide for myself an' my own."

"And you would have if circumstances had not changed, circumstances beyond your control."

"Circumstances beyond my control," she repeated slowly.

"Yes, Jane, you're not the only person that this sort of thing has happened to. There are times in the lives of all of us when we need help and we can't be too proud to accept it."

"You ever had that happen to you?"

"I've been in a position where I've needed help and had to accept it when it came. When I first started teaching out here, I found I couldn't control some of the older boys. They were disrupting my classes and there was nothing I could do about it, because they were bigger than I. So Davy came along and helped me. I didn't like it, I wanted to be able to do it by myself, but when I found I couldn't, I accepted his help and later, I was glad I had. It made it possible for me to continue teaching out here and to make a success of it and feel good about it. If I hadn't accepted Davy's help I would have had to admit failure and go away beaten."

I rose and poured two cups of coffee and brought them to the table.

"It ain't quite th' same thing, though, is it?" she asked, doubtfully, picking up her cup.

"I don't see the difference. Help is help, whatever form it takes. You have to think of your boys, Jane, and what's best for them, and of this new baby. You have to keep yourself healthy so you can have a healthy baby. You don't want a defective child. Think of the burden, the expense of something like that."

" 'Spect maybe you're right, but it goes against th' grain, I can tell you, 'specially since I got myself in this mess. Seems like I oughta be th' one to get myself out of it."

"You didn't get yourself into this mess 'all by yourself,' you had plenty of help. The question now is how are we going to go about getting you the help you need to get past this crisis? I could drive you into town."

"Won't put you to that trouble," she said rising and pushing her chair back under the table. "My brother'll be out in th' next day or so. I'll have him take me, but I thank you jist the same. S'spect I best be gettin' back. My boys'll be drivin' Miz Proctor up th' walls by now."

"I'll drive you home."

"That'd be right nice, if you're sure I ain't puttin' you out."

"You aren't putting me out, and you keep your chin up, Jane. Things are bound to get better."

"Can't get much worse, that's for sure, but I do feel better for havin' talked to you. I'm thankin' you for that, an' for the coffee."

"You're welcome. If I can be of any further help, you be sure and let me know."

CHAPTER TWENTY-SEVEN

A Real Country Girl

*I*t was the first of July and the weather was hot and sticky, but the cabin stayed relatively cool because of the shade trees and several electric fans inside. I had been doing some canning every day so the top shelves in the closet in the utility room were slowly filling with jars of vegetables. We were finished with the peas and I had put up all the beets I wanted and was starting on the green beans. The peaches on the Hilton's trees were ripening and we had begun getting a few tomatoes from the garden. After that would be pickles and corn. There seemed to be no end to it.

It was a lot of work for me, but not overwhelmingly so because I was doing small amounts each day, but Clemmy seemed to slave over her hot stove constantly. I tried to get her to come to my house to do at least part of it, but she didn't want to. She was used to the old ways and accepted it as her responsibility without complaint. I helped her as much as I could in preparing the vegetables but I couldn't stand the heat in her kitchen during the actual canning process.

Today she was going to take me blackberry picking. Blackberries grew wild and were plentiful in the woods. Clemmy canned them for cobblers and made jelly from them. I was not particularly fond of blackberry cobbler because of all the little gritty seeds, but Davy liked it and we both were partial to blackberry jelly.

Clemmy was coming about ten. She had instructed me to

wear pants and a long-sleeved shirt and boots and to put a bonnet or something on my head. Mosquitoes were sometimes bad and there was always the danger of stepping on a snake.

The thought of snakes frightened me, but I'd learn to be a real country girl or die in the attempt. Davy didn't seem too concerned when I mentioned it to him, so perhaps there really wasn't that much danger. For Clemmy and Davy and others here, the woods held less danger than crossing a city street. Perhaps in time I'd be able to feel the same.

It was an hour until Clemmy was due, so I decided to make myself a bonnet. Clemmy had given me an old bonnet of her own to guide me and a piece of blue-flowered material. I sat down at my machine and in a matter of minutes had the bonnet made. I tried it on before a mirror then went to find Davy. He was in the pump house tightening a loose belt.

"Well, what do you think?" I asked, standing before him.

He straightened and looked me up and down, an amused smile playing about his lips. "Dunno," he said. "Who is it, anyway?" He reached out and tilted the brim of the bonnet up. "Oh, it's you, is it? For a minute there, I didn't recognize you."

"I made it all by myself," I said. I took the bonnet off and held it by the strings. Davy went back to working on the pump and I stood and watched him, thinking of something Sue had told me the day before.

It seemed that Goldie Sutton was spreading the rumor that Davy was unhappy with me and regretting our marriage. According to her, I hadn't turned out to be the kind of wife he wanted, it had been infatuation on his part, nothing more. He was beginning to realize he should have stuck with his own kind, implying that she was his own kind.

Sue assured me that, of course, she didn't believe it and neither did anyone else. Everyone knew she'd been after Davy for years and he hadn't been interested. It was the jealous reaction of a woman scorned, but Sue felt I should know in case the rumor got back to me and I was taken unaware.

"Somethin' botherin' you?" Davy asked, pausing and looking at me. I gave a little start, I had been so preoccupied with my disturbing thoughts. I shook my head. "Still worrin' about snakes?" he persisted.

"No. If your mother isn't afraid, then I won't be either."

"Jist keep an eye out for them, that's all. Will you be home for lunch?"

"I don't know. If I'm not, there's plenty to eat in the refrigerator."

"If you're not home by then, I'll come looking for you."

"I'm sure we'll be fine. Well, see you later."

I went back into the house to wait for Clemmy. A few minutes later I heard Davy calling to me. I stuck my head out the back door.

"What is it?"

"Get your rifle an' come out here," he called back.

I went into the bedroom and took the rifle Davy had given me from the rack on the wall. I took a handful of shells and went out to where he waited.

"What is it?" I asked.

"Look up there," he said, pointing skyward.

I looked up and saw a large bird slowly gliding around in a circle overhead.

"Is it a hawk?" I asked.

"Yep."

"But what's it after?"

"Watch it an' see what you think."

I watched. The bird seemed to be circling directly over the puppy's pen. I looked from the bird to the pup to Davy.

"But surely it isn't after Brownie. He's too big."

"Maybe this hawk's got big ideas. Load up an' see if you can get him."

I loaded the gun as Davy had shown me. I lifted it into the air and sighted along the barrel until I felt I had the bird in my sights. I pulled the trigger, then lowered the gun to look. The hawk still circled, unafraid. Evidently I hadn't even come close.

"Try again," Davy said.

So I tried again, and then again. The hawk turned and soared away in a leisurely way. Davy stood looking at me, shaking his head.

"Well," I said defensively. "At least I scared him away."

"He didn't look too scared to me."

"I guess I'm not cut out to be a crack shot like the rest of the Hiltons."

"You need more practice. Oughta practice ever' day. Never know when you might need to hit somethin'."

I sighed. He leaned over and kissed me on the cheek.

"Never mind," he said. "You'll get th' hang of it one of these days. I'll clean this gun for you. Thought I saw Mom comin' up th' path. You be careful now."

"I will."

I went back into the house and through to the front door to let Clemmy in. I'd never seen her in anything but a dress before, but today she was dressed in a pair of Mr. Hilton's pants under her dress and one of his shirts unbuttoned over her dress. She had rubber boots on her feet with the pant legs tucked in. Her bonnet was on her head and she carried two buckets, one inside the other, in one hand, and a garden hoe in the other.

"What's the hoe for?" I asked.

"Snakes," she returned. "You ready?"

"Yes. I made myself a bonnet. How do you like it?"

She looked it over rather critically, then nodded.

"I have a couple of buckets. Do I need a hoe, too?" I asked.

"No. One'll be enough. We'll prob'ly be able to pick up a big stick along th' way."

"For what?"

"For pokin' around th' bushes to make sure there ain't no snakes in there."

We started out, Clemmy leading the way. We didn't have far to go until we came to a big thicket of blackberry bushes. Clemmy took the stick we'd found and probed around in the dried leaves at the base of the bushes. When she was satisfied there were no snakes, we moved in with our buckets and began picking. I discovered blackberry bushes were as full of thorns as any rosebush. I kept pricking my fingers and getting my clothes caught in the brambles. My hands were soon stained purple and the sweat was running down the middle of my back. A mosquito buzzed persistently around my face, but I kept doggedly on. I was determined to stick it out as long as Clemmy did.

We moved on to another thicket. The blackberries were succulent and sweet. I ate so many I began to feel a little sick. When Clemmy decided it was time to quit, the buckets were filled to overflowing.

We started for home, Clemmy holding the metal part of the hoe in one hand as well as a bucket, letting the handle drag along behind her so that it was rather slow going.

When we came out of the woods we separated and she went on to her house and I went to mine. Davy met me at the door, a grin on his face. He took the buckets from me and put them on the kitchen table. When he came back I was struggling with a knot in my bonnet strings. He took it from me and worked it loose and removed the bonnet. With a finger under my chin, he lifted my face and stood looking down at me, grinning, then he laughed.

"What's so funny?"

"You," he said and bent to kiss me. "Mm-m, blackberry flavor."

"Davy, I'm all hot and sticky," I protested.

"That ain't all you are either," he said, and turned me to face the mirror on the wall. I gave a little horrified gasp.

My hair was plastered to my head, my lips and teeth were purple and I had purple streaks across my face.

"My goodness," I said. "I hope it comes off."

"It will, in a week or two. Don't you wish your mom an' dad an' your city friends could see you now?"

"I'm profoundly thankful they can't. Your mother didn't look like this. Davy, you go ahead and have lunch. I'm going to try to soak some of this off."

"Need any help?"

"I think I can manage," I said dryly. "My goodness, what it must have taken to be a pioneer woman. I'm all scratched and snagged and bitten and purple. I never dreamed there was so much work involved in doing everything from scratch."

"You're not overdoin' it? I don't require you to do all th' things you been doin' lately, you know."

"I know. I want to do it."

"I don't want you wearin' yourself out."

"I won't. Go have lunch, Davy. I'm not hungry. I'll have something later."

I went into the bathroom and ran water into the tub. I brushed my teeth and was relieved to find that most of the purple came off. I stripped off my clothes and stepped into the tub. I sighed and leaned back and relaxed. Pity the pioneer woman who couldn't indulge in this kind of luxury. Pity poor Clemmy, too, going to work immediately, I was sure, in that hot kitchen of hers.

CHAPTER TWENTY-EIGHT

Being a Neighbor

"**Y**ou got anything special you was plannin' on doin' today?" Davy asked me.

It was Saturday morning and we had just finished breakfast and were having a second cup of coffee.

"Nothing special," I answered.

"Want to go in to town after lunch? We could do a little shoppin' then have supper an' maybe go to a show or somethin'."

"That sounds like fun. Yes, I'd like to do that, Davy. I could use a little change."

"I think you got yourself jist about wore out. I want you to take it easy th' next few days."

"I don't do nearly as much as your mother does."

"She's used to it, you ain't. Besides, I ain't too sure she does do more, with you runnin' to check on Sue an' Calvin an' Granny an' Jane all th' time."

"I am rather tired. An afternoon and evening in town sounds good."

"We'll go right after lunch then. I got some things to do this mornin'." He rose and leaned over to kiss me.

"Are you going to see Lewis this morning?" I asked.

"Not plannin' on it. Why?"

"Perhaps I'd better run out and check on Sue before we go. I'd hate for her to be left without transportation if she should go into labor."

"Ain't time yet, is it?"

"Just a week or two now. She's really been feeling miserable in this heat. I wish they could get a car and a better place to live. It's too bad they can't buy Jim's house."

"They could if I'd co-sign a loan at th' bank. I have been thinkin' about that some. What do you think?"

"I have no objection. In fact, I'm all for it. Sue hates that old house they're in so much."

"Lewis has talked about it some but he's leery of goin' in debt that much jist before th' baby comes. Never know how much that'll end up costin' him."

"I know. Well, maybe when the baby gets here he'll feel differently."

"Jim's gonna have to put it in th' hands of a real estate agent if he don't sell it soon."

"And that will increase the price, won't it? Can't you talk him into holding off for awhile?"

"Don't think it's my place to do that. He seems anxious to get it settled. You seen anything of him since he went to see your sister?"

"No. He hasn't been here."

"I seen him once. Think he's got it bad. He's talkin' about sellin' both places an' movin' closer to town."

"Seriously?"

"Seemed like it."

"Then that takes care of our plans to get Todd and Evelyn in to meet the high school bus. Well, we'll just have to come up with something else. I'm determined that those kids are going to high school, if I have to take them myself."

"Don't see how you could do that an' still get to th' school on time."

"I don't either, but I'll think of something."

"I gotta get goin'. See you at noon," he said.

I cleared the table and did a few things around the house before I got in the car and drove to Sue's. I found her lying on the sofa, hot and miserable and almost in tears.

"I'm fine," she said dolefully. "Just uncomfortable and hot and so tired of this place. Lewis and I went to see Jim's house again and it's so roomy and airy and clean. I begged Lewis to buy it, but he won't. He's afraid of going into debt, but I'd almost sell my soul to live there. He doesn't understand what it's like to be cooped up in these dingy little rooms all the time. He's out of here as soon as the chores are done and breakfast is over, and he doesn't have to come back to it until evening. Sometimes I think I'll go out of my mind, and I hate the thought of bringing up a new baby here."

"You'll have something better one of these days," I said inadequately. "Lewis is cautious, but you know the reason why, and it's understandable, isn't it?"

"I suppose so," she sighed. "I shouldn't complain. Things are so much better for us than they were a year ago, but it seems as if I'll never get away from here. I'll be stuck here the rest of my life." Slow tears slid down her cheeks. She wiped them away. "So you and Davy are going in to town?" she asked with an attempt at lightness.

"Yes. I wanted to make sure you were okay before we started. I didn't want you left without transportation. Tomorrow, Sue, I'm going to bring my car out here and leave it just in case you go into labor in the middle of the night or something."

"But you won't need it?"

"No, I won't be going in to town again for awhile and Davy has the truck. I'm getting quite good at driving the mules, too. At least I'm not afraid of them anymore."

"You're a good friend, Anne. I don't know what I'd do without you. Is — are you and Davy all right?"

"We're fine. Why?"

"Lewis was upset with me for telling you what Goldie was saying. He said it might cause trouble between you."

"I'd already heard something of it before you told me, so don't worry about it. The local gossips have had a field day with Davy's marriage to a city girl. Hopefully, they'll tire of it one of these days and find something more interesting to talk about." I rose to go. "Take care of yourself, Sue. You know, it would be much cooler out under a shade tree than in here. Shall I carry a chair out for you?"

"If you'd like. I don't feel like doing a thing, but I can at least keep an eye on the girls out there."

I carried the chair out and left her sitting under the shade of a large oak. Since I was so close I thought I'd drive on to Jane's and see how she was doing. I'd been thinking about her quite a lot in the past week.

She was in the garden and the boys were with her. They were picking green beans and they were all hot and perspiring. Jane straightened with a little groan and put a hand to her lower back.

"I just stopped by to see how you are," I said.

"We're makin' it," she said. "My brother took us into town yesterday an' I went to that welfare place an' signed up. It'll take them awhile to check us out, but I'm hopin' by wintertime I'll be gettin' commodities, at least. That'll help. At least we won't starve to death. Will you come in for a minute?"

"I really can't, Jane. Davy and I are going into town this afternoon and I have to get home. I just stopped to check on Sue."

"She's doin' all right?"

"Yes, just hot and uncomfortable. Should you be out in this hot sun like this? I'm afraid you may be over-doing it."

"A body's gotta do what a body's gotta do," she said.

"Are you feeling any better?"

"Sicker'n a dog ever' mornin' but it passes after a hour or so."

"It's for certain, then?"

" 'Fraid so."

I was silent. I didn't know what to say. There should be some way I could help her more.

"Well, I suppose I should be going. Is there anything you need from town?"

"Don't know of anything."

"Jane, have you ever thought of going to the Goodwill store to look for clothes for the boys? I've heard that sometimes you could find some pretty nice things there at a very reasonable price."

"I been there before but ain't no point in goin' now. Don't matter if it don't cost much. I jist ain't got it."

"I'm sorry, Jane. I wish there was something I could do."

"I jist can't send them boys off to school lookin' like they do an' with no shoes or nothin'," she said with a little stubborn tilt to her chin.

"Don't worry about it. Something will come up, I'm sure."

"More'n likely it will, but it won't be nothin' good, way my luck runs."

I hated to see her feeling so depressed. I put my arm around her shoulder and her chin wobbled a little and tears sprang to her eyes.

"You keep your chin up, Jane," I said bracingly. "Things will get better. I know they will. We all have to stick together and help each other. I'll see that the boys have clothes for school."

"I don't want you spendin' your money on me."

"Who said anything about spending money? You just leave it to me, but you make plans to send those boys to school, Jane. They have to go. And now I've got to run. Davy will be in for lunch and no lunch ready. You've got food, Jane?"

"Food ain't no problem now, with th' garden an' the' chickens layin' good. It's th' winter I'm worrin' about."

"Winter's months away. Don't start worrying about that yet. Don't stay out in this hot sun too long. You look so hot."

"Bless you, worrin' about me like that. I been workin' out in th' hot sun all my life. I know when to quit."

"I'll see you later then, and if there's ever anything you need help with, you let us know. That's what friends are for."

I went home and took a bath and got dressed. When Davy came in I was putting lunch on the table. He paused in the kitchen doorway and looked at me.

"I think marriage to me must be agreein' with you," he quipped. "You get prettier ever' day."

I looked up with a smile, putting my more somber thoughts away for the moment. "Well, if that's true, then a lot of the credit has to go to you," I said lightly.

"That's what I said. I don't appear to be doin' such a bad job of this husbandin' business."

"Not bad at all."

"I better get myself cleaned up or you won't want to be seen with th' likes of me."

He went off to the bathroom and when he came back he was freshly shaved and dressed in clean, new blue jeans and a soft blue shirt. He looked very handsome and smelled faintly of a good shaving lotion. I went to him and put my arms around his neck, and smiled up at him.

"You look nice, Davy," I said.

"Think it'll do?"

"Definitely you'll do."

I kissed him and he held me close for a minute, but my mind was more on Jane than it was on my husband. When we sat down at the table, I broached the subject to Davy.

"If you don't mind," I said, "I'd like to stop at the Goodwill store on the way into town."

"Didn't know we was that hard up," Davy said quizzically.

"It's for Jane. I want to see if I can get some clothes for her boys, but don't tell anyone about it, okay? She's proud and she doesn't want me to spend any money on her, but those boys have got to go to school this year, and she won't send them without fairly decent clothing. I feel so sorry for her. She had such big plans for the summer. She was going to raise hogs and chop cotton and sell eggs, but because of that no-good husband of hers, she hasn't been able to do any of it. He came home just long enough to get her pregnant again, then he took off with everything of value she had. How a man could do that and still call himself a man I'll never know. I'd like to get my hands on him. If I thought there was the least little chance of success, I'd get the law on him for taking Rosy."

"Wouldn't do no good."

"I know. We've got to do something to help her, Davy."

"Don't mind helpin' her, but don't mind tellin' you she scares th' life outta me. Surprises me you like her so much."

"She's out-spoken and forthright and honest, and she has a lot of courage. I guess that's why I admire her."

"She reminds me of one of them barracudas I seen pictures of."

"Why Davy Hilton! What a terrible thing to say. I'd trust Jane a thousand times more than I'd ... "

"More than you'd what?"

"Nothing," I said, hurriedly reaching for my glass of milk. I was not going to discuss Goldie Sutton with him. "As I was saying, I'd like to see if I can find some school clothes for Jane's boys, and Davy, I'd like for you and Lewis to chop a load of wood and take it over to her. I noticed she's almost out and she's trying to do a lot of canning. She has no business trying to chop wood while she's pregnant."

"I'll have Lewis do it."

"Are you chicken?"

"Sure am. Ain't goin' near her place 'less you're there to protect me."

"That's what you get for being so good-looking. She admired you and she said so. What's wrong with that?"

"Ain't what she said as much as it is th' way she looked.

I was afraid I was gonna be another Jonah an' get swallowed by a fish."

I laughed. "You're silly. Jane's nice. She and Sue are both good friends of mine."

"By th' way, don't go out walkin' very far from th' house for awhile. Heard this mornin' there's a pack of wild dogs runnin' loose over near th' ridge. Ain't likely they'll end up around here, but you can never tell about wild dogs. Might be a good idea if you start carryin' th' rifle with you in th' car, too."

"Wild dogs? But where would wild dogs come from?"

"Sometimes a dog'll turn wild if he's mistreated or sometimes people from town will bring a dog out to the country an' dump him 'cause they don't want him anymore. They go wild an' they start killin' chickens an' things to eat, an' sometimes they'll band together to do their huntin'. They say this is a big pack, about seven or eight an' their leader is a big German shepherd. Wild dogs get real vicious. They're worse'n wolves as far as I'm concerned, 'cause they don't have th' fear of man that wolves have. They'll come right out in th' open in th' daytime. Ain't nobody safe from a pack of wild dogs, 'less he's got a gun an' knows how to use it."

"That excludes me then, but Davy, what about the children?"

"They're tryin' to warn ever'one an' th' men are gettin' a group together to hunt them. Dad's one of them. He's got a repeatin' rifle so he'd be able to get more'n his share of them, prob'ly."

"Does Calvin know?"

"I went over an' told Granny an' Calvin myself."

"Oh good. Thank you. Does Lewis know?"

"Yes. I even told him to go over an' warn your friend Jane."

"That's good. I just hope Calvin realizes the seriousness of it and doesn't go wandering off by himself the way he's used to doing."

"I told him to stay close to home. You see that you stay close to home, too."

"I will. They'll have to get them before school starts, otherwise it won't be safe for any of the children."

"They'll get them before then. Dad's a good tracker. He'll find them if nobody else does. You 'bout ready to go?"

"As soon as I get the table cleared and the dishes done."

"I'll help you."

CHAPTER TWENTY-NINE

The Birth

*I*t was early afternoon of the Monday after Davy and I had gone to town. Davy had been in for lunch and had gone out again. He and Lewis were clearing a piece of land at the far side of the farm and cutting the trees into logs to haul to the sawmill located further back in the hills. I had been canning tomatoes all morning and I was tired. Not that canning tomatoes was all that hard. Of all the things I had canned so far, tomatoes were the easiest, but the heat was oppressive and I had had a very busy summer. I decided to rest awhile before I went to Granny Eldridge's in mid-afternoon to help sort out more of Calvin's possessions. We hoped to have him moved in with us by the time school started and that was only four weeks away.

I took one of the electric fans into the bedroom, aimed it toward the bed, then stretched out on top of the quilt. I must have fallen asleep almost immediately because when I woke my head felt fuzzy and groggy and I was aware of some kind of disturbance. I struggled to a sitting position, trying to figure out what it was. It was a car horn. I got up and looked out the window. My car was there in front of the cabin with the door open on the driver's side and Sue Proctor was hanging onto it, bent over as if in pain. I came fully awake and rushed to the door and out in to the yard.

"Sue!" I cried. "What is it? Is it the baby?"

She nodded, her face contorted, her breath coming in little gasps.

"Get back in the car. I'll just grab my purse — "

"No, no! There's no time. I'm going to have this baby right now," she panted.

"But you can't! Sue, I can have you at the hospital in less than an hour — "

"It's not going to be an hour and I'm not having this baby by myself in the back seat of a car."

"But Sue — "

"Please, Anne, help me. I need to lie down. I tell you this baby is going to come right now."

I felt panic welling up in me. I didn't know what to do. I caught a glimpse of the scared faces of her two little girls in the back seat. I jerked open the back door.

"Girls, run to Clemmy's, that house down there, and tell her I need her right now. Tell her your mama is at my house and she's having the baby and I need her, and hurry."

They were out of the car and off with flying feet. I took hold of Sue's arm and helped her into the cabin. It was slow going because the pains were coming fast and hard, but finally I got her to the guest room. I stripped the quilt off the bed in one motion and quickly spread a clean sheet, still doubled, over the middle of the bed.

"Newspapers," Sue gasped. "The book said spread some newspapers under the sheet."

I ran into the living room and grabbed an armload of newspapers and ran back to do as she had said. I helped her into a clean nightgown of mine, then helped her into bed. I ran to the kitchen to put a pan of water on to boil. I was almost praying that Clemmy would hurry.

When I got back to the bedroom, Sue's hands were locked on the metal bars of the headboard behind her, her face was red and straining, her body rigid.

"Don't push, Sue," I pleaded. "Please wait just a little while 'til Clemmy gets here."

"I have to," she gasped. "I . . . have . . . to."

I looked and saw the baby's head. I took Sue's feet and held them in a firm grasp because they kept slipping down on the sheets.

For what seemed like ages, the baby didn't move in spite of Sue's pushing and straining. I felt panic again. What if the baby got stuck and wouldn't come out? What was I to do then?

Sue gave a mighty push that ended in a long moan of pain and the baby suddenly shot out between her feet where I was still holding them.

I stared in fear at the baby. It was a boy, but it was a strange blue-black color and it didn't move. I thought it was dead.

"My baby?" Sue asked in beginning fear. "My baby?"

I let go of her feet and reached for the baby. I didn't know whether to spank it or hang it by its feet or stick my finger in its mouth to clear the mucus away, but I had to do something and do it quickly.

Just as my hands touched him, he moved convulsively and began to cry, a strong lusty boy cry. Right under my eyes, his skin color began to change to a healthy pink. I was almost faint with relief and I could hear Sue laughing and crying at the same time.

"It's all right. It's all right," she said, and then, "It is all right, isn't it?"

"It's fine," I said with profound relief. "You've got your boy. Can't you tell by his voice?"

"Oh, thank God, thank God," she breathed. "I was so afraid when I knew I had waited too long. I was afraid something might go wrong with the baby and I'd never be able to forgive myself. But he is all right? You're sure?"

"He's fine, as far as I can see, but the question is, are you? Sue, I don't know enough. I can cut and tie the cord, but I don't know what to do for you. Here's Clemmy. Maybe she'll know what to do."

Clemmy came in, took one look and set to work. We cut the cord and tied it and I brought a clean soft towel to wrap the baby in. He was still crying lustily so I took him in to the living room and sat in the rocker and rocked him gently until he quieted.

Clemmy bathed Sue and then the baby. She seemed to feel everything was all right. The baby was crying lustily again after his bath. His sisters had been allowed a good look at him, then I took him in to Sue and laid him in her left arm.

She unwrapped the towel and looked him over to make sure he was healthy and whole, then she held him to her breast. He took hold almost immediately and began to nurse. Sue winced a little. She had bottle fed the two girls, but had decided to nurse this one because of the expense of buying formula.

"I went off without a single thing and I had my suitcase all packed, too," Sue said. "I did remember to leave a note for Lewis, though."

"Sue, if I thought you did this on purpose, I'd be very angry with you," I said rather severely.

"I didn't. Truly I didn't. I was having these funny little crampy feelings in my lower back off and on, but it didn't feel like labor pains, not the way it did with the girls. Then all of a sudden my water broke and the hard pains started. I was afraid I wasn't going to make it here, even. I'm sorry I put you through all that, Anne, really I am, but I'm so glad I had you to turn to. You were wonderful."

"Wonderful! I was scared silly and I didn't do anything. It all happened so quickly, which is a good thing. I don't think I could have lasted much longer."

"You couldn't have lasted any longer. What about me? I thought I was going to be torn apart. Thank goodness it was quick. It was much longer with both the girls. By the way, where are they?"

"In the living room. Subdued but proud. Clemmy, do you

think I should go and phone the doctor?"

"Might be a good idea, jist to be on th' safe side," she said. "I'll stay here while you're gone."

"All right. I won't be long."

"I wonder where Lewis is," Sue said a bit wistfully.

"Shall I go look for them?"

"Would it be too much trouble?"

"Not at all. I'll enjoy seeing Lewis's face when I tell him, or shall I not tell him? Would you rather do that yourself?"

"Tell him, otherwise he might panic. Tell him he's got a son, David Lewis Proctor."

"David?"

"You don't mind? Davy has been so good to us. You both have, and if it had been a girl, we were going to name her Anne. But since it's a boy, his name will be David. That is, unless you object."

"Of course I don't object and I'm sure Davy will be pleased. David is a beautiful name, I think. Someday ... Well, never mind. I'll go find Lewis, then I'll go to the Miller's and phone the doctor. You have his name and number?"

"Yes, in my purse, if I remembered to bring my purse. I think I left it in the car."

"I'll get it."

I went out and got the purse and brought it in to Sue. She fished in it until she found a folded piece of paper and handed it to me.

"I may be gone awhile because on the way home I need to stop at Granny's. I was supposed to be there about three so I need to stop and tell them why I didn't show up. Get some rest, Sue. I'll be back as soon as I can and I'll bring Lewis to you."

"If that doctor can't come, you maybe oughta try callin' Dr. Phillip Connors," Clemmy said. "He's been our doctor for years an' he knows th' way. Some doctors don't like to come all this way out here, but he's done it lotsa times. He's gettin' old an' don't do a lot of doctorin' now, but he's a good 'un. Tell him Clemmy Hilton sent for him."

"All right, Clemmy, I'll do that."

I started out again, but suddenly remembered Davy's advice to carry the rifle with me because of the pack of wild dogs. Since I was going to the woods and might possibly have to get out to look for Lewis and Davy, I thought I better follow his advice, if for no other reason than to prevent his being angry with me. I got the rifle from its rack on the wall, took up a handful of shells and was on my way.

CHAPTER THIRTY

The Wild Dogs

I had a general idea of where the men were working and as I drew nearer I could hear the whine of the chain saw. I followed the sound and soon saw the wagon and mules. I drew nearer and stopped a few feet from the mules and got out. I could see them working in the distance, bent over a fallen tree, Davy sawing the limbs off with the chain saw and Lewis dragging the limbs away. When the saw quieted for a minute I leaned into the car and honked the horn. Both men lifted their heads, then started toward me, Lewis in the lead.

"What is it?" he called while he was still some distance away. "Is it Sue?"

I waited until he was closer before I answered.

"Congratulations," I said lightly. "You have a son."

"A son?" he repeated, bewildered. "But — I was just there at lunch. She didn't say anything about — "

"It happened very suddenly."

Davy had come up now and was standing a little behind Lewis.

"But — is she all right?" Lewis stammered. "Where is she?"

"She's fine and she's in our spare bedroom. There wasn't time to get her to the hospital. She drove to our house and the baby was born about ten minutes later."

Lewis passed his hand over his hair in a distracted manner. "You say it's a boy?"

"Yes, a fine, healthy, lusty little boy, from the sound of him."

"So you've added midwife to your list of accomplishments," Davy said softly, grinning at me.

"I didn't really do anything. I didn't have time to do much, other than help her into bed. She and the baby did the rest, then your mother came over and finished up. She's with them now and she wants me to call the doctor and ask him to come out and check them over, just to be sure everything is all right. I'm on my way to call him now, but Sue wanted me to find you first. Do you want me to take you up to the cabin, Lewis?"

He was still looking rather dazed but he nodded his head and went to the car. Davy leaned forward and gave me a kiss.

"My wife, the little wonder woman," he said. "I'll be comin' in jist a little while with th' mules."

"Perhaps we should just run by your house first," I said to Lewis when we were on our way. "Sue came away without anything and the baby needs some clothes. She said the suitcase is just inside your bedroom."

"I should clean up," he said slowly.

"Why don't you just grab some clean clothes and take a bath at our house? It would be quicker."

"Okay. The girls?"

"They're fine. She remembered to bring them along, at least."

We stopped at his house and he was in and out again in a matter of minutes, carrying the suitcase and a change of clothes for himself over his arm. I drove on to the cabin and he was out of the car before I had it properly stopped. He leaped up the path and disappeared into the house. I decided to go in to make sure everything was still all right before I went on to the Miller's.

Lewis was standing in the doorway of the spare bedroom

looking at his wife and child with tear-wet eyes. Sue was asleep on her side and so was the baby, nestled at her breast. Clemmy sat nearby in a chair keeping watch. The girls crowded around their father, wanting to be a part of things. Lewis put his finger to his lips to quiet them.

"Make yourself at home, Lewis," I said, low-voiced. "Have that bath and then you can hold your son. I'll be back in a little while."

I drove to the Miller's and phoned Sue's doctor. I was cooly informed by the receptionist that the doctor did not make house calls that far out in the country, so I borrowed a phone book and looked up the number of Clemmy's doctor. I delivered her message and was told that Dr. Connors would be on his way within the hour.

I thanked the Miller's for the use of their phone and stayed to visit for a few minutes. They were an older couple and didn't seem to mind the use of their phone by the Hilton family. I had just recently found out that Davy supplied them with half a beef once a year as compensation, though they did not require it.

It was after four when I was back in my car and headed for Granny's house. She met me at the door.

"Where's Calvin?" she asked with a touch of concern. "Didn't he come back with you?"

"What do you mean, Granny? Calvin isn't with me. I haven't seen him today. Isn't he here?"

"He got to frettin' when you didn't show up an' went lookin' for you."

"But Granny, the dogs."

"Thought it'd be all right," she said, worried now. "In th' middle of th' day an' all. 'Sides, we ain't seen no signs of th' dogs 'round here, but if he ain't showed up — "

"Now don't get upset, Granny," I said quickly, remembering her bad heart. "I left my house nearly an hour ago, so I must have missed him. How long has he been gone?"

"Pert near an hour."

"Then he's probably at my house right now, but I'll keep an eye out for him as I go along. He usually goes around by the school when he comes to see me, doesn't he?"

"Think so."

"All right. I'll go by there. Now don't worry, Granny, I'll find him. I'm sorry I didn't come when I was supposed to, but Sue Proctor had her baby at my house this afternoon and I couldn't get away."

"She had it right at your place?"

"Yes, a boy, and they're both fine. Calvin is probably there now. When I find him I'll bring him back to you, so don't worry."

I hurried back out to the car and turned it toward the school, more than a little concerned myself. The men had not yet been able to track down the pack of dogs, though they had been seen several times. It was unlikely that they would be hunting in this close, but still Calvin should not be out wandering around alone like that. The sooner he came to me and Davy, the better, I thought. Granny didn't keep a close enough watch on him, as far as I was concerned.

When I rounded the corner by the schoolhouse I saw no sign of Calvin, but just beyond I saw a number of dogs lying under a slender oak tree. One of them was leaping against the tree and barking. I stamped on the brake and froze. The dogs lying there looked peaceful enough but there were so many of them, and for that one to be leaping and barking as he was, there must be something up in the tree.

I had stopped several yards away. Some of the dogs turned their heads and looked at me, otherwise they paid no attention. They didn't look vicious. They just looked like ordinary dogs of varied breeds.

Cautiously I opened my car door and got out. A big gray German shepherd rose and took a couple of steps toward me, the hair standing up on the back of his neck, a low growl in

217

his throat. At the same time I heard a strange little frightened cry from up in the tree. I hurriedly got back in my car. More of the dogs were up now, a couple of them leaping at the tree again at the sound of the voice. The big German shepherd had stopped, his head down, looking at me with strange, wild eyes.

"Calvin?" I called through my half open window. "Calvin, hold on. Don't let go for anything, or try to move. Sit very still and hold on tight. I'm going to help you. Calvin, are you all right?"

"I'm okay," his voice came back with a sob in it.

"Just hang on. I can't get out but I have my rifle and I'm going to shoot at them and try to scare them away. Don't let it scare you and don't let go or slip and fall. Stay there until I say it's all right to come down."

I turned and reached for my rifle in the back seat. I loaded it and tried to aim at the dogs through the open window, but I was parked at the wrong angle. I laid the rifle on the seat beside me.

"Calvin," I called. "I have to move the car so I can aim, but I'm not going away. Don't worry. Everything is going to be all right."

I started my car and moved it so that my window faced the dogs. They were not afraid. The big German shepherd still watched me. I took up my rifle again and aimed through the window straight at the German shepherd and pulled the trigger. I missed him but a smaller dog behind him yelped and leaped into the air and fell. Two of the dogs sniffed around the fallen dog but they didn't run away. I hadn't succeeded in scaring them.

I reloaded and pointed my gun at the mass of dogs without aiming and pulled the trigger. At that close range I could hardly miss hitting at least one of them, I thought. Another dog yelped but didn't fall. They were all on their feet now, snapping and snarling, turned toward me. A cold chill went up my spine. Suppose Calvin were to slip and fall or his arms go numb or something? He'd already been up that tree for close to an hour. I was suddenly angry and my anger made me brave. I couldn't aim properly sitting in the car. I reloaded and carefully opened the door again and stepped out. I was going to have to get that German shepherd, the leader of the pack, before I could scare the others away.

I lifted the rifle to my shoulder. The dog was advancing slowly toward me, crouched low to the ground, the growl low in his throat. Before I could pull the trigger, there was the report of another rifle and the big dog sank in a heap on the ground.

"Git back in that there car," someone yelled and there were several rapid shots in a row. I had just a moment to fear for Calvin up in the tree if one of the shots should go astray. I looked to my left and saw my father-in-law, rifle at his shoulder spitting fire. He picked the dogs off, one by one. None of them escaped him. Instead of getting back in the car as instructed, I started toward the tree.

"Hold on there," Mr. Hilton shouted. "Them dogs may not all be dead."

He was coming rapidly toward me. I waited where I was. He reached the tree and prodded the prostrate dogs with his boot. His rifle pointed downward and exploded one more time. Then he propped the gun against the tree and turned to me, a half grin on his face.

"Thought you'd get ahead of th' fellas an' take on th' whole pack by yerself, did ya?" he chided.

"No," I said, my voice shaking. "Calvin is up in that tree."

"Heh?" he exclaimed, startled. He turned and looked up in the tree. I looked, too. Calvin was sitting on a limb, arms and legs wrapped around the trunk of the tree, tears and dust streaking the face that looked back down at us. I had just a moment to wonder how Mr. Hilton was going to react before he spoke.

"Come on down then, boy," he said, not unkindly. "They're all deader'n doornails."

For a minute Calvin didn't move, then slowly his arms loosened their grip. He moved from the limb but his arms and legs must have been stiff from sitting so long. He lost his grip and came plunging and sliding down the tree trunk. Mr. Hilton caught him before he hit the ground and set him on his feet. He turned to me, crying again, and I put my arms around him and held him tight.

"Enough of that," Mr. Hilton said rather roughly after a few minutes. "Ain't no need cryin' over it now. It's done an' over an' th' men are comin'."

I bristled with resentment but Calvin straightened, wiping his hands across his face, smearing the dust and dirt that much more. I let him go and we both looked toward the sound of several men coming.

"Me an' th' little teacher here done beat you to it," Mr. Hilton greeted them with wry humor.

"You got 'em all?" one man asked in awe.

"Yep, ever' one, me an' th' teacher together. Had th' boy here treed an' th' teacher happened along an' spotted 'em. I was passin' by on my way to meet you all on th' ridge an' heard her shootin' an' come on down to help her out, in case she didn't get 'em all."

"But I didn't — " I started to say, but Tom Hilton interrupted me.

"Who'd a thought it?" he said in a drawl. "Ain't there nothin' you can't do, Teacher? Hear you jist delivered th' Proctor baby up at your place, too."

"But I didn't — "

"Davy sure got hisself some kinda woman, ain't he?" joked another man. "Reckon he'll be able to handle her all by hisself?"

There was laughter and more joking and I wasn't able to say anything. Mr. Hilton seemed determined to give me more credit than I deserved and the men seemed to be trying to make me into some kind of heroine. I looked down at the dead dogs at my feet and felt sick. At one time all these dogs had belonged to someone, perhaps had been a pet, and now because of neglect or abandonment, they had come to this. The German shepherd had been a magnificent animal. What a shame he had been killed. I was upset, too, because the men could stand there in the middle of this slaughter and laugh and joke.

"Come on, Calvin," I said, my hand on his shoulder. "Let's take you home. You're worn out and Granny is worried about you."

We got in the car and left the men standing there. I would not look down at the dogs again. I suppose they would bury the bodies or dispose of them some way. I left Calvin with Granny, her fat arms around him, and drove on home. When I stepped inside, Davy came forward and kissed me on the cheek.

"Here's our little wonder woman back home again," he said proudly. Something inside me snapped.

"But I didn't do anything," I said, tears welling up in my eyes and a sob in my throat. "It was your father. I only killed one of the dogs. He got the rest."

"Dogs? What are you talkin' about?" Davy exclaimed.

"You know," I sobbed, tears spilling down my cheeks. "The dogs! They had Calvin treed near the school and I shot at them to scare them away but they wouldn't scare, then your father came and killed the rest of them. I only got one and why everyone wants to make such a big deal of that I don't know. To have to shoot a dog is not . . . is not . . . "

My voice became totally suspended. Davy had his arm around my shoulder and everyone else seemed to be staring at me open-mouthed.

"You're talkin' about that pack of wild dogs?" Davy asked.

"Yes," I sobbed. "There were eight of them and one of them was a big, beautiful German shepherd. Oh Davy, I think I'm going to be sick!"

He swept me up in his arms and he carried me into our bedroom. "Lay still," he said. "I'll get th' doctor."

"Doctor! But I don't need a doctor."

I said it to the air so I closed my eyes and tried to relax. A moment later Davy came back with an older, white-haired man beside him, a black bag in his hand. I struggled to sit up.

"But I don't need a doctor," I said. "It was Sue — "

"That young lady's just fine," he said soothingly. "And so is the baby. Lie back down and just relax. What seems to be the trouble?"

"I'm fine, really. I just . . . killed a dog."

My voice ended on a sob, fresh tears poured down my cheeks and into my ears.

"She canned tomatoes all mornin'," said Davy's voice. "An' this afternoon she's delivered a baby an' rescued my nephew from a pack of wild dogs."

"But I tell you I didn't," I sobbed.

"There, there, just relax," came the doctor's soothing voice. "Just let me take a quick look at you since I'm already here."

I felt his stethoscope on my chest and gave it up. I was so tired.

"She's pretty well wore herself out," I heard Davy say. "An' I think killin' th' dog upset her. She don't like killin' things."

"Can't say I blame her," the doctor said. He took the stethoscope away. "She's all right, just tired and a little hysterical, with good reason, I'd say. It's been quite a day for you, hasn't it, young lady?"

I nodded and sobbed at the same time.

"I'm going to give you something to help you relax and maybe make you sleep a little, then I want you to stop worrying about things and stop thinking about them, too. If you'd bring a glass of water, Davy."

I sat up and took the capsule he gave me and swallowed it with some of the water. Then I lay back down and closed my eyes.

CHAPTER THIRTY-ONE

The Girl of His Dreams

I became aware of hands at the neck of my blouse, unbuttoning it. "What're you doing?" I objected drowsily.

"I'm goin' to undress you an' put you in your nightgown so you'll be more comfortable," Davy said.

"I have to get up."

"No you don't. Ever'thing's taken care of."

"What time is it?"

" 'Bout nine o'clock. No you don't," he said, his hands holding me. "Lay still."

"But I have to fix supper."

"I already done it."

"You fixed supper?"

"Yep. Well, you said I might have to sometime, so this seemed like one of them times."

"What did you fix?"

"Opened a couple of them cans of chicken noodle soup you had in th' cabinet an' we had that an' th' rest of th' tater salad an' a whole loaf of your bread an' th' rest of th' cookies. Here, put your arm in here."

"Sounds like quite a meal."

"Wasn't bad."

"Is Sue all right?"

"Jist fine an' th' baby, too."

"Did she tell you she was going to name him David?"

"Yep, she did."

"I should just get up and see if she needs anything."

"She don't. Lewis is lookin' after her. Got him bedded down on the sofa an' th' girls on a couple blankets on th' floor. Now you jist relax an' go back to sleep. Ain't nothin' you need to do till mornin'."

I snuggled down in the bed with a sigh of content and closed my eyes. "Are you coming?" I asked drowsily.

"I'm comin'."

A minute later I felt the bed give under his weight. He reached for me and I snuggled close and went to sleep.

I woke to the sound of a baby crying and for a minute couldn't think where it was coming from. It was early morning and I was still in Davy's arms. Memories flooded back and I lay quietly, thinking about the events of the previous day and listening to the baby cry. Perhaps I should get up, but I was so comfortable and Davy was still asleep. If I moved I would wake him. Besides, it was Lewis's baby. He could help Sue with it. Davy stirred beside me and raised his head.

"You awake?" he asked softly.

"Yes."

"How you feelin'?"

"I'm fine, Davy. I'm sorry I went all to pieces like that yesterday."

"S'all right. Like th' doc said, you had reason. Ouch! My arm's gone to sleep."

I lifted my head so he could remove his arm and rub the circulation back in it.

"Davy?"

"Hum-m?"

"I've been lying here trying to figure out why your father tried to make me into some kind of heroic person to the men yesterday. Do you have any ideas?"

"Dunno. Ain't been able to figure out what exactly what happened yesterday."

225

I told him in detail. He was silent for a minute.

"Dad always has admired grit an' determination. Maybe that was it," he said then.

"I've been wondering if it might be because he didn't want to take credit for rescuing Calvin. Of course, he didn't know Calvin was up in that tree, but when I told him, he was kind. He even spoke directly to Calvin and he caught him when he would have fallen."

"Dad ain't a monster, jist got his own ideas 'bout what's right an' what ain't."

"I know but it's a little hard to figure him out. All the time he kept calling me 'th' little teacher.' You'd never know I was his daughter-in-law. I suppose it's about the same thing as my calling him Mr. Hilton, though. We're still almost complete strangers."

"Takes time to get to know Dad."

"I suppose so. I've been wondering, too, Davy, how Calvin's coming here to live with us is going to affect your father's attitude toward you. He won't disown you or anything, will he?"

"No. He'll prob'ly jist ignore Calvin like he ain't there for awhile an' then gradually he'll jist accept him as part of our family. If you noticed, Dad don't pay much attention to none of th' gran'kids. He's a real loner."

"Yes, I had noticed. I'm glad you're not like that, Davy."

"Mighta been someday, if you hadn't married me. I got it in me to be a loner, too."

"Have you?"

"Yep. Course, you put a stop to all that."

"I'm glad. See that it stays that way, will you?"

"Ain't no danger of that now."

I snuggled close to him again. "But your dad had your mother," I said, after a moment's thought.

"Things change. Used to be th' man went off huntin' or to th' fields an' th' woman stayed home an' took care of th' house an' kids. It was a pretty lonely business, wasn't much talk or companionship, least not between my folks. Mom had us kids an' a few neighbor women an' Dad had his friends an' his dogs an' they both seemed satisfied with that. Least if they wasn't, I didn't know about it."

"It sounds like a lonely life. I wonder if your mother didn't sometimes feel like rebelling?"

"Didn't know it if she did. You ever feel like rebellin' an' goin' home to your mama?"

"Home is here in the hills with you now, Davy, and no, I don't ever feel like rebelling, except of course that one time when I had that little run-in with Tom. That reminds me, Tom was there yesterday with the men that were going to hunt the dogs. He already knew about Sue's baby and it had only been about two hours. It has been puzzling me for some time. How does news travel so fast out here with no phones?"

"Beats me, but it always does. Can't do nothin' without ever'one for miles around knowin' it within a day or two."

"It's strange," I mused. "Well, I suppose I ought to get up and start breakfast. I'm starved."

"No wonder. You didn't have no supper, but I thought you needed th' rest more."

"I guess I did. I feel wonderfully refreshed this morning."

"You take it easy for a few days anyhow. Ain't no point in wearin' yourself to a frazzle tryin' to be th' world's greatest wife an' housekeeper."

"You think that's what I'm tryin' to do?"

"Seems like it sometimes. I'm afraid you're gonna burn yourself out. Forget th' cannin'. We got enough an' if we don't, we'll buy what we need. Forget th' dustin' an' sweepin' for a few days, too, an' jist rest up."

"I was thinking of asking Sue and the family to stay for a few days until she's strong enough to take care of herself and the baby. It would be a whole lot easier than having to run out to her house to help her."

"Ask them to stay if you want to, but you let Lewis wait on her. He can take off work a few days. Ain't nothin' urgent needin' to be done right now."

"Did he take that load of wood to Jane?"

"He done that yesterday mornin'."

"Good. I know she was needing it. Well, I guess I'll get up. What would you like for breakfast?"

"How 'bout pancakes?"

"All right, with scrambled eggs and bacon or sausage or both," I said, getting out of bed.

"You are hungry, ain't you?" he said with a grin, propping himself up on his pillow, his arms behind his head.

"Starved," I said.

I dressed in a cool cotton dress while Davy lay and watched me, then I left the room and went into the living room to get to the bathroom. The little girls were still asleep on their blankets on the floor. The door to the spare bedroom was closed and I could hear the murmur of voices behind it. The baby was no longer crying.

I washed my face and brushed my teeth, then went to the kitchen to start breakfast. I put the coffee on to perk, then put bacon on to fry. I mixed the pancake batter and scrambled the eggs and by that time the coffee was ready. I poured myself a cup and took a sip. I heard a door open and close softly and Lewis appeared in the kitchen doorway.

"Good morning, Lewis," I said. "Coffee?"

"Please."

I took down another cup, poured it and handed it to him. "How is Sue this morning?"

"All right, but tired. She's going to try to go back to sleep for awhile."

"And the baby?"

"Sleeping finally. He decided to cry an hour or so earlier."

"I heard him."

"I'm sorry if he woke you."

"He didn't. I woke because I was hungry. I'll bet you're hungry, too, aren't you? Davy told me about the meal he served you last night."

Lewis grinned. "It tasted pretty good even if it was a little unusual, but I am a little hungry."

"It'll be ready in a few minutes. Sue and the girls can eat later."

"Anne."

"Yes?"

"I really don't know how to thank you for what you did for Sue yesterday."

"I did very little, actually. I was there and that's about it."

"Sometimes that's the most important thing, just being there."

"I suppose."

"I'm not a man who goes around hugging other women, but somehow words don't seem adequate this time. Do you mind?"

He came over and put his arms around me and hugged me tight. I hugged him back; he was such a nice person. He was just releasing me when Davy walked into the room.

"Hey, what's goin' on?" he asked in a mildly complaining voice.

"I was just trying to thank your wife for what she did yesterday."

"Did you have to hug her to do it?"

"Yes, I did actually."

"Seems like half th' men in these hills is in love with my wife. If I was a fightin' man now, I'd be invitin' you to step outside."

"Stop teasing, Davy," I said, handing him a cup of coffee. "Lewis is not in love with me and you know it. He was just thanking me, and you're welcome, Lewis. I'm glad I was here. Now sit down and I'll have breakfast on the table in just a minute."

"Anne tell you she wants you an' th' family to stay here with us for a few days?" Davy asked, seating himself.

"Are you sure it won't be too much trouble?"

"It won't be too much trouble, Lewis," I said. "We'll enjoy having you."

"It won't be too much trouble 'cause she won't be here," Davy said matter of factly, helping himself to a piece of bacon. "You're gonna be housewife an' I'm takin' Anne out with me to chop wood."

Lewis looked at me and I looked at Davy. "Oh really?" I asked a little dryly.

"Yep."

"And I don't have anything to say in this matter?"

"Nope, not this time. You need a change an' Lewis needs to be with his wife, so — "

"But I don't know anything about chopping wood."

"Time you learned."

I lifted my eyes and looked at Lewis. He gave me a small grin. Davy was nonchalantly buttering his pancakes. I sat down and began to fill my own plate.

"The master has spoken," I said. "Today I learn to chop wood."

"Might pack a few sandwiches an' somethin' to drink in case we don't get back for lunch," Davy said, lifting a forkful of pancake to his mouth.

"You can manage?" I asked Lewis.

"I can manage."

"There's plenty of food in the refrigerator for lunch. Will I be home in time to fix supper, your royal highness?"

"Prob'ly. If we ain't back, Lewis'll jist have to manage th' best he can. I'll take care of your chores on th' way to th' woods. Anything special needin' to be done?"

"No, I left the calf in with the cow so you won't need to bother with milking. You probably wouldn't have to go by at all."

"We'll check, jist in case."

"Shall I do your chores this morning?"

"I'll do 'em while Anne's gettin' things ready. We'll leave th' car, case you need to go anywhere."

"Thanks."

"You won't mind havin' a day off, will you?"

"I appreciate it."

"Sue an' th' baby all right this mornin'?"

"They're fine."

"I'll get at th' chores." He pushed his chair back and rose, taking the milk bucket as he went toward the door.

"Well," I said. "Life is full of challenges, isn't it? I hope he's not counting on me for too much help. I've never pictured myself as a wood chopper somehow."

"You'll enjoy it. There's something very pleasant and peaceful about being in the woods. I think Davy's a little afraid you've been overdoing it lately. He was really worried about you last night."

"I'm sorry I went all to pieces like that."

"I'm just sorry we contributed to it."

"You didn't, it was killing the dog that upset me. I've never killed anything before. Well, I suppose I'd better see about those sandwiches. Will you be able to fix breakfast for your family, Lewis, if I leave the rest of the pancake batter? There's plenty of eggs and bacon, too."

"I can manage. I do a little cooking now and then."

"Just make yourself at home. I feel badly about running out on you like this. I can stay if you think you might need me."

"We don't need you, but thanks."

I fixed sandwiches and wrapped them in waxed paper.

There was cold tea already in the refrigerator so I poured that into a gallon thermos. Davy came in and I strained the milk and refrigerated it while he went into the bathroom to wash up.

I was in the bedroom changing into jeans when he came in, clean shaven and smelling of after shave. I put my hand up to his cheek.

"I thought we were going to chop wood," I said. "You look good enough to be going out on a date."

"Might do both," he said. "We've been out on th' town together a few times. Thought it was about time we had a day in th' country together."

"But we've been together every day in the country."

"Yes, but jist around here. You ain't hardly seen none of th' rest of th' farm."

"What shall I wear?"

"Blue jeans an' a long sleeve shirt. Hurry up. It'll be gettin' too hot to work 'fore long."

I dressed quickly in jeans and a tank top, with a long sleeved shirt on over it. I wore sturdy shoes and carried my straw hat and an old pair of jersey gloves. We went in Davy's truck since his father was using the mules to go to town.

We stopped by the Proctor's house but the cow and calf were out in the pasture and there was a pond, so they were taken care of. Davy made sure everything else was in order before we drove on down to the woods where he and Lewis had been working.

"Thought I'd jist saw up some of this little stuff for firewood today," Davy said, taking the chainsaw from the back of the truck. "Won't be too long 'fore it'll be time to get a stove set up in th' house. You wantin' to buy one or would a homemade one be all right?"

"One you make will be fine, Davy. What do you want me to do?"

"Nothin' till I get this log cut up, then when I move on to the next one, you can pick up th' wood and throw it in th' back of th' truck."

The chainsaw started with a roar and I stood back while he cut a small log into pieces. When he moved on to another log, I picked up an armload of wood and took it over to the truck.

We worked without pause for about two hours. It was getting hot and my back was beginning to ache. My shirt was unbuttoned and hanging open and I took the two sides and flapped them to create a little breeze, then bent to wipe my face on my shirt tail. The chainsaw stopped at last and I was relieved. The noise was starting to get on my nerves. Davy came and put the chainsaw back in the truck.

"Gettin' tired?" he asked, wiping an arm across his face.

"A little."

"I'll help you pick up th' rest of th' wood, then we'll take a break."

"Lewis said you were afraid I was overdoing it and wanted to give me a rest. Is this what you call a rest?"

He grinned and reached out and pulled my hat down over my eyes. "Ain't what you been doin' restin'?" he teased.

"Not so that I've noticed it."

We finished picking up the last of the wood and threw it into the truck, then we sat down on a fallen log in the shade.

I took my outside shirt off and Davy's was unbuttoned and hanging open. Except for a slight rustling of leaves in the trees and the twittering of birds, there was utter silence. It was peaceful and very restful. I was beginning to see what Lewis meant.

"Rested up yet?" Davy asked.

"I suppose so," I answered reluctantly.

"Then let's go."

He was on his feet reaching a hand down to me. I took

his hand and he hauled me up. He led me to the truck, opened the door and took our our sack lunch and handed it to me. He took the Thermos himself and closed the door.

"It isn't lunch time yet, is it?" I asked.

"No, but it will be when we get where we're goin'."

"Where are we going?"

"For a walk in th' woods."

"Oh. Could I have a drink of tea first? I'm thirsty."

He paused and poured the cap of the Thermos full of tea. I drank it, then he refilled it for himself and drank. He put the top back on then, still holding my hand, he led me into the woods. I felt a little apprehensive as the woods were quite dense here, but I didn't say anything. I knew Davy would take care of me.

We walked side by side. Dried leaves and small sticks crunched under our feet, a crow cawed raucously from a tree and flapped his wings and flew away. Smaller birds twittered and fluttered overhead, a breeze soughed through the trees, otherwise there was silence. A deep peace began to steal over me.

There was a rush of sound and something shot off into the wood beside me. I gave a little gasp of fright and Davy's hand tightened on mine.

"Jist a cottontail," he reassured me.

"Oh."

Silence again. I drew a little closer to my husband.

"Been roamin' these woods ever since I can remember," Davy said, his voice hushed, almost reverent. "Long about th' time I was sixteen or seventeen, I guess, I started thinkin' how nice it'd be to have a girl with me. She'd be little an' pretty an' cute. She'd have laughin' eyes an' smilin' lips an' she'd b'long jist to me, not to anybody else. When I got a few years older, I stopped jist dreamin' 'bout her. I started lookin' for her. After ten years or so, I was 'bout ready to give it all up an' jist settle for whoever I was able to get. Then you come along."

I didn't say anything but I was touched. Was he trying to tell me I was the girl of his dreams?

"First time I seen you I thought, 'There's my girl'."

"You did not," I said softly, mockingly. "The first time you saw me, you didn't like me. You treated me like I had leprosy or something."

"That's 'cause I was scared. I did, too, think of it. You come to the door of th' shop to tell me supper was ready. Th' sun was shinin' in your face an' you put your hand up to shade your eyes an' looked up at me, an' my heart jist about jumped outa my throat. But then you said you was th' school teacher an' that's when I got scared. I thought that since you was a educated city girl you wouldn't want nothin' to do with th' likes of me."

"Did you really, Davy?"

"I did. I had experience with educated city girls before an' I saw what Jim was goin' through an' I thought, 'I gotta stay away from her, else I'm gonna end up gettin' myself in a heap of trouble.' I tried to do it, too, but it didn't work out too good. Seemed like things was always throwin' us together. Wasn't too many weeks after you come that I knew I was a gonner."

"Are you sorry?"

"Not for a minute. Best thing ever happened to me. I told you before we was married you was th' only girl for me. I meant it then an' I still mean it, an' here I am walkin' in th' woods with you jist th' way I dreamed about it. Sure am glad I waited an' didn't jist settle for whoever I could get."

"I'm glad, too, Davy," I said, hugging his arm to me. "So very glad. Thank you for telling me."

I thought of Goldie Sutton and the gossip she had been spreading about Davy's disappointment in me as a wife.

It was just a fleeting thought, though. I wouldn't mention it. I didn't want her intruding on this tender moment with my husband.

We walked on, silent again, but it was a silence of peace and love and trust. I was a very fortunate woman indeed.

CHAPTER THIRTY-TWO

Conspiring for a Home

"**W**ell, how did the wood cutting go?" Lewis asked.

I was standing in the doorway of the room where Sue was lying, my hat in my hand, my shirt on again but hanging open. I was hot, dusty and tired. I had sunburned my shoulders and the end of my nose, but I had never been happier.

"It was wonderful," I sighed.

"First time I ever knew wood cutting to put stars in a person's eyes like you've got," Lewis said with a little gleam of humor.

"We went for a long walk in the woods and we had our lunch by a little lake and Davy told me ... "

"Davy told you?"

"I can't tell you. It's too personal," I said dreamily.

"Oh. Did you get any wood cut?"

"Quite a lot actually. Davy is unloading it now. How did you get along here?"

"We were fine," Sue said. "Lewis took good care of us. He bathed the baby and I had a long soaking bath in the tub. It felt so good."

"I'm glad because I'm going out with Davy again tomorrow."

"Like wood cutting that much, do you?"

"Love it. I'm thinking of giving up housekeeping and teaching and becoming a woodsman. Woodswoman, perhaps

I should say. I never knew it could be so peaceful and wonderful out in the woods."

"Depends a lot on who you're with, I'd say," Lewis said dryly.

"Yes. Well, I'd better get a bath and start supper, I suppose. The baby is doing all right?"

"He's fine, and you don't have to worry about supper. I made some stew," Lewis said.

"You did?"

"Yes, with a few suggestions from Sue, of course. I told you I can cook some."

"How nice. I'll admit I'm glad I don't have to cook supper tonight. I'm going to soak in the tub for half an hour, then I'm going to lie down for a few minutes, then I'm going to let you serve me supper."

The stew was good and I was hungry. Sue got up and came to the table and ate with us. We had a pleasant meal, then Sue went back to bed and I did the dishes while Davy and Lewis went off to do their chores. Lewis took my car since it was some distance to his house.

He hadn't returned when the baby had a crying spell. Sue seemed tired so I took him and sat with him in the rocker and sang softly to him. He soon quieted and went back to sleep. I looked up to see Davy watching me over the top of the newspaper. I smiled at him.

"Davy, I want one," I said softly.

The newspaper came all the way down. "Now?" he asked, startled.

"Yes. Unfortunately we can't, though. I've signed a contract to teach again next year, but do you suppose we could plan on having one about next October or November? That way I'd only be four or five months along by the end of the school year and maybe it wouldn't be so noticeable that anyone would object."

"What if you was sick?"

"Maybe I wouldn't be if I took good care of myself ahead of time. Some people aren't, you know."

"I'm willin', if you are."

"I am. I never knew tiny babies could be so sweet."

"Better'n baby pigs or puppies?"

"Oh, much better."

I held the baby awhile longer then took him back in to Sue. She was half asleep so I laid him beside her and quietly closed the door behind me.

I got out the quilts and made up a bed for the girls on the floor. It was close to nine o'clock and they were yawning. Davy took his newspaper into the kitchen and I turned the lights out in the living room when the girls were in bed. I said good night to them and went into the kitchen to join Davy.

"You'll make a good little mama," Davy said. "You like kids, don't you?"

"Very much." I went to him and clasped my hands behind his head. "Davy, thank you so much for my lovely day."

"You liked it then?" He laid the newspaper on the table and drew me down on his lap.

"I loved it. I think it's been about the nicest day of my whole life. Was it special for you, too, Davy?"

"You bet it was. I had my dream girl with me an' she was for real, not jist a dream."

"I love you so much."

"Not as much as I love you."

Lewis cleared his throat from the doorway and I jumped a little. I hadn't heard him arrive and I didn't think Davy had either.

"I'm sorry," he said. "I didn't mean to intrude, but there didn't seem to be any other place I could go. Is my whole family asleep?"

"Yes, they are. Sue and the baby went to sleep awhile

ago and the girls just in the last few minutes. They wondered where you'd gotten to."

"Do you mind if I come in?"

"Of course not." I tried to slide off Davy's lap but he held me there. Lewis came on in to the room.

"I feel like I'm intruding on a honeymoon," he said.

"You're not," I said just as Davy said, "You are." I gave a little laugh and felt my face flush. "Davy's teasing," I said. "You aren't intruding. Davy, let me up."

He released me and I went and sat in another chair. Lewis pulled out a chair and sat down, too.

"I wonder if I might talk to the two of you," he said, his face serious.

"He's heard you're threatin' to take over his job," Davy said in an aside to me. "She really took to wood cuttin'," he told Lewis.

"I noticed. But that isn't what I wanted to talk to you about. I wanted to talk to you about Jim's house. Being here today and seeing and experiencing the contrast between this house and ours has been an eye-opener. Sue hates our old house but I've more or less been shutting my ears to what she's been saying. After today I don't think I can do that anymore.

"There's such a thing as being too cautious, I guess, and I've got to face the fact that we'll have to move sooner or later, if for no other reason than the place is going to fall in on us someday. Sue's hating the thought of taking the baby home there, so I've been thinking." He paused and I gave a little jump of excitement.

"Wouldn't it be wonderful if you could take her home to Jim's house?" I said.

"The key word is if," he said. "If I can get a loan, if I'm going to have a steady job, if I can make the payments. That's why I wanted to discuss it with you two. I've been over there tonight talking to Jim. He'd like to see us have it, if the details could be worked out, and I think the price he's asking is reasonable. What do you think, Davy?"

"I doubt you'll ever get a chance at a better deal," Davy said. "It's a good house. I oughta know. I helped build it."

"I know it's a good house. The question is, will I have a steady job for the next few years, at least?"

"If you want it. There's plenty of work, a man can work 'bout as hard as he wants to. There's logs to be cut and hauled to the sawmill, there's a market for as many cabinets as I can make an' you can help me there, might even learn how to do it yourself. There's firewood to cut an' sell an' there's always farmers needin' help with this an' that. I can keep you busy as long as you want to be kept busy, or you can branch out on your own."

Lewis drew a deep breath. "There's also the matter of a loan," he said. "I doubt I'd be approved on my own. Would you be willing to co-sign with me?"

"Told you I would a long time ago."

"You haven't changed your mind?"

"No reason to. You don't make your payments, I jist hold up your paycheck. Ever thought of that?"

"I've thought of it."

"If somethin' happens an' you couldn't make th' payments, I'd have to make them an' th' house would be mine. Ain't that much of a risk to either one of us, far as I can see."

"Then I can go ahead with it? I have a little money saved, since Sue didn't have to go to the hospital. I can use that as a down payment."

"Sounds good."

"It sounds wonderful," I said.

"Don't tell her," Lewis said. "If something happened and it fell through she'd be just sick. Besides, I want it to be a surprise."

"I won't tell, but it won't be easy," I said.

"I told Jim I'd talk to you and if you were favorable, I'd

come back and make some kind of arrangement to meet him in town tomorrow to get things started. Do you think you could go along?"

"Not tonight. Jist tell him I'm willin' to co-sign. He'll take your word for it."

"But will you be able to go into town tomorrow?"

Davy glanced at me.

"Do go, Davy," I said. "We can go back to the woods another day."

"Okay," Davy said. "Make your arrangements an' let me know in th' mornin'."

"Thanks. No man has ever had better friends. I don't know how to thank you."

"Might start by takin' yourself off to Jim's," Davy said with a whimsical grin at his friend. Lewis rose immediately.

"I'll do that," he said. "Good night, both of you, and I'll talk to you again in the morning."

"Good night, Lewis. I'm so glad. Sue will be so happy."

"Don't tell her," he warned me again.

CHAPTER THIRTY-THREE

Jim and Liz's Surprise

"**S**tay just one more day, Sue," I said.

"But we've been here a whole week already."

"I know, but we've enjoyed having you and you haven't minded it too much, have you?"

"Minded it! I've reveled in it, but I'm getting spoiled rotten. I'm going to hate going back to that old shack of ours, but I have to go sometime."

"You can go back tomorrow."

"All right, if you're sure you don't mind."

"Would I be asking you if I minded? May I hold little David?"

She handed him over and I took him and sat in the rocker, gently rocking him.

"You should have a baby of your own, Anne," she said, watching me. "You'd make a very good mother."

"I'm going to," I said. "One of these days. But I want to teach school at least one more year."

"You're a good teacher, too. Maybe you could do both."

"When I have a baby, I'll want to take a couple of years off from teaching, at least. Then perhaps I'll go back to it, I don't know yet. I'll just have to wait and see. Well, I promised your girls we'd make cookies this morning, so I'd better get at it. Here's your son."

Lori and Becky and I were in the kitchen, the recipe book open on the table, when the door opened and Calvin came in. He took one look at the Proctor girls and scowled.

"Hello, Calvin," I said. "How are you?"

"Okay."

"Say hello to the Proctor girls."

"Hi," he said grudgingly.

"We were going to make some cookies. Want to help?"

He came on into the kitchen but hung back from coming right over and joining us.

"How about if you read off the instructions, Lori measures out the ingredients, and Becky stirs? Come and wash your hands first."

He came over to the sink and I turned the water on for him. I put my arm around his shoulders and kissed him on the cheek.

"I'm glad you came," I said. "How is Granny?"

"Okay. How long they gonna be here?" he asked, low-voiced, jerking his head in the directions of the girls.

"They're going home tomorrow."

"When am I gonna be comin'?"

"In about two weeks. That will give you a week to settle in before school starts. I'll be over next week to help you pack up the rest of your things. Will that be all right?"

He nodded, reassured, and dried his hands on the towel I held out to him. He went over to the table and stood before the recipe book.

"First thing is one-half cup shortenin'," he read in a loud voice.

"Let's double the recipe, Calvin," I said.

"Then one cup of shortenin'."

It seemed to take Lori forever to measure out the shortening. Calvin began to look impatient, shifting from one foot to the other, but at last it was done.

"Two cups sugar," he said then. Lori measured the sugar. "Cream together shortenin' an' sugar. Where's th' cream?"

"It means mix it together, Calvin. That's your job, Becky."

Becky mixed with vigor and some of the sugar flew out of the bowl on to the table.

"Not that hard, dumbbell," Calvin said.

"Calvin! You don't call anyone dumbbell. Now you apologize to Becky."

"Sorry," he mumbled. "Two, no, four eggs, beaten."

"Break them into a bowl, Lori, and beat them with a fork before you add them to the shortening and sugar."

The door opened again and my father-in-law came in. I was surprised. He rarely came over.

"Davy around?" he asked.

"No, Mr. Hilton. He's off with Lewis somewhere but he should be home at noon."

He nodded, his eyes on Calvin. "You ain't gonna make a sissy out of that boy, are you?" he asked bluntly. "Here tell 'bout all he does is read books an' write stories, now you got him cookin'? Oughta be out learnin' how to plow a field an' shoot a gun."

"Well, since I know for a fact that you're the best shot around, why don't you teach him to shoot a gun? Davy will teach him how to plow a field."

He looked at Calvin a minute longer, then turned without another word and left. I shrugged and turned back to the cookies.

"Go ahead, Calvin."

"Two teaspoons vanilla."

Since it looked as if the cookies were going to take the rest of the morning, I thought I'd go ahead and get started on lunch. I would invite Calvin to stay since he would soon be a permanent fixture and I felt it was time he got used to being around other people.

He stayed until mid-afternoon. He and the girls even went out in the back yard and played together. He seemed to have gotten over his initial jealousy. Poor little boy, I thought, so hungry for a mother's love. I was anxious to get him under our care, so he could have the attention he craved.

About mid-afternoon I put a pot roast on the back burner of the stove, then went to talk to Sue. She was just waking from a nap.

"I'm going to drive Calvin home now," I said. "I may be gone until supper time. Will you be all right?"

"I'll be fine. Is there anything you want me to do while you're gone?"

"You might check on the pot roast in an hour or two, otherwise, there's nothing. The girls are out in the back yard. Shall I call them in?"

"No, leave them there. I may even take myself and the baby out for a few minutes."

"I'll be back about six or so then."

I called Calvin and took him home, then drove on to Jim's house, though I'd have to stop thinking of it as Jim's house now. Lewis had bought it. Davy co-signed at the bank and he and Jim had rushed the deal through, so that Lewis would be able to move his family in when Sue was ready to go home. That would be tomorrow. I was meeting Davy and Lewis there now and we were going to clean and arrange things. Earlier, Lewis and Davy had hauled all their personal belongings from the old house and put them in a back room. I would help sort out and put at least some of the things away so that Sue could get by with doing very little at first. Jim's house was furnished. Neither he nor Sally had wanted to take any reminders away with them. The furniture had been included in the price of the house.

After two hours, most of what I could do was done, and the house was neat and clean, except for that one room. Davy and Lewis went out in the back yard to trim some bushes, while I washed up all Sue's dishes and arranged them in the cabinets. I had bundled up their soiled clothing to take home with me so that Sue and I could get it washed before she came home.

It was getting close to six o'clock, past time I was getting home. There was a quick knock on the door and Jim came in. He bounded over to me, grabbed me in a bear hug, and gave me a loud smacking kiss on the lips.

"Jim!" I protested, drawing away.

"Sorry, couldn't help it. Had to kiss somebody or bust," he said. "Congratulate me, Teacher. Me an' your sister is gettin' married."

"Jim! Really? When did this happen?"

"Jist happened today."

"Liz is here?"

"Nope. Talked to her on the telephone. Set down an' I'll tell you all about it."

We sat on the sofa, he at one end and I at the other. He looked excited and happy, his sandy hair was almost standing on end where he had been running his fingers through it.

"Well, since Lewis started sayin' he wanted to buy th' house, I started gettin' this idea. Thought maybe with neighbors like th' Proctors close by an' you close, too, I might be able to talk Liz into marryin' me an' tryin' livin' in my ol' shack, jist for th' winter. Then if she couldn't stand it, when spring come we'd move in closer to town, but I wanted her to at least try it out here. So when th' papers was all signed I called her up an' jist asked her straight out. Course I told her how I was a pinin' away for her out here."

"Of course," I said.

"Anyhow, she wouldn't give me no answer right away, said she'd have to think about it. So today she calls me at work an' she says yes. I give such a whoop, nearly scared all th' customers away. I'm goin' up to see her this weekend an' buy her a ring an' settle on th' day. We want you an' Davy to stand up with us."

"Congratulations, Jim. That's wonderful."

"You don't sound too sure. Ain't you happy for me?"

"I'm happy, Jim. I guess it just still seems a little soon to me."

"How long you an' ol' Davy know each other 'fore you got married?"

"Four months."

"Well, time we get married, your sister an' me'll know each other 'bout th' same length of time. It's long enough. I been goin' in to see her ever' weekend."

"So that's why we haven't seen anything of you for so long."

"That's why."

"I am happy for you, Jim. I'll have to call Liz and talk to her."

"An' you'll help me see that she's happy out here? Cause I sure would like it fine if we could live here. I could have Davy build us a house like yours someday."

"I'll help you all I can, Jim; but winter is the worst time to bring someone out here. It can get so terribly lonely."

"Not if you're on your honeymoon."

"No, I guess not."

"Liz wants to get herself a job in town, too, so she'll be goin' in to town with me ever' day an' she won't be left out here alone."

"That's wise, I think. Will you still be able to give Todd and Evelyn a ride in to meet the bus?"

"I will till spring, at least."

"Good. I was a little worried about that."

"You gonna like bein' my sister-in-law?" Jim asked, his eyebrows lifted rather quizzically.

"Oh, I think I'll probably get used to it," I answered in the same vein.

"Think maybe there's somethin' I ought to tell you."

"What is it?"

"There was a time there, quite a long time, in fact, when

I thought I was in love with you. Bothered me a lot, I can tell you, thinkin' I was covetin' my best friend's wife. But then I met your sister an' I fell for her like a ton of bricks first time I saw her. Didn't even think about you for days on end. That's when I knew I wasn't really in love with you, it was jist that other thing, what do you call it?"

"Infatuation?"

"Infatuation! That's it. Guess I was jist lonely and you was so pretty an' sweet an' kind, made me want th' same thing ol' Davy had. Knew I wasn't really in love with you the minute I laid eyes on your sister. Relieved my mind a whole lot, I can tell you."

"I'm glad, Jim."

"Did you think I was in love with you, too?"

"No," I said not quite meeting his eyes. "I knew you were just lonely and alone, but I think Liz was a little concerned about it."

"We talked about it. She understands."

"That's good. Well, I'm very glad for you both. I hope you'll be very happy."

"Me, too. Worries me some though. When you got one failure behind you, kinda shakes you up about tryin' again, but it's different this time. Me an' Sally was a mistake from th' start, couldn't seem to agree on anything. Liz an' me get along real good."

"Do you like her, Jim?"

"Like her? Jist told you I'm crazy 'bout her."

"It's not the same thing. You love her, but do you like her? Physical attraction can be very strong, but sometimes it doesn't last. It's the liking, the friendship that makes a marriage last, at least that's my opinion. Do you and Liz have that?"

"Yes, we do. At least, I think she's jist th' sweetest, prettiest little thing, don't you? When I'm walkin' down th' street with her, I jist feel so proud. She's smart an' fun to be with, too. She laughs at th' same things I laugh at, an' gets mad at th' same things that make me mad. She's jist about th' best little friend I ever had."

"Then I think you'll be all right, Jim, but remember, she's very young."

"No younger'n I am. I been feelin' about seventeen these last few weeks."

"Yes, I've noticed. Well, I'm glad you've told me. It's exciting news. I have to get home now and get supper on. Would you like to come and have supper with us tonight?"

"Don't think I will, but thanks. Think I'd rather be alone this evenin'. Davy around?"

"In the back yard with Lewis somewhere."

"I'll go find him. Wonder how he's gonna like bein' my brother-in-law."

"He'll like it fine. Tell him supper will be on in half an hour, will you?"

"Okay. Uh, don't tell Liz I kissed you, will you? She says I can't do that no more, but I forgot."

"I won't tell her." I solemnly held out my hand and he took it and shook it. Then his face broke into a grin, he bent and kissed me on the cheek, then turned and with a jaunty step, headed for the back door. I went out the front door and got into my car. I still felt a little concerned for the two of them but it was not something I was going to interfere in. I had said what I could; I wouldn't say anything more.

CHAPTER THIRTY-FOUR

A New Family

"**W**here are we going? I thought you were taking me home," Sue said when I turned off in the opposite direction from her old house.

"I am. I just thought I'd go a different way."

"But . . . well, you're the driver, but I don't see how you expect to get there this way. Our house is in the other direction."

"Tell you what. You close your eyes and leave it to me and I just might surprise you."

"Close my eyes? But why should I?"

"Because I asked you to. Do it to humor me. You don't think I can get you home this way, I say I can. So sit back and close your eyes and I'll prove it to you."

"If you say so, but it doesn't make any sense. Oh, all right. They're closed."

"Keep them closed tight. I'll have you home much sooner than you could ever imagine."

I drove on to Jim's house, or rather to the Proctor's new house and stopped before the door.

"We're here. You can open them now," I said.

She opened her eyes, saw the house and her mouth flew open. "Why did you bring me here?" she asked bewildered.

The door opened and Lewis stepped out and came toward us. Sue stared at him. He opened the door on her side and reached for the baby.

"Welcome home, Sue," he said softly.

"But . . . but what do you mean?" she asked.

"This is your home now. We've bought the place and it's all ready to move in to, thanks to Anne and Davy and Jim. Get out and come on in, Honey."

Her face puckered, tears rolled slowly down her cheeks. She stumbled getting out of the car and Lewis took hold of her arm and helped her. I got out and opened the back door for the girls.

"Go in and see your new house," I told them, "but take one of these sacks with you."

I gave them each a sack to carry, then set about unloading the rest of the things. Lewis was fully occupied with Sue and the baby, and the girls were running excitedly through the house. I set things just inside the door and left. I knew Sue needed time to get herself together, and she would do it better alone with her family.

I drove to Granny Eldridge's and went in to help sort out some more of Calvin's belongings, a task that had been interrupted by the advent of Sue's baby.

I spent several more afternoons there. Granny was a collector. I don't think she ever threw anything away. She had evidently saved all Calvin's clothes from the time he was a baby. I packed them all up and took them home with me. I spent one whole day washing and mending them, and when I put them with the things I had picked up at the Goodwill store, they made a sizable pile, several changes for each of Jane's boys. There were even coats, gloves, socks and a smaller assortment of shoes. I packed them away in boxes, ready to take to Jane the first chance I got.

Time seemed to speed by, there was so much to be done before school started. Davy mowed the school yard and I cleaned and aired the inside. I was able to replace some of the older books on the shelves with newer ones. There were also new maps and a new blackboard. I was beginning to feel

the little stir of excitement I always felt when the beginning
of a new school year rolled around.

Calvin moved in with us on a Friday, ten days before
school was to start, and Granny moved into town with her
daughter. They both took the separation with very little
show of emotion, but I felt sorry for Granny. She took little
with her, just her clothes and a few personal belongings. All
the collecting she had done in the fifty years of living there
was just left behind. I thought it must be very hard to be
uprooted at her age, but if it was, she didn't show it. I
promised her that I would bring Calvin to visit her from
time to time.

Calvin and I spent the afternoon arranging his things in
the spare bedroom. He was quiet as usual but he didn't seem
upset or disturbed. Toward evening he went out into the
back yard to play with the pup while I started supper.

I knew Calvin liked pork chops and mashed potatoes so
I fixed that for supper, along with sweet corn on the cob and
sliced tomatoes. He ate well then helped me with the dishes
while Davy went to do the chores. After that we all sat in
the living room and read. Davy read the newspaper and I
read a magazine with an article that interested me and
Calvin had a book. It was a quiet evening, but companionable.

"Bedtime," I told Calvin at nine. Obediently he rose, his
finger keeping his place, and went to his room. "I'll be in to
say good night in a few minutes," I told him.

"Good night, Cal," Davy said.

"Night."

A few minutes later I knocked at his door and went in.
He was in bed but the light was still on.

"Would you like to read in bed for awhile, Calvin?" I
asked. "Sometimes it's a little hard to go right to sleep in a
strange bed."

He nodded, pulling his book out from under the sheet, a small half-sheepish grin touching his lips. I smiled and reached down to tousle his hair.

"Good night, Calvin," I said. "I'll be right in the next room if you need me."

"Okay," he said, opening his book.

When I looked in on him half an hour later, his book had fallen to the bed and he was asleep. I put the book on the night stand and stood looking down at him for a few minutes before I switched off the light. I didn't feel he was going to intrude much on our lives.

The next afternoon I loaded the boxes of clothes I had collected for Jane's boys in the back seat of my car and Calvin and I drove to her house.

"Calvin is my husband's nephew," I explained to Jane. "He's going to be living with us now. His grandmother had all kinds of clothes packed away that he's outgrown and we have no use for them and no place to store them, so I washed them up and brought them to you. I thought perhaps your boys might be able to use them."

"Well, sure," she said slowly. "If you're sure you can't use them."

"I'm sure. Granny was a collector. I don't think she could have ever thrown a thing of his away, from the amount of it. I think there's something there for all your boys. Calvin, will you help me bring the box?"

"That much?" Jane asked almost suspiciously when we brought the large box into her living room.

"Yes. As I said, Granny never threw anything away. By the way, Jane, school starts a week from Monday, you know, so I'm planning on being at the schoolhouse Friday afternoon from about one until about four, if anyone wants to come and talk to me. I thought it would give the first graders and other new students a chance to look around a little so they won't feel so strange on the first day of school. Will you come and bring the boys?"

"There's clothes in here my bigger boys might wear?"

"Yes. Enough to start school on, at least. I'm not too sure about the shoes, there are not many of them, but there were several pairs."

"Won't need shoes for a month or so yet anyhow," Jane murmured, starting to look through the clothes. "Land sakes, some of these things look almost brand new," she exclaimed.

"Some of them are in good shape, others not so good. Will you come Friday, Jane?"

"I'll be there."

"Good. Then I'll be running along. I just came by to bring those things and tell you about Friday. I'm glad to see you looking better. Are you feeling better now?"

"Lots better. I'm pretty well over th' mornin' sickness now. You might like to know I got my first commodities from them welfare people and they say I can expect a check, too, one of these days, so I'm feelin' considerable better in lots of ways. Tell your husband I could jist kiss him for that load of wood he sent over. I was sure needin' it."

"I'll tell him," I said, suppressing a smile.

"Maybe I'll be able to pay him for it one of these days."

"It didn't cost him anything, Jane, just a little time and work. There's no need to pay him."

"Well, you tell him how much I 'preciate it anyhow, an' I'm thankin' you for these things, too. My boys can wear these an' not have to feel 'shamed to be seen. You been powerful nice to me. Maybe it'll mean my luck's gonna turn at last."

"Maybe it will. We have to go now, but we'll see you and the boys on Friday afternoon."

We left her looking through the clothes and went back home.

CHAPTER THIRTY-FIVE

Home in the Hills

*T*here were few occasions for socializing in these hills, so perhaps that was why so many families took advantage of the opportunity to gather at the schoolhouse on Friday afternoon. At any rate, by two o'clock, the room was pretty well filled with little groups of people talking and laughing.

I concentrated most of my attention on the students who were newcomers. That included Jane's two boys, Johnny and Jimmie, and Davy's sister Maggie's oldest son, Timmy. There was also another Baxter starting first grade and another Anderson. The rest of the children I already knew.

When I glanced up and saw Goldie Sutton saunter through the door, I felt myself stiffen with resentment. She had as much right to be there as anyone else, I supposed. She had two brothers in school, but there was no sign of them. She was alone. She walked past me without speaking. I had a crazy impulse to put my foot out like a naughty child and trip her as she passed. I knew where she was going.

She made straight for Davy, who was standing toward the back of the room talking to a couple of men. When she reached him, she put her hand on his arm. There was a sudden hush in the room. All eyes were turned on my husband and Goldie.

Davy very deliberately removed her hand from his arm and stepped back. "S'cuse me," he said politely. He turned and came toward me. Goldie stared after him.

"Lo, Maggie," Davy said to his sister who was standing beside me. His arm slid around my shoulders and stayed there. "Timmy startin' school already?"

"Yes. He's five now, you know," Maggie answered.

"Guess he is. Time sure flies, don't it? You feelin' any better?"

"Lots better."

"Mom's been worryin' about you 'cause you ain't been by for awhile."

"I'll come when th' two older ones get back in school. Seems like such an effort to drag them all along."

Davy turned and spoke to another friend, but his arm slid down and he clasped my hand in his and held it. Goldie made one more attempt to approach him, but I took the initiative this time.

"Was there something I could help you with, Miss Sutton?" I asked.

"No," she said bluntly, coldly. "I was wantin' to talk to Davy."

Davy turned and looked down on her. He was not smiling. "I don't think we got anything to talk about, least not anything that can't be said in front of my wife, 'less you'd be wantin' to apologize to her for th' lies you been spreadin' around."

Her face flushed unbecomingly. She gave me a baleful glare and flounced from the room. There was a sudden flurry of conversation in a room that had been almost silent. I squeezed Davy's hand.

"Thank you, Davy," I said softly.

By four o'clock, everyone was gone except Davy, Calvin and me. Calvin went out to the swings and I sat down at my desk to organize a few papers. Davy sat before me on the long bench.

"Can you b'lieve it's been a whole year since you come out here to teach this school?" he asked me.

"It doesn't seem that long, does it? It's been a very different and challenging summer for me and I've enjoyed it, well, at least most of it, but I'm glad to be behind this desk again. I love teaching, particularly this school."

"Why this school?"

"I suppose because I feel needed here. There's so much to be done and I can help do it. It's almost as if I belong."

"You do belong. You're married to me, ain't you? That makes you one of us."

"Yes. Pretty smart move on my part, wasn't it, marrying you?"

"I thought so. Is it home, Sweetheart?" he added, a bit anxiously.

"It's home. Your father was wrong when he said city girls don't belong out here. Some city girls do. And Goldie Sutton was wrong, too. By the way, if she ever comes and puts her hands on you again, I may be tempted to scratch her eyes out, right in front of everyone."

"Don't think she'll do that again."

"No, I don't think so either. Thank you, Davy. Everybody heard what you said. That should help to stop some of the rumors that have been floating around. I didn't know if you'd heard about them or not."

"An' I didn't know if you did. You never said anything."

"It didn't seem important enough to mention."

"It wasn't."

"Davy, did you notice how ragged and dirty that little Anderson boy was? That family worries me. I'm afraid those children are being badly neglected. They're not being taught anything in the earlier years and that is so important. I've heard the father drinks a lot and the mother is . . ."

"Is what?"

"I won't say it. There are always extenuating circumstances but — I'm going to have to do something, what I don't know, but something. There are so many of them, and if I'm not mistaken, she's expecting again. I think the Decker family and the Anderson family are my next two projects, and I'm much less concerned about the Deckers than I am the Andersons."

Davy sighed. "More projects, huh? You're makin' me jealous."

I looked up, surprised. "Why do you say that, Davy?" I asked.

"Cause when you get back to teachin' again an' get all these projects goin', you ain't gonna have much time for me."

"I will, Davy. We'll have the evenings together the same as before. I love you very much. You're the very best husband in the world. Can't I keep what I have with you and still teach, too?"

"Maybe I oughta start back to school an' you could teach me how to talk right an' maybe I'd get a chance to be teacher's pet, you think?"

"I'm afraid that might not work, but I could give you private lessons and you could be teacher's pet then. As a matter of fact, Davy, I've been thinking — "

"Oh, oh," he said mournfully. "Figgered this'd happen sooner or later."

"What do you mean?"

"Figgered soon as th' honeymoon was over, you'd start tryin' to reform me, tryin' to teach me how to talk proper."

"But you brought it up," I said, a little disturbed.

"I know. I'm surprised you let me get by with it long as you have. Guess maybe you been too much in love to notice, is that it?"

"It isn't that I haven't noticed, Davy," I said with a softening smile. "It's just that I've been too much in love to do anything about it."

"And now you ain't?"

" 'And now I'm not,' Davy."

"I was afraid of that," he said, hanging his head.

"Silly, I was just correcting your grammar. You should say 'are not' or 'aren't' instead of ain't. Ain't is not good grammar." I paused and studied his face for a long moment. He was looking sober, but his eyes were twinkling. "Davy," I said slowly, "I won't nag you about your grammar if you don't want me to. I love you very much. I wouldn't change a hair on your head, except — "

"Except for my grammar?"

"Yes, but even that isn't important enough to make an issue of if it's going to bother you."

"I've been studyin' on it an' I figger it this way. Th' teacher's gonna have a hard time teachin' th' kids good grammar if she can't teach her own husband. Bet, too, when we have kids, if they start tryin' to talk like me, they'll get theirselves in a heap of trouble with their mama, am I right?"

"Probably."

"Then I reckon I better have them private lessons, but jist remember, I get to be teacher's pet, an' I'm gonna expect to get a little better reward than jist a 'you done good today.' "

"For a start you can stop saying 'you done good' or you done this or that. Say 'you did well' or if you have to say done, use have, has or had with it. 'You have done well,' or 'you did well.' Say it, Davy."

"You have did well," he said solemnly.

"Wrong. 'You did well,' or 'You have done well.' Try it again."

"You done well. You done good."

"Davy, you clown, you're not even trying. You know how to use good grammar if you'd just get into the habit of it. Just for that, you don't get your reward," I said rising and gathering up a few papers to take with me.

"I didn't know I was gonna get a reward," he complained, rising also. "I coulda done it if I knew that. 'You did well', 'You have done well.' How's that, Teacher?"

"You're impossible," I said, unable to suppress a laugh.

"What's th' reward I get?"

"You don't get one now. You didn't cooperate."

"I'll cooperate. Come on, Teacher, I want my reward."

His hands were at my waist. I looked up into his smiling eyes and had to smile back at him. I put the papers on the desk and lifted my hands to his face and put my lips on his.

"I love this place," I said softly in a little while, my head on my husband's shoulder. "There are so many happy memories. You kissed me for the first time here, do you remember?"

"I remember. You nearly slapped my head off."

"And it was here that you told me you loved me and asked me to marry you."

"I was awful afraid you was gonna say no."

" 'Were going to say no', Davy."

He sighed and released me. "Yes, Teacher," he said humbly. "You ready to go home?"

"Home," I said almost dreamily. "It's a good word, isn't it, Davy? It suggests warmth and comfort and rest after a hard day's work, and love and companionship. I love the home we're building here in the hills together. I love everything about my life out here. I'm so glad I had the good sense to say yes when you asked me to marry you."

"Me, too. Let's go home, Sweetheart."

We went out together and I padlocked the door. Calvin was still on the swings. I called to him and he came running. Davy took my left hand and Calvin took my right, and together we started for our home in the hills.

THE END